"**TROIKA** is literary gold, and
Adam Pelzman is a shooting star."
—BOOKREPORTER.COM

"A glorious testimony to the way damage
can become a lovely destiny."
—SUSAN CHEEVER

"A surprisingly poignant meditation on love in all of its forms...
The sort of book you'll miss long after it's over."
—*FLORIDA BOOK REVIEW*

"So beautiful and powerful...Pelzman's talent
and vision are formidable."
—*PUBLISHERS WEEKLY*

"An electrifying read. Pelzman plunges us deep into the lives of his characters, makes us feel their joys and sorrows on a visceral level, and beautifully renders the mysteries of love."

—Alice LaPlante, *New York Times* bestselling author of *Turn of Mind*

"I. Love. This. Book. It's fucking fantastic. Poignant, painful, impeccably realized and ultimately joyful. I am so grateful to Adam Pelzman for creating this gem of a world."

—Ayelet Waldman, author of *Love and Treasure*

"Pelzman's story is a beautifully painted mural that twists together the many different colors of people's lives into one magnificent experience. He varies the perspectives every chapter, stringing you along every important moment right when it was needed. His characters bleed through the pages, and their energy reaches into your body . . . *Troika* was instantly impressive in the way it presented itself. The characters will stay with me long after the book is layered in dust on my bookshelf. My ideas of love were challenged by themes and topics it explored. I was glued to every detail, and this world became my own. *Troika* is literary gold, and Adam Pelzman is a shooting star."   —Bookreporter.com

"What a great gallop through the landscape of the human heart, what a brilliant, astonishing modern love story, what a beautiful pair of heroines, what an amazing journey from the plantains of Little Havana and a Fort Lauderdale strip club to Fifth Avenue and East Hampton, what a ride to a complex and satisfying redemption, what a glorious testimony to the way damage can become a lovely destiny, what a book!"   —Susan Cheever

continued . . .

TROIKA

ADAM PELZMAN

BERKLEY BOOKS
New York

THE BERKLEY PUBLISHING GROUP
Published by the Penguin Group
Penguin Group (USA) LLC
375 Hudson Street, New York, New York 10014

USA • Canada • UK • Ireland • Australia • New Zealand • India • South Africa • China

penguin.com

A Penguin Random House Company

Berkley trade paperback ISBN: 978-0-425-27536-8

The Library of Congress has catalogued the G. P. Putnam's Sons hardcover edition of this title as follows:

Pelzman, Adam.
Troika / Adam Pelzman.
p.   cm.
ISBN 978-0-399-16748-5
1. Cuban Americans—Fiction.   2. Stripteasers—Fiction.   3. Orphans—Russia—Fiction.
4. Rich people—Fiction.   5. Triangles (Interpersonal relations)—Fiction.   I. Title.
PS3616—E443T76   2014   2013036209
813'.6—dc23

PUBLISHING HISTORY
G. P. Putnam's Sons hardcover edition / May 2014
Berkley trade paperback edition / April 2015

PRINTED IN THE UNITED STATES OF AMERICA

10 9 8 7 6 5 4 3 2 1

Cover design by Jason Gill.
Interior text design by Michelle McMillian.

For Jonathan Spencer Newman, my brother

Of all forms of caution, caution in love is perhaps the most fatal to true happiness.

—BERTRAND RUSSELL

I am ashamed—ashamed to admit that I am so unattractive that I have never kissed a girl. That's not true. I did once, when I was eight, before the girls knew what ugly was. That was a bright-life moment. But soon the fist of hierarchy squeezed tight and rammed me to the underworld.

My great loves have been unilateral and unknown to all but me. That is why I write, to create voices, back and forth, with Her, where only a muffled soliloquy once existed—a maddening, tortured, silent scream.

Sometimes I dream about a blind girl, but fear that her sighted friend—the one she's known since third grade— would tell her she'd made a terrible mistake. He's hideous, she might whisper, just hideous. Or maybe the friend would have mercy on me. Do you think she would? Have mercy?

I once asked a man, my father, if mercy exists. Yes, he said, mercy abounds. And he gave me a tap on the top of my head, a loving yet hollow tap that foretold both the tragedy of a child and the powerlessness of a father, the awful soul-sickening impotence of Our Father. Yes, He repeated, mercy abounds.

But I'm not so sure. I was born in Mercy General, says it right here, right on this piece of paper. But that's as close as I get.

—JULIAN PRAVDIN

PERFECT DARKNESS

He comes in the first time, eight o'clock on a Tuesday night and it's real slow. White, maybe forty, real handsome in an odd way—unusual—with a crooked nose like some Irish boxer. He's got sharp clothes and messed-up hair, not sloppy but sort of stylish, and a fancy watch, blue face with gold around the edges, and I'm thinking *ooh, that's a pricey watch.*

First thing I do when they sit down is I sit right next to them before the other girls get there, and that's what I do with Julian. When I started out, I wasn't so aggressive and all the other girls got the dances and the tips and I ended up spending the whole shift running from table to table—like some dolled-up little girl in her mama's clothing—late for the party and not making any money. But after a few weeks I learned how it worked. That's when the girls found out I wasn't fooling around anymore and stood way back when I was on the move.

So, he comes in and sits down a couple feet from the stage. I see Lopez eyeing him, and she's a nasty slut. She's one of those inked-up burlesque girls, with the Betty Boop haircut and the black eyeliner and pierced everywhere. And I know what she's gonna do to this guy, 'cause Lopez is a skanky bitch and a hustler and she keeps going until she gets their stats and God forbid they're rich or famous or in politics, 'cause then she holds them up until they pay her off. But I throw her a glance, a mean stare, and Lopez freezes like she's some animal in the night that just got lit up—she's all bark and no bite with me—and that's my opening.

I sit down next to him and say, real confident, my name's Perla, what's yours? He tells me Steve, but I know from doing this a thousand times that the way he's saying it doesn't ring true, like he hesitated just a second to give it some thought. It's the smallest details I'm always seeing. But that's the thing about first names. We use them so much, people always calling us by them, that when someone asks what it is, then no reason to have to think about it. What's your name? Bob. What's your name? Rick. What's your name? Joe. See, it's real fast. Bob, Rick, Joe. Question, answer. Question, answer. Question, answer.

But a zodiac sign? That's another thing. There's so many of them, twelve actually, and sometimes it's hard to remember them all. When I was little, I wanted to be a Capricorn, the sea goat, 'cause both my parents were born on January third, which I always thought was strange, both of them on the same date. I mean, what are the odds? Turns out it's one in three sixty-five. Except if it's a leap year, then the odds are a little worse. But I didn't get a Capricorn birthday. I ended up Sagittarius, the one that's half horse and half archer. Which is fine with me.

So I say no way you a Steve. And he looks all nervous and sweating a bit, especially on his forehead, and he smiles and says you got me, it's Julian. And the way he says it, real fast and self-assured, I know he's telling the truth. Pleasure to meet you, Julian. And I lean over and give him a playful little peck on the cheek, my signature move, fun and sophisticated, to show him that I got a little personality, a little class, not like the other girls. I look up and Lopez is glaring at me all angry, I guess 'cause it's a slow night and we're not making much money and she sees a nice-looking man with a fancy watch.

I ask Julian if I can buy him a drink, which is what I do sometimes when it's real slow and I got a handsome guy. That's the opposite of what the other girls do. They're always begging the guys for a drink, which I don't think is a good idea 'cause it puts the guy on the defensive, makes him think you want something from him. Which of course you do, and he knows it, otherwise what's he doing here in the first place? But why wouldn't you just pretend sometimes that's not the case. Seems like a good strategy to me. And the truth is, he's gonna pay for it one way or the other.

Anyway, he says I'd love a water. A water, I want to know, you don't drink? Nope, he says, I used to but not anymore. And something about the way Julian speaks makes me think that maybe he's not from here—and I don't mean from some place like the Panhandle or Alabama. I mean from another *country*. I can't pick up the accent, but I can tell the pronunciation's just too perfect, all proper and smart, like he learned it from those language tapes or from watching the evening news.

I wave over to the waitress. She's a white girl in her forties, a lady really. Jade's her name and she used to dance here, but it's too late for that now. She's had two kids—actually, two pregnancies and one kid—and her body's all stretched out, red marks around the hips. I hope the same thing doesn't happen to me, being a cocktail waitress in a place like this at an age like that. So I wave her over and get Julian a bottle of water and get myself one too, 'cause I don't drink either, and not 'cause I got a problem, but 'cause I need to be in total control of myself at work, reduce the chance that I make a mistake and put myself in a bad situation. Sometimes I treat myself to a ginger ale with an orange slice, but I stick with water this time.

When Jade comes back with the drinks, Julian says thanks for the offer, Perla, but this round's on me. And that's the best possible result, when I offer to pay but the guy pays anyway, 'cause I get credit for being generous but it doesn't cost me a dime. Julian turns to Jade and asks how much and she says a hundred dollars. She gives me a little wink 'cause this is our inside joke, where she makes a new guy think he's getting jobbed. And you can see on his face that he's shocked, and you can also see him look over to the bouncer near the stage, whose name is Schultz—yes, Schultz—and who looks like something you'd see in an old horror movie that takes place in Transylvania or Bavaria or some other spooky place like that. And I guess Julian decides that even though a hundred's a crime, he's out of his territory and it's better than having to fight Schultz.

So he opens his wallet and takes out a hundred-dollar bill, hands it to Jade. Well, damned if she ever had someone just hand over the money without a big production, and she laughs and says I'm just screwing with you, sweetie, it's ten for the two. Well, Julian gets all red and embarrassed and he looks at me, then Jade. He smiles and says I knew you were screwing with me, which of course he didn't, but keep the hundred anyway. Jade's shocked and she leans over and gives him a big wet kiss on the cheek, not like my classy peck.

With a certain type of guy, the talk's awkward, and that's what it's like at first with Julian. The drunk college guys, they just jabber away with nonsense and they're so excited to be near a nude girl that the words just flow out their mouths, like their entire system's flying. The locals, the burnouts who hang around every night, they don't say much, don't even seem too interested in the girls, like we might as well be a piece of old furniture that you throw your coat and keys on at the end of the day. But the mature ones, the ones with some substance, especially the new ones, they're hard to crack. With them, it's not all *hey, baby, show me some ass*. With a guy like Julian, you gotta talk all grown-up, which isn't easy for a girl like me. I can do it and all, but that's not a place I like to go in the club. Outside, fine, but not in the club.

He isn't much for taking the lead, so I start with the usual. Where you from? What do you do? First time here? You married? Got kids? Julian downs half his water before he can answer a question, and when he does answer he's so vague that what's the point? I'm from up north, he says. Where, I say? Orlando? No, New York. What sort of work? I'm in business up there. Business? I say. Well, that could be anything, right? What's *not* a business? And no, he says, I'm not married. So I take his left hand and hold it up to the light. There's no ring, that's for sure, so I'm looking for the indentation. You know, lots of times they take it off right before they come in and the mark's still there. But if he's got a mark, I sure can't see it.

Then he starts asking me questions, most of the same ones I asked him, but it's worse when it's the man asking the girl. It's worse 'cause I've answered the same questions a thousand times and the guys really don't care what I say, and it's hard as hell to pretend I care. And the worse thing is you know exactly what they're doing.

They're acting all interested in my life, but they're really trying to figure out how a girl like me, all pretty and innocent and I don't have any tattoos or piercings, how I could do this type of work.

There's also something voyeuristic about the questions, like they're trying to get into my world, peer inside. Do you enjoy it? Do guys ever get rough? How much a night do you make? Your family know what you do? They want to know the secrets. But the funny thing, funny to me at least, is that they don't need my answers to get in my world. They're already *in* my world. These fools are part of it. And not only are they part of it, but it's them, not us, who are the real actors, the *lead* actors. Me? I only got a supporting role. If it's not me, it could be anyone. So when a guy like Julian starts asking me questions about the darkness of my life, it's like a tourist, a foreigner, standing on Broadway and Forty-fifth Street and asking a local for directions to Times Square. And the New Yorker looks around at all the bright lights and the theaters and thinks *what the* . . . ?

Now, the only reason I know that's how it works in New York is 'cause my dad took me to the city when I was little, just a couple of years after we left Cuba. It's the only time he ever did take me on a trip up north, and we were standing right in front of the Shubert Theatre and damned if he didn't walk right up to a taxi driver having a smoke and say sir, you be kind enough to point me and my daughter in the direction of Times Square?

So how does this place work, Julian asks, my first time here. You got three choices, I say. You can sit here with me and talk for free until I get bored and go find someone else who will pay me. How long until that happens? he asks. Five minutes ago. I smile. Or we can go in that room over there with the drapes, that's the VIP Room. That's fifty for the house and fifty for me. There's some privacy there, more than out here on the floor. And then over there, that's the Champagne Room, behind the black door. And what happens there? he asks and downs the rest of his water. That's a hundred for the house and a hundred for me, and we got lots of privacy. How long? he wants to know. About fifteen minutes—and I adjust my top to get him focused on my tits. Could be a little more if I like you. Or a little less if I don't.

Julian takes out his wallet again and hands me two hundreds, one for me and one for the house. Champagne Room it is, and I lead him to the back. There's a low chair against the back wall. I sit him down then close the door. I stand over him and look down at his face, and he's got that damned look that drives me nuts, all serious, like it's the first time he's ever seen a pair of tits. So I take my top off and hang it on a little hook on the wall that they put up after we complained about not having a clean place to put our lingerie. I get up on top of Julian, straddle him and start doing my thing.

Now, there's a few ways this can go. There's some guys, usually the younger ones and real drunk, who can get pretty aggressive. They'll be grabbing my ass hard, pulling on my nipples, trying to get their hands under my panties, which they're not allowed to do. That's against the rules—at least *my* rules. Then there's the nerdy types, so shy and nervous that they can't even look me in the eyes, looking like they'd rather be anywhere else but next to a pretty, naked girl. Then there's guys who are just so plain middle-of-the-road that it's real easy. One song, two songs, three songs, four. They move a little, groan a little, rub your tits like they're petting a puppy or something, and then it's over. That's easy money. But every once in a while there's a guy like Julian, and that's the most dangerous kind.

I had him pegged for the plain vanilla type, an easy hundred. But first thing I notice about him is the way he touches me, not too hard and not too soft, but right in the middle. Like he doesn't want to lose me but also afraid he's gonna leave a bruise or something. He's holding me the way a boyfriend would hold me, a *good* boyfriend. Then he starts on my tits with his mouth. Not biting or nibbling, but brushing his lips real tender across my nipples. Now, I got a rule, which is this. If there's ever a moment that I start to feel good, start to feel a little, well, you know, then I shut it down right then and there. I get back to business.

But I'm feeling a little something with Julian, not just between my legs, but in the chest too. And not in the chest like my skin feels funny, but inside, down near my lungs. That's happened to me a few times over the years, and like I said, I just shut it down, which is what I do with him. And I'm back to doing my thing, flicking my hair across his face all playful, shaking my ass, even nibble on his ear a bit. But next thing I know, he puts his hands between my legs and presses strong against me, not under the panties but on top, and there it goes again but even worse this time. And he knows just how to touch a girl. Some guys are too clumsy down there, like they're trying to crush a grape. But Julian? Julian knows how to rub it perfect, just enough pressure and just the right angle. I press my face into his neck. I start feeling tingles in my thighs and then I feel it coming on, an orgasm, so big and deep, so unexpected that I think I'm gonna break apart.

Now, that's another thing I don't let happen. All this time at the club, I never did come once. A couple of times I got real close, right to the edge where it almost feels like an orgasm but isn't, just a little flutter, a tease, and not very satisfying. But I never did make it all the way no matter how close I got. I always, how do they say? Detach. I detach and that makes it stop. I get the hell out of the moment. But with Julian I don't have time, 'cause it happens so fast, and the problem is that once you cross a line—it's different for every girl, that line—but once you cross a certain line there's not a damn thing you can do to cross back. And that's what happens. So I dig my face real deep into his neck, bite him a little bit 'cause my body's not following orders.

The whole thing lasts just a minute or so, but who knows for sure 'cause it's hard to judge time when your body doesn't behave. But when I'm finished, I go real still, still like a corpse. And that's the moment when Julian surprises me again, 'cause most guys right then will start pressing against me, grab my hand, rub it over their pants until they get off. But Julian does something different. He puts his arms around me, around my back, and strokes my skin with his fingertips, so light and airy that I get little bumps all over and I feel the tiny hairs stand up straight. And the chills, little shock waves, run through my entire body, and even though the music is pounding loud and our time's up, I just want to fall asleep right there with the man.

I try to fight the sleep, but it's hard to do with the orgasm running through my blood. And I'm already so damn tired from being on my feet all day, dancing in these ridiculous heels, that I close my eyes. I rest my head on his shoulder. I go limp and drift off. I don't sleep long, but real fast and deep, just a minute of perfect darkness before I wake up, before Julian taps me on the shoulder and whispers something in my ear I don't understand. Just a minute of perfect darkness before he pulls me out of a place I really had no business going.

BLINK, THERE I GO

I'm young, just turned twenty-three, so I've only worked a couple clubs so far. There's different types of places down here in south Florida. There's the real high-end clubs, like Pink Flamingo or Jubilee, with valet parking and the best DJs, top-shelf liquor and lots of pretty girls—Russians, Colombians, Brazilians, and gorgeous black girls. And those places are sort of intimidating for me. Seems like most of the men who come in are either real rich or pretending they're real rich, and a lot of those men, for reasons I just don't understand, are not too nice.

The other reason I don't like those clubs, the fancy ones, is 'cause I got the wrong look. I mean I'm pretty and all, and I never had a problem attracting men. I got a body that's better than ninety percent of the girls out there, but compared to the girls in a top place, the girls who are on the circuit, who fly around the country from club to club, compared to them I don't quite cut it. First thing is I got small tits, and that's the way I like it. Most of the girls got fake ones, and that's what the customers want. So when they see me, and I'm standing next to a girl who's got DDs and they're pointing to the ceiling, well, there's no way they go with the girl with the B cups, 'cause that's what they get at home.

And I got a pretty face, no doubt about it, but a customer once told me it's not *stripper pretty*. I didn't know what he meant when he said it, and I'm still not sure what it means, but I think what he was getting at is that I don't have a slutty look, don't look like I'm gonna get down on my knees and suck their dick. What I got is a look clean and serious that says *boundaries*, which some guys seem to like 'cause it's safe for them. And not just safe, but a challenge too. But most guys when they come to a strip club they're not looking for boundaries. They're looking for green lights.

At the bottom are the hole-in-the-walls, clubs that are real dark and skanky. All the men in these places are felons. The staff *and* the customers. They're huddling in the corners, in the dark, exchanging little bags, whispering, maybe showing off the handle of a gun. Every girl in one of these dumps is a hot mess: crack whores, meth sluts, whatever. They dance for a guy, get a twenty, go to the back lot, hand the dealer the cash, and smoke a rock next to the Dumpster. Sometimes a nice guy walks in, doesn't understand the place, and he walks out without his wallet, his money, sometimes his teeth.

The place I'm at, Paris Nights, is somewhere in the middle, and that's how I like it. Not too fancy and not too sleazy. It's a small place right off the highway, a few miles from the beach. Best thing I like about it is Schultz, 'cause he's good with the girls. Lots of places, the head bouncer's got his hands all over you, groping, grabbing, slapping, asking for a blow job, demanding it really, and threatening your job if you don't give it to him. But not with Schultz. The man's a gentleman.

But it's not perfect, of course. I mean, with this type of job, even at its best, how good can it be? The place is filled with smoke so thick that sometimes it's hard to see the other side of the room. Now, I don't smoke, but I'm inhaling that crap eight hours a day, six days a week. Another problem is that they keep the place freezing, blasting the AC, and I'm always chilly, goose bumps everywhere. And it's not like you're working in a library, so forget about putting on a sweater or a long-sleeved shirt. But the smoke and the cold, that's not only for Paris Nights. It's like that at all the places, though I hear Pink Flamingo just got a new ventilation system and you can't even smell the smoke there.

And at most of these clubs, even the high-end ones, there's girls who do a lot more than just dance. Now, I'm a stripper and that's it. No sex, no hand jobs, no blow jobs, nothing. They can touch my tits and grab my ass, and that's it. But some of the other girls do more than strip, and they're nothing but low-rent hookers. They go to the Champagne Room or the back lot and get a guy off. The girls who are tricking usually got their pimps right in the club with them, and most of the out-of-towners don't know what's really going on. They don't know that the guy sitting by himself in the corner sipping on a soda, checking his phone constantly, keeping his eye on just one girl, maybe two, they don't realize that this guy's looking after his investment. And those are guys you don't want to cross. Heartless, every one of them. The pimps are always recruiting, trying to pick up new girls to work for them, so a girl like me has to be careful. I stay clear of them, don't give them even the smallest opening, and once they learn there's no chance, they leave me alone. One time, I had a pimp get aggressive with me, so I just had Schultz give him a little talk, man to man, and that was the end of that.

Like I said, there's all types of customers at the club, some types you never knew existed, and there's times when I think it's interesting, this job, 'cause I get to see more of the world than anyone else, except for maybe a pilot or a diplomat. The other day a guy comes in wearing a white turban, mid-fifties is my guess, proud-looking with a long white beard and gold rings on each pinky. I can tell the second he walks in that there's something regal about the man, and sure enough it turns out he's a wealthy Sikh. Well, I see Lopez eyeing him, but I'm always one step ahead of that bitch, and I slip my arm around him before Lopez can even get her bony, tattooed ass off the bar stool.

I introduce myself, say my name's Perla, it's a pleasure. Now, most strippers use a stage name, and there's a few reasons why. First is, maybe their real name isn't so sexy. If you were born with a name like Bertha or Harriet, one your parents gave you when you were a baby and they had no idea you'd end up in this line of work, then I don't care how hot you are 'cause you're just not making as much money as a Crystal or a Jasmine. That's Marketing 101, and you don't have to go to business school to know that. But Perla's my real name, I was born with it and it's just fine for stripping and it's also good for the real world, so there's really no need to make a change.

Next thing is some girls change their name for privacy. Now, that's something I never did understand. True or fake, you're only giving out your first name, no last names, so how this gives you any more privacy I got no idea. And if someone from your neighborhood happens to walk into the club and sees you shaking your booty on the stage, then it doesn't matter what you call yourself 'cause they know exactly who you are. Some of the girls even use a few different names in case there's another dancer in the club with the same one. It happens all the time. You just can't have three Crystals tripping over each other on the way to the main stage—but that would be real funny to see, a bunch of strippers in their high heels falling over each other, money flying everywhere. So you always need a backup to avoid the confusion.

So, this man in the turban puts out his hand and shakes mine, tells me his name is Singh, and I don't know if that's his first name or his last, but I can tell by the way he says it, real quick and proud, that he's telling the truth. Not that I care, but it says a lot about a man when he tells you his real name. Anyway, I say Singh, it's your lucky day, 'cause this pretty girl is buying you a drink. And even though he's got dark skin, I see him blush a bit and he says thanks but I don't drink. So I laugh. You mean you never drink alcohol or you never drink *any* liquids? In which case you've got some issues you need to be dealing with, serious medical issues. And he smiles and says of course I drink—water, juice and tea.

I wave to Jade and she walks over to our table and says what can I do for you? I give Singh a peck on the cheek and say my turbaned friend here would like a bottle of water. And I shake my head in a way that says Jade, if he offers to pay, please don't play the hundred-dollar joke on this man, 'cause I don't think he can handle it. Jade knows exactly what my look means and she nods and says two waters and they're on the house.

Singh is awkward in the way that an older guy gets around a hot, young girl, and it's hard for him to make conversation. I see this a lot, so I try to loosen him up, ask him where he's from. Kashmir, which he says is a region in India or Pakistan, depends on who you ask. You married? He shakes his head, twists his lips and I get no response.

You got kids? Singh's face lights up and he says three, two girls and one boy, the oldest girl in medical school and the two younger in college and getting straight A's. His boy's on the squash team at Harvard, which even a girl like me knows is enough to make a father proud. Though God knows there's tons of assholes from Harvard and I've met my fair share, even fucked one once. (He was a lousy lay, not that he had a clue.) The younger girl's studying economics in London and has a boy-friend that Singh tells me is too ambitious by half. Too ambi-tious by half? I ask. And Singh smiles and says the boy just wants too much out of life, never satisfied, and a man like that scares us. He pauses, mumbles something I can't hear and bites his lower lip. Then he corrects himself. *Me*, that scares *me*.

That little slip-up with *us* and *me* makes me think there used to be a wife. Now, I want to ask him about her. Did she leave or did he leave or did she die? But there's certain things a girl like me doesn't ask. I got my boundaries and the men got their own boundaries and it's my job to know when to stop, and something about the man makes me back off. A tremble in the lip when I asked the question, vague answers, the mistake with *us*. I catch everything, you know, but something makes me think that she died and it was probably real recent and maybe unexpected, or maybe it was after a long illness and they saw it coming.

I feel some compassion for the man and I ask him if he wants to go to the VIP Room, maybe even the Champagne Room. I point over to the far wall and tell him I'll make him feel real good, even give him a couple of songs for free, which isn't something I normally do. Singh smiles, scratches his beard and says I already feel real good and I have you to thank, and he takes out a hundred and hands it to me, slow and careful, like that kids' game where you carry an egg on a spoon. And then he gets up, bows real respectful and walks right out of the club. Just like that, he's gone.

Now, I've never been to India or Pakistan, never even been out of the country except if you count Cuba, which I don't 'cause that's where I'm from, not where I went. So here I am, getting to meet a real live Sikh and have a nice conversation with the man. And in some weird way I get to travel around the world—virtual travel like in some sci-fi movie. Blink, there I go. Blink, I'm back. Blink, gone. Blink, back. Blink, blink.

SOME FOOL

After that first night in the Champagne Room, I don't see Julian for I'm guessing two months. And even though we had a real intense moment there, I try to forget him the second he leaves the club. That's how I do it. I shut it down fast, 'cause most of the time you never see the good ones again. The creeps, for some reason they're regulars. There's a smelly lawyer who comes around every damn night it seems, stained pants and bad breath with teeth all crooked, but he's got tons of money, so what can you do. But for a guy like Julian, you know it's just a little escape for him, gets him fixed up and sets him off on the road all clear and focused. It's like getting a B-12 shot, but even better.

Then one night Julian walks in a few minutes before my shift ends, around quarter of nine. I'm on the stage, tired from working all day, barely moving, and everything's looking foggy around me. I usually wear these grips on the soles of my platforms so I don't slip on the stage. But both of them fell off—they don't last too long—and now sure enough I'm sliding around like I'm on an ice rink. I'll get new grips tomorrow, but the best thing I can do for now is stay close to the pole, keep my balance, and that's what I do. But when I see Julian come in, it's like a current runs through me, takes me out of my funk and suddenly I got my bounce back. There's a big smile on my face and looks like he's got one too, though it's hard to tell 'cause of the lights and the smoke and the darkness.

He walks over to the edge of the stage and I put out my leg. He holds my leg, my lower leg, and he pulls out my garter and wraps a one-dollar bill around it. Now, I know it's a joke and he knows that I know it's a joke, which makes it even funnier. He snaps the garter real hard against my thigh, like a rubber band, and ooh, it hurts in a nice way. And that snap on my flesh makes my mind real sharp and alert.

I finish up on the stage 'cause it's time for the new girl, Shanna, to come up. Shanna's the flavor of the month, black girl, little tits, real ditzy like a blonde on a sitcom but she's not blonde, and I like her. She's impossible not to like. So I put my clothing back on, though there's not much of it really so it doesn't take long, and sit down next to Julian. I give him a playful peck on the cheek, my signature move, and he puts his hand down on my thigh real nice. Then I pick it up, his hand, and hold it to the light to see if he's got the indentation. All clear, I say, and he smiles 'cause he knows exactly what I'm doing. But part of me doesn't believe the guy, 'cause he's so cute and seems like he's got some money, so what's he doing without a ring and a wife?

The clock on the wall—that's the one they go by for figuring out the shifts—says five minutes before nine. And that means I got to be off the floor real quick or I'm paying for more time. That's how it works here. The girls pay a house fee to dance, seventy-five bucks a shift, and if you go over, you're coughing up more dough. Be right back, I say, don't go anywhere 'cause I'm just getting my stuff. I make a run for the changing room and Julian taps his seat like he's staying, then I say on second thought meet me in the lot out back, that's where I park my car.

Now, there's some girls who think twenty steps ahead, always playing things out in their mind and preparing for all sorts of different outcomes. But right now, I'm not that girl. And I'm not even thinking *one* step ahead. The only thing I'm thinking is that I'm just real happy to see Julian, I've been real lonely lately, and maybe we can go get a bite to eat and talk a bit, something normal. Since I started dancing, there were only a couple of times I met a customer outside the club. Real sweet guys, both of them, and that's the only reason I did it. Nothing much happened with either of them, just a nice meal and some good conversation—two people making a little connection for a couple of hours then going on with their lives. But you have to be real careful 'cause there's some serious freaks out there, and it's rare for me to get such a good sense about a guy that I'm open to taking a chance.

First girl I see when I get in the locker room is Lopez, the nasty bitch, and a new girl from Poland or Ukraine or someplace like that. I got a problem with those girls from Eastern Europe, all stuck-up and gold diggers, every one of them. I move real fast, get my civilian clothes on: jeans, T-shirt, flats. I've been wearing platforms with five-inch fuck-me heels, so there's no way I can do anything but flats outside the club. I brush my hair out, a bit of mouthwash, some eyeliner and I'm done.

In the back lot, which is where they make the girls park, I'm half expecting not to see Julian, but there he is leaning against his rental car, a white boxy thing that looks like something an undercover drives. And I'm thinking maybe he parked in back by mistake or maybe parked here on purpose 'cause he didn't want anyone seeing him out on the front lot, which is right on a main road and real visible. Or maybe he just pulled around quick while I was getting ready. Anyway, he's got his arm resting on the roof and he's got a funny look on his face. He pats the roof with his hand and says sexy wheels, right? Damn right, I say, hotter than a Porsche. I lean close, press up against him real tight and give him a hug.

Julian leans back against the car and he does this thing with my hair, wraps a strand around my ear, fixes me up. What did you have in mind? he asks. And I say, Julian, I'm a little hungry, haven't had a bite to eat all day, and maybe we can go find a place and have some food. He nods, looks at me likes he's thinking hard, like he doesn't know if he should say what he wants, something real risky, or if he should play it safe. Some food? Julian asks. Yup, and I wink, just some food and nothing else. Then he takes a big breath and lets it out, smiles, sort of embarrassed, and says I was thinking that maybe we could go back to my hotel, hang out and get some room service. He waits a sec to see my response, which is nothing. And I promise to be a gentleman, I swear.

I give him a look that says *you can't be serious.* Go back to your hotel room? He nods. And you'll be a gentleman? Nods again. A *perfect* gentleman? Yes, yes and yes, he says. Now, normally there's no way I'm going back to a hotel with a customer, 'cause you never know. I remember Jackson, she was young and didn't know shit. She did the same thing, went to a motel with a guy, and damned if anyone ever saw her again. Now, that doesn't mean she's dead. Maybe she's happy somewhere. Or maybe she just had enough, got some sense and gave up the grind, but who knows.

Anyway, going back with a guy isn't something I do, and I know damn well that if I get in that room we're doing a whole lot more than just having some food. But I start thinking about that night in the Champagne Room, when Julian made me come and was all tender after. And I'm thinking that I've been on a cold streak lately, haven't had sex in months and I'd like to feel close to a man again. I'm not picking up any creepy vibes from Julian, just a lot of sweetness and smarts and a guy who knows how a girl works. So I say sure, what the hell, but I'm texting my friend Carolina, telling her where I am and if there's any crazy shit from you then her and her boyfriend, Dino—he's Dominican and he's insane—they're coming over and you're a dead man. Got it? And Julian nods, sort of cocky, like he's not too afraid of Dino or anyone else, and he says I got it, there'll be no crazy shit from me. I pull out my phone and point the lens. Smile, I say, and he does. And I take a picture of him and send it to my friends just in case.

We take separate cars over to the hotel, that way I can get the hell out if I want. It's a real nice hotel, one of the new ones they built by the beach, with a pretty lobby and a trendy bar and lots of nice-looking people. He takes me up to the room, fourteenth floor. There's a big bed and a table to eat at and a view of the ocean, which is tough to see 'cause it's dark outside. I'm out of sorts, nervous, and so is he, which I can tell by the way he's biting at his lower lip and tugging on his ear. Feel free to take a shower if you want, he says, not that you need it, I mean, but you're more than welcome, and he points to the bathroom door.

Well, after dancing for eight hours, sweating and guys all over me, damn right I need a shower. So I go inside, throw my purse on the counter, my clothes on the floor and turn on the water. And it's a great shower with two heads and lots of pressure and all sorts of pretty-smelling gels, shampoos, soaps. I'm in heaven, 'cause I don't have this in my place. I just got a thin stream of water that's warm, not hot, and it's okay for cleaning, but it's not too good for relaxing. I'm loving the shower and the bathroom's filled with steam, and when I peer past the curtain I can barely see the mirror, it's so foggy. But then I feel a little draft, chilly, and first thing I think is Julian opened the door and he's coming in and I'm in trouble. But instead he calls out Perla, take all the time you need in there, no rush, you've had a long day. And I'm thinking, well, this is a guy who sure knows how to treat a girl right.

When I come out in my robe, a fluffy one from the back of the door, Julian's sitting on the bed with a menu. He looks up and smiles. Room service, and he waves the menu. I think I'm getting the burger, the sweet potato fries and a club soda, how about you? I bounce down on the other side of the bed and grab the menu from him. There's so many things on there and I wonder if a hotel can really make all this fancy stuff, Cajun salmon, tuna with Asian greens, or if it's better to play it safe. I'll have the same as you, but eighty-six the club soda, just a ginger ale with a slice of orange.

Julian gets up off the bed and says he's going to take a shower too, real quick. And I'm thinking wow, I can't believe he's leaving me alone in the room with all his stuff—his wallet, keys, phone—and that he either trusts me or he's not too sharp. When he closes the door and I hear the water, I walk over to the dresser and look at his wallet, at the pricey gold watch. I keep an eye on that bathroom door. I put the watch on my wrist, and it feels heavy, the gold. I admire it, move it back and forth so that the ceiling light shines on the blue face, wonder how much it costs, then take it off and place it back nice and soft on the dresser. Then I'm on to the wallet, which is some sort of hide, alligator or ostrich, I don't know, but it looks expensive and it's thick, so I'm thinking that it's filled with cash 'cause he's not the kind of guy to fill up a wallet with old receipts and discount cards. I start lifting up the edge to see who this Julian really is, how old, where he lives, what he does.

But before I open it up, I wonder again, is he a trusting guy or some fool? I take my hand off the wallet and climb back on the bed. I grab a magazine off the side table, check my nails that are all cracked and remind myself to get a manicure. I hear the water stop, a few seconds of soft sounds like he's drying off, then the knob turns. Is he a trusting guy or some fool? Either way, I'm happy I didn't look at the wallet, proud even, 'cause it's not just bad but maybe even a sin to look, a terrible sin, 'cause you can't punish a guy for believing that a girl's good. And you also can't punish him for not being smart enough to know maybe she isn't.

THE HUNTER'S SON

Julian Pravdin's room in the Siberian orphanage was small, and there he lived with two other boys, one named Petrov and the other Volokh. The three boys shared one mattress; nothing but a misshapen rectangular sack, it was filled with bedbugs and had weird bulges sticking out in the strangest places.

A small window faced south over the bay. There was a substantial hole in the glass that the boys stuffed with rags to repel the incomprehensible Siberian winter; when the weather turned warm, they removed the rags, welcoming the moist, cleansing salt air into their dreary chamber. There was the hot plate that the boys sometimes used to cook food. But because they rarely had food and electricity at the same time, it remained mostly unused on the top shelf, the cord dangling, swinging like a noose, taunting them, reminding them how little they really had. And then there was the toilet in the side yard, a small wooden hut with two holes cut in a rough plank and a shallow pit below, a frozen stew of feces and urine, a soiled rag hanging from a nail.

Julian was lithe, thin and twitchy like a borzoi, with bad vision and shiny black hair. His father, Ivan, was a legendary hunter who knew every foot of the Stanovoy Range, from Lake Baikal all the way to the Sea of Japan. In what one witness described as an epic and harrowing battle, Julian's father was killed by a tiger in Khabarovsk Krai. The local paper wrote that the wild cat was a mythical beast twenty feet from snout to tail and five feet high at the shoulders, and the villagers said that when the tiger was finished, there was nothing left of Ivan but a hand and a boot. Even the man's gun, the legend goes, had been devoured. After Ivan's death, Julian's mother suffered a clean and rapid break from her principled past. A local doctor called it a severe psychiatric episode; a shaman from her home village, an ancient man with a feathered hat and a painted face, called it the work of a malevolent spirit. Either way, the pain of her loss, of *Julian's* loss, forced her first into alcohol, then heroin and then, by financial and chemical necessity, into prostitution.

In a gray metal box with his other precious things, Julian kept a photo of his parents; there, in a thick forest, his father, strong and rugged, stood with his arm around the shoulders of a slender girl, pink cheeks and white skin, her eyes offering a hint of Asian narrowness that revealed her connection to the village near the Mongolian border. Her shy smile suggested unexpected happiness, as if she had stumbled upon some treasure that she knew must one day be returned to its rightful owner.

Like most of the orphans, Julian didn't receive visitors. But there was one time, it was the only time, when his mother came to visit. The head of the orphanage, Krepuchkin, knocked on the boys' door one morning before chores. The three of them stood at attention, lined up like soldiers. Krepuchkin was a repellent old man with hunched shoulders and a flaccid paunch that hung low over his belt. As though he could not distinguish one from the next, Krepuchkin scanned the boys' faces. He settled on Julian and pointed at the boy. Put on a clean shirt, he barked, your whore mother is going to be here in an hour. And with that, he slammed the door.

Petrov and Volokh turned to their friend. Julian's lower lip trembled. He darted to the cabinet and removed the only nice shirt he had, the one he kept clean and folded for the governor's annual visit or—his deepest hope—a visit from his mother. Julian unfolded the shirt and held it up to his shoulders. Satisfied that it still fit, he then dipped a comb in a cup of water and straightened out his unruly hair.

The three boys stood by the window quietly, looking down to the trash-covered courtyard below. In his damp hands, Julian held the photograph of his parents. Every few minutes he stared at it, as if to remind himself what his mother looked like. He held the photo up to Petrov and Volokh and pointed to his mother's image. They nodded, comforted him that they too were keeping a vigilant watch for her, that she would not slip by undetected.

At noon, the grub bell rang and howls filled the hallway, the howls of animals—the other orphans running to the dining hall for lunch, fighting for the front of the line so they would not have to settle for scraps. The three boys did not move, for they would not eat lunch on this day. Just then, a truck with a broken windshield lurched up the cratered road and stopped in front of the orphanage. The boys leaned forward, pressing their noses against the cold glass. Out of the driver's seat stepped a man, hunched and elderly, who hobbled to the back of the truck and removed a stack of wood. Disappointed, Julian dropped his head. To get a better view of the road, Volokh used his sleeve to clear a circle on the glass that was fogged from their breath. "Over there," Petrov yelled, pointing to a figure approaching on foot from the east.

Walking along the side of the road was what appeared to be an old woman. Despite the cold, she wore high heels and her ankles buckled in the pitted road. Over her head was a scarf—not the thick wool babushka favored by the women of this region, but a bright silk scarf, yellow and blue. As she approached to within fifty feet of the courtyard, the boys could see that she was not an old woman at all, but a young woman who walked with the tentative deliberation of the aged. Julian gasped. He tapped the window. "That's her," Julian whispered. "That's her." He handed the photo to Volokh and ran out of the room, down the stairs.

Volokh carefully returned the photograph to Julian's box, and he again assumed his position at the window—Petrov by his side. Below them, Julian burst through the front doors of the orphanage. He stood in the courtyard, wind whipping papers and aluminum cans across the surface. He bit the fingernails of his left hand and shielded his face from the wind with his right. The woman stood at the front gate and peered through the rusted metal. Before her stood her son. She choked on the phlegm in the back of her throat. Her lips moved. She removed a kerchief from her pocket and wiped the lipstick off her mouth. Julian smiled wearily. He waved.

Maria Pravdina stepped through the front gate. As if to nor-
malize the syncopation of her heart, she placed her right hand
over her chest and pushed down hard. Julian and his mother
now stood twenty feet apart but remained still, unsure of their
next steps, unaccustomed to each other. Maria began to cry, a
soft whimper. Slowly, she fell to her knees and bowed her head.
Julian ran to his mother, threw his arms around her neck, held
tight. He, too, cried—the tortured howl of a child abandoned,
reunited.

Maria wrapped her arms around the thin waist of her only
child. "Sorry, Julian, sorry," she whispered. "I'm sorry."

Julian struggled to breathe. "It's okay, Mom. I understand."

"I wanted to come, my love. It's just that they wouldn't let
me, that I lost the legal right once I signed the papers." Julian
nodded. "And then I had some trouble with the law, and
Krepuchkin said I was unfit."

Julian held tight and whispered into his mother's ear, "You're
not unfit, Mom."

Maria smiled, kissed her son on the forehead. "Thanks, love."

"But at least they let you visit today, which is a great thing.
How did it happen, Mom, that they let you come see me?"

Maria turned away from Julian. She watched as the old man
returned to his rusted truck and drove away. "I worked out
something with Krepuchkin. I figured out a way."

Julian reached for his mother's hand. "Come see my room,
Mom. Meet my friends, the ones I wrote you about. I told them
all about you. And Dad, too."

Maria and the three boys spent the day in the small bedroom.
They plugged in the hot plate and popped a fistful of corn that
Julian's mother brought with her; they sipped with delight from

the two cans of cola that she carried in her purse. For each boy, she'd brought a small toy. Julian got a model World War II tank. Petrov, a plastic dinosaur. And Volokh received an action figure—a Viking with a horned hat and a tiny plastic sword. Maria asked the boys about their lives: when they arose, what they ate, what they did for exercise, their favorite subjects. She asked if they had girlfriends, a question that made the boys giggle with shame. She told them to stay strong, be honest, pray to God. She said that if they did these things, they would be happy and free.

At five-thirty, the dinner bell rang, and the howls of the other children again echoed through the halls. Julian shuddered. A look of deep, unreachable pain crossed his face. He reached for his mother's hand. "It's time, my love, it's time," she said.

Julian shook his head. "Please, no," he begged. Petrov and Volokh stood back, uncomfortable.

Maria shook her head and approached Petrov. As she leaned down and kissed his cheek, the boy inhaled her sweet perfume. She ran her fingers through his hair. She then approached Volokh and gave the boy a kiss on the top of his head.

Maria turned and looked at her child. Trembling, Julian approached his mother. "Stay," he pleaded. "Or take me with you. I've got a bag all ready to go." Julian pointed to a canvas satchel on the floor. "We can sneak out. Krepuchkin can't catch us. We can outrun him. And you can take me home, Mom, take me to your home."

Julian's mother pursed her lips. "No, love, no. It can't be, at least right now. I'm sorry. I am not fit." She held her son's cheeks in her palms. She kissed him on the lips. She withdrew—and before Julian could reach for her, before he could anchor himself to his past, his future, she was gone.

The boys stared at the closed door. Then they darted to the window and looked out to the courtyard. A sickly fluorescent light flooded the rotted concrete. Below them, Julian's mother stepped out of the front door and looked about as if she were searching for something, someone. Just then, Krepuchkin emerged from behind the gate. He approached Julian's mother. She bowed her head and glowered at him, empty, detached. Krepuchkin extended his hand. At first, Maria did not move. She stared at the wrinkled hand. Krepuchkin barked something, and through the window Julian felt the force of the old man's rage, his sense of entitlement. Julian's mother reached out and held his hand, leading him to the far end of the courtyard, behind a twisted, dead oak.

Krepuchkin opened his long coat. He unbuckled his belt. His pants fell down around his ankles. With his right hand, he tapped Maria's shoulder, pushed her down to her knees. Julian's mother complied, and as she did so, she glanced up in Julian's direction—praying that her son would not witness her degradation.

"What . . . what . . ." Julian mumbled, gripping Petrov's arm. "What . . ." Volokh and Petrov turned away from the revolting scene below. "What!" Julian screamed. He turned to his friends. "What is happening? What is he doing? What is *she* doing?" He looked down to the courtyard and saw the movement of his mother's head, Krepuchkin grasping her shoulder tightly. Julian scanned the room. The hot plate—still warm from popping corn—sat on the shelf. He pushed his friends aside, grabbed the hot plate and reached for the door. But before he turned the knob, he stopped, lifted the satchel from the floor and threw it over his shoulder. "Leave me be," he directed as he fled the room.

Volokh and Petrov returned to the window. They watched anxiously as Julian emerged. They watched him cross the courtyard, the hot plate under his right arm. He approached the lifeless oak—slow, steady, powerful like a wild cat. He peered around its gnarled trunk. He approached Krepuchkin from the side and raised the hot plate. He eyed Krepuchkin's temple. And the moment before he split the old man's skull, Julian's mother looked up to her son—a tear in her eye. But there, amid the horror, a sly smile crossed her face, a recognition that her dead husband's predatory stealth, his primal rage, his willingness to kill, all lived on in their little boy.

Krepuchkin lay on the ground, motionless, dead. Gray matter, bloody pulp spackled the ground. Julian's mother stood. She wiped her mouth with her sleeve. She rubbed her sore knees, and she again placed her palms on her son's cheeks. She nodded and smiled. Julian smiled in return, filled with the pride of a child having pleased his parent. He looked up to the window and waved good-bye to his friends. And then he bowed at the waist, dramatic and proud, like Yevgeny Svetlanov after the final note of *Die Walküre*.

Julian and his mother skipped through the front gate. They looked right, then left. They hesitated for a moment, wondered which way to go, then turned east toward the coastal road, toward the bay, the young boy—*the hunter's son*—guiding his mother with acute instinct through the magical Siberian night.

GIRL, YOU SEE
THINGS CLEAR

It gets to be a regular thing with Julian. He comes down every month or two, doesn't give me notice, just shows up at the club five minutes before nine. He sits down near the stage, gives me that nice smile of his. Sometimes he comes in a little early and there's time to go over and give him a dance, pretend he's just another customer, which is something that gives me a little thrill. Pretending I don't know him.

One night, he shows up when I'm dancing for another guy, a cute guy who comes by now and then. And I don't get close to getting off with this guy like I did with Julian in the Champagne Room that night, but this one sort of turns me on, nice-smelling, makes me laugh and always gives me a big tip. This one doesn't even pretend he's not married, wears a thick gold wedding band and there's nothing wrong with that. Fact the opposite, I say. He's right out there with it, tells me that his wife knows he comes to the club and she doesn't mind, as long as he comes home to her at the end of the night. He says it even turns her on, so much that one night I had this glitter body spray all over my tits and he said rub those babies on my face, get that glitter all over 'cause it's gonna drive my wife wild. So that's what I did, glitter all over his lips and cheeks, and you should have seen him when the strobes went off and his face lit up like a disco ball!

So Julian comes in and sees me dancing with the glitter guy and damned if I don't see a look on Julian's face like he just caught his wife screwing around. Now, I'm not his woman and he's not my man and there's no way I can tell after all these months if he's single or married. There's no way he's got any say in how I spend my time, make my money.

After I finish up with glitter guy, I put my clothes back on and walk over to Julian. He's got a bottle of water and he's squeezing it so hard that it's crushed and almost falling over, it's so crooked. I say good to see you, baby, but he won't even look up, just bites at a cuticle like he's real stressed. So I put my hand on his thigh and try to give him a peck on the check, my playful little kiss, but he pulls away. And I'm thinking, well, *here's* a side of this man I haven't seen before.

What's wrong, baby? Nothing from him but silence. So I ask again, what's wrong, baby? Still nothing. And now I'm getting a little pissed 'cause what the hell have I done wrong? I'm the one who has no idea when he comes, when he goes, just follow him back to the hotel after my shift and order burgers and watch TV and fuck him, which is real nice, and then I leave first thing in the morning. There's no way to call him, don't even have his number, don't know his last name and I never did open the wallet, never asked for a single penny. I even offered to buy the burgers once, which I thought was real nice, but he wouldn't hear of it.

He finishes the water, which isn't easy 'cause there's lots caught in the bottom of the bottle, which is all crushed, so he has to keep turning it back and forth, spinning it around to get all the water out. Nothing's wrong, and he holds my hand, says let's head back to the hotel. Now, truth is I got a date, not a guy I met at the club, but a civilian. But I'd rather be with Julian, which tells you a lot about me and my shitty decisions, so I text the guy and tell him I got cramps and can't make it. After I press the send button, I say to myself *cramps?* What are you doing telling a man you got cramps? It's no wonder I don't have a guy, I guess. But sometimes I do stuff without thinking things through, which a guy I used to love, the only one really—that's what he told me is my best trait. Right after my ass.

Now, we're back at the hotel and Julian's on the bed. He's in a better mood for some reason, maybe 'cause he's got me to himself, and he's flipping through the menu like he's never seen it before, like he doesn't order the same damn thing every time. Let me guess, I ask, you having the burger and a club soda? And he looks at me and smiles and says matter of fact, I'm having the sesame crusted tuna with bok choy. I smile and say what the hell is bok choy? He pulls me close and says leafy greens, I think it's some sort of Asian leafy green, you getting the burger? And I grab the menu, take a look and say if you're gonna be radical tonight, then so am I. So get me the Cajun salmon with wild rice. And a ginger ale, with a sweet cherry this time.

After he calls room service, I rest my head on his chest and he puts his arm around my shoulder, strokes my face with his left hand. And I'm real happy, peaceful, 'cause I'm in a nice room with a guy who isn't mean to me and I'm about to have Cajun salmon, and I never did have that before. And I look up at his hand as it passes my face, and from underneath I see his ring finger and right there on the bottom, on that little pad of flesh on the bottom, I see what looks like a shadow, a line, an indentation. And I gasp, not loud enough that he gets scared, but loud enough that he squeezes me tight, like he senses I'm off.

I don't know why I gasp 'cause look where I met him. Most guys in the club they're either married or no way anyone's ever gonna marry them. And more than that, Julian never promised me anything and I never promised him anything, so why I get a reaction I don't know. I'm a realistic girl, that's what my dad always told me. Girl, you see things clear, real clear, he used to tell me.

But still, I feel a little something when I see that line on his finger or what looks like a line on his finger. His hand's a few inches from my eyes and I squint 'cause of what I think I see. And, yup, it's still there, a straight thin line, sort of gray, sort of red. So I reach out for his hand, turn it just a little so it hits the light, and when it hits the light, the line goes away, just goes from barely nothing to nothing at all. And I wonder if I'm seeing things, if my mind's playing tricks on me. And I wonder if I should keep my mouth shut, not pry. Just like the wallet, leave it alone. But then this urge comes up, like a kid grabbing for a piece of candy or something shiny, and I can't control myself, and I say Julian, are you, tell me straight up, 'cause I'm cool with it either way, are you . . .

And he looks at me real nervous, a little cross-eyed, and it occurs to me that there's something so pure about him, so much pain maybe, that I don't have the courage to ask the question. I bring his hand back down to my shoulder, close my eyes real tight, and ask him, baby, are you gonna get dessert, 'cause if so, if you're gonna get something sweet, then I want the chocolate pie. Whipped cream on top.

THE SOFT PURR

There was the death: it occurred at home, in the cold room that Julian and his mother shared in a dilapidated boarding-house. During the six transcendent months after their escape from the orphanage, after the destruction of Krepuchkin, Maria worked at a fish market on the wharf. She walked right up to one of her old customers—a humble, sad man who ran the shop—and requested a job. The man looked to the back of the shop. He watched his obese wife toss fish heads into a bucket, a tuft of wiry hair sprouting from her chin. Understanding Maria's implicit threat, he shrugged his shoulders, handed Maria a soiled smock and quietly returned to his work.

Maria used to joke that she took to this job the way a fish took to water. She discovered great satisfaction in preparing the fish for sale: whitefish, salmon, perch, grayling, lenok, muksun, dogfish. She dressed them with the skilled hand of a surgeon, laying the fish out on beds of ice, decorating them with local

flowers—yellow poppies, spring beauties, purple larkspurs—
bringing a dash of color and sweet smells to the dismal market.

To evade any authorities who might be searching for him,
Julian enrolled at school under the assumed name Ivan
Bezdomny, an inside joke from his mother's favorite novel by
Bulgakov. Bezdomny, the principal laughed when Julian showed
up the first day. *Homeless.*

During those six months, Julian and Maria would eat breakfast together every morning—usually dried fruit and cereal and
a cup of black tea. Maria would walk her son to school in the
morning, drop him off at the front gates, and place her hands on
the boy's cheeks—a ritual that memorialized their connection
to each other but also evoked in them the terror of their separation. At the end of the day, Maria would walk from the slimy
wharf back to the school in the center of town and pick up Julian.
Each day, she brought a small treat for him: a piece of candy, a
marble, a colorful string. Julian, with a hunter's eye, would wait
outside the school, scanning the street, the distant wharf, the
sea—nervously awaiting his mother's arrival.

Her body ravaged by disease from years of shared needles
and degrading sex, Maria's decline was fast and precipitous.
First, there was a rapid wasting away of the flesh, as if the sub-
cutaneous fat had been heated, liquefied, absorbed into her core.
And then came the purple blotch across her chest—deep and
royal like the ribbon on a general's uniform. Finally, there was
the coughing, so wet and so rough, with each spasm expelling a
fine mist of blood.

Julian sat by his mother's bed. He held her hand. He cried
until he realized that his pain, the *expression* of his pain, was
torturing his mother, destroying what little remained of her

fractured soul. He composed himself. He told his mother stories about Petrov and Volokh, how they had once stolen Krepuchkin's watch and sold it in the market. Maria smiled. Julian told his mother that he was proud of her, that he had no regrets. He told her that she should have no regrets, that a life isn't defined by mistakes, but by whether you recognize them, own them, fix them.

"You fixed everything, Mom," he said. "Everything."

Maria squeezed Julian's hand. "I love you."

"No, Mom, no," he pleaded, struggling to breathe.

Maria held her index finger to her lips. "Two things you must do, son. Promise me." Julian nodded. "First, you must go to Frankmann, the old Jew, the one who trades pelts. You know of him, with the office on the wharf. Right across from the butcher. He will make sure you get to the States. I spoke to him and everything is taken care of. He owes me."

Julian swallowed. "The *United* States?"

"Yes, that is where I want you to be, to start fresh, away from the stigma. Away from *my* stigma."

"Okay."

"And second, you must promise me this. . . ." Julian's mother paused.

"Anything, Mom."

"You must promise me, Julian, that you will submit to no man. You are your father's son. Sometimes predator, sometimes protector. Only you will know when to be one and when the other." Julian recalled the fatal blow he delivered to Krepuchkin's skull. He shuddered.

Maria motioned her son to come close. She extended her lips, cracked and dry. Julian kissed his mother, smelled her bitter, infected breath. He pressed his ear to her chest and listened. There was a rattle from deep within, mechanical and slow. Then the rattle stopped, replaced by something that sounded like the soft purr of a sleeping cat, and finally, a rush of air through his mother's lungs, out her mouth, her nose—a hissing through her eyes, her ears, the pores of her skin.

The room was quiet. Julian looked around. He felt tiny, impotent, untethered. The immensity of his solitude threatened to overwhelm him. He again struggled to breathe. I submit to no man, he said. He reached for his mother's hand. I submit to no man, I submit to no man. He repeated the mantra one hundred times, his resolve growing with each recitation. I submit to no man—a primal, rageful howl that caused the pedestrians on the street below to stop in their tracks and gaze in terror at the building above.

PURGATORY

Julian's down for work again and comes by the club. I'm real perceptive, always picking up on the smallest things, and I can tell as soon as he sits down that there's something wrong with him, something that's different than before. He's still put together all nice, but the man looks tired, frail, his shoulders slumped a bit. So I sit down on his lap, rub his thigh, wrap my arm around his neck, give him a peck on the cheek. What's wrong, baby, you looking exhausted. And I'm not just saying it to make conversation, 'cause I really am concerned about the man. Julian looks at me, not straight on but out of the side of his eye, and then lowers his head and looks at the floor.

Now, I've been doing this long enough to know when a man's under pressure, when he's all out of answers, and that's when a man usually shuts down, goes deep inside and keeps the world at a safe distance. So I reach for his hand, his left hand, and squeeze real tight. And when I squeeze, he winces just a little bit, not 'cause I hurt him, but 'cause I'm doing just the opposite. A man feeling this bad about himself can't stand any kindness, especially from a woman.

But when I squeeze tight, I feel something cold in my palm, something thin and hard, and my heart pounds real fast. I open my hand and put my thumb and index finger around his wrist and lift it up to the strobe light. And there it is, blinking in the light, on-off, on-off, on-off, a platinum wedding band, clear and bright like a priest's collar.

I lean back and look at his face, focus from a different distance, like I'm trying to figure out if I made a mistake. Maybe I sat down on the wrong guy's lap, but sure enough it's Julian. He shrugs his shoulders, and I'm not sure if the shrug means *you caught me* or if it means *damned if I know how this got here.* I open my mouth, not sure what I'm gonna say or how I'm gonna say it, either real mad or real hurt or real professional. His hand is around my ribs, he's holding real tight, and as I open my mouth to speak, he releases—and something about the way he lets go tells me that a break just occurred, that we're not connected anymore. And I can feel myself floating away, up toward the ceiling like a balloon. And I swear I can see his eyes moving up too, following my flight.

The first word is about to come out of my mouth. I'm deciding between *I* and *you*, and I think I'm gonna go with *I* 'cause in some way this is more about me than it is about him. But just before the first word comes out, Schultz gets on the speaker and says in his deep voice that always makes me laugh 'cause he sounds like a game-show host, he says Perla to the main stage, let's welcome the fabulous Perla to the main stage. That's my cue to stop what I'm doing and get up and dance.

Got to go, I say to Julian. I'm done in fifteen minutes and then we can talk about this. And I grab his wrist and hold his hand up to the light again and the ring is glowing and flickering in the strobe. Julian nods but still doesn't say a damn thing, and the fact that he can't seem to speak gets me angry. Fifteen minutes, I say, then the set's over and we can go to the Champagne Room and talk. I push down on his shoulder and jump up off his lap.

I climb the three steps to the main stage, which is nothing more than an elevated platform twenty feet long and maybe four feet wide with two poles and some little white Christmas lights around the base. I pull a few antibacterial wipes from a box on the corner of the stage and clean off the poles, 'cause God knows what kind of nasty stuff is on them. The times when I go on after Lopez, I wipe down the poles twice just to be sure 'cause that is one skanky bitch. I take a deep breath, which is what I do for anxiety and I say to myself here we go again. I take off my top and toss it to the floor, put my hand up high on the pole, wrap my lower leg around it and look over to Julian. But he's not there. He's gone.

I wait for the music to start. I stand on the stage in silence, just the chatter of the locals at the bar and the girls flirting with different accents. South American Spanish, Russian, Gulf Coast. I'm cold up on the stage. A cloud of cigarette smoke drifts my way, a storm cloud that's dark and thick, carried by a blast from the AC. As it reaches my face, I close my mouth and hold my breath, 'cause to inhale the smoke would mean to inhale this place, this life, to bring it deep inside me, mix it with my blood and my organs. To breathe in this smoke would be suicide. Please, please start the music, I say to myself, to Schultz, as the cloud consumes my head, hovers for a few seconds, surrounds me, and then, caught again by a draft, moves past me, past my face, and toward the bathrooms.

I stand on the stage, exposed and naked and staring at the empty seat. I curse myself for being such a fool, and all along I thought *he* was the fool. Schultz comes on the speaker and he says one minute, Perla, there's trouble with the music, one minute. So here I stand, waiting for the music, waiting for my life to start again, frozen, caught in this purgatory, which is something I learned about in Catholic school. And sometimes I feel like it's happening to me right here on earth, right here in this club. I'm stuck on this stage, right in the middle between heaven and hell.

And just then, when my mind's about to take me to a dangerous place, the music starts. Boom, boom. Then a pause. Boom, boom. Another pause. And I'm back.

AREPAS AND
SWEET CORN

After I finish my shift, there's two ways I can go. I can pack up my stuff, go home and have dinner with my mom, which is either gonna be chicken with rice and beans or shrimp with rice and beans. My mom's name is Carla, and she's forty-two, had me when she was real young and she's just about the hottest mom a girl could ever have. She's a great cook and sometimes for dinner she'll make up some sweet plantains, which I love, hot and steamy and all gooey with a crust of caramelized brown sugar on top. The other thing I can do is go to the hotel and see Julian, get the story behind that ring. But I'm so damn mad, so hurt even though I've got no right to be, that I decide I'm gonna make a good decision for once in my life and go home, have a quiet night and see my mom.

I stand in the parking lot and there's a tiny space maybe six inches wide where I can stand up on the curb, up on my tiptoes, and from there I can see a clip of 95 through the buildings. It's pouring rain and I get up on the curb, my purse flat against the top of my head, and I can see the freeway and the red lights glowing in the mist, the cars all backed up. There's the flicker of emergency lights bouncing off the green sign, and the traffic looks like hell getting back to Miami.

So I'm thinking I should stick to the surface streets, make my way south and west, avoid the bad neighborhoods, which in this part of the state can pop up out of nowhere. One second you can be in a real safe area, lots of middle-class homes, cute shops, a bicycle just lying on a lawn and no one's even thinking about stealing it, nothing to worry about. And then the next minute, maybe you make a wrong turn or you're daydreaming about being loved or famous and you don't see the red flags, some graffiti on a wall, a woman on the corner smoking a cigarette, she's wearing a short skirt and a pink halter top, holding her fingernails up to the light, a pack of kids on bicycles looking over their shoulders, puffy jackets even though it's hot as hell outside. So you make that wrong turn, and you're only a quarter of a mile from the nice place, but you make the wrong turn and there you are and damned if you can't remember how to get out. Was it left, right, left? Or left, left, right?

You panic and start to sweat, and you can feel it under your arms, the dampness, the fear. It happens to me like that sometimes, and not just in a car driving around. Sometimes I'm daydreaming and I'm not paying attention to what's really happening, I'm somewhere else, and even though it feels good for a few minutes, the fantasy, it turns out to be just the opposite. It turns out that I'm not escaping at all, that I just got myself into deep trouble, and I can feel the sweat coming on, my body's way of telling me that I made a mistake and I'm going, again, in the wrong direction.

I look at my watch and it's nine-thirty and I figure it's gonna take me a good hour, hour and a half to get home in this weather. I think about Julian and the ring on his finger and that sick feeling in my stomach when I saw it. I think about the anger I felt when I got up on that stage, looked down and found myself staring at an empty seat. I jump inside my car and close the door, toss my purse on the passenger seat and gather myself, the rain coming down hard on the metal roof—plunk, plunk, plunk—and it feels nice and cozy.

The sound of the rain on the roof makes me think about my father, the camping trip when I was a little girl. Me and him in a canvas tent on a beach near Nibujón, the east end of the island, and the rain crashing down just like now, with me and him all safe inside, eating pastries and listening to salsa on the radio. Tito Puente, Celia Cruz, Willie Colón.

I ache for him and try not to think of his death, try not to think about how things might have been different for all of us. Him, my mom, me. How so many lives can change 'cause of just a few seconds, maybe a fraction of a second, an inch or two, even a small change in speed or direction. Everything has to come together perfect to end a life before it's time.

There's my father, Rafael was his name, standing on the beach. He's a few feet from our tent, casting a line into the water, a white straw hat on his head and his thin body twisting in the hot wind, proud and determined to catch our dinner. And there's me, his little girl. And I'm watching him in awe, wondering what will end up on his line, maybe a wahoo or a snapper, which is delicious. And there he is now, the pole bending, something big and strong on the hook, and my father digs his bare feet into the sand, pulls hard and arches his back.

I see him struggling to keep his balance, so I run over, put my hands around his waist and hold tight. I try to pull him away from the water, to stop the fish from pulling him into the surf, away from me. And the two of us are sliding in the soft sand, sliding toward the edge of the water, then catching ourselves and back a few feet toward the dunes. Every time we take a step toward the water I feel a panic in my chest, like I'm about to lose everything. Every step back, away from the surf and whatever creature is pulling us into the dark blue, every step away brings me comfort and slows the thump of my heart.

Hold on, baby, my father yells, and his hands grip the pole so tight I can see the veins popping out through his smooth, tan skin, and I hold on tight as I can, so tight around his waist that he gasps for air and says not so tight, baby, not so tight. But I don't listen to him and don't let up a bit. He's pulling in the line a few inches at a time, but the pole is bent so much, like a half circle, that I can't imagine what in God's name he's got on the other end of the line, maybe some sea monster or a whale. And we're making our way, half step by half step, up toward the dune while my father works the reel. And then my heel hits something hard, a burned log in the sand. I trip and fall backward and, with my hands around my father, I pull him down to the beach with me—and before we hit the ground the pole breaks in half, shatters right in the center from the force of our fall, and the top half flies out into the sea and disappears into the water, attached to the sea monster. The bottom half stays in my father's hands, a piece of broken wood attached to nothing.

I'm afraid my father will be angry with me, that he will blame me for the fall and the broken rod and the lost dinner, and the dampness under my arms gets worse. But instead, my father puts his arms around me and gives me a kiss on the forehead.

You all right, Perlita, you all right? And I smile and tell him I'm fine and sorry for falling. Don't worry, baby, don't worry. And then he lifts me up off the ground, brushes the sand off my bony shoulders, holds my hand and we walk down the old beach road, where there's a few goats and men selling trinkets and necklaces. We find a little stand and we get grilled meat and arepas and sweet corn and take it back to the beach and talk about the past and the future, and we watch the sun set, amber and purple and thin lines of yellow.

I'm in the car, driving in the Florida rain, but I'm really on the beach with my father and tears are running down my cheeks. I'm not aware of the road around me and I almost run through a red light, and an old woman with powder-blue hair in a big old Cadillac, there's lots of them down here, the Cadillacs *and* the old women with blue hair, well, she gives me the finger and points to her temple like she's telling me to use my brain, and she mouths the word *stupid*.

It's that woman calling me stupid that snaps me out of my state, bittersweet thoughts of my dad, and it's only then I realize that I'm not driving toward Miami. Turns out I'm driving *east*, toward Julian's hotel. I'm going past the dead strip malls, leftovers from a crazy time when it seemed that anyone who wanted to put up a building could do it. There were some girls from the club, two from Latvia and one from Baton Rouge, who got together, started a company called Brass Pole Development— yup, that's the real name—pooled their money and built a little apartment building in Pompano Beach with four units and a wading pool in the back. They rented it out quick and figured they were real smart. But then the market crashed, the tenants didn't pay and the girls couldn't make the mortgage payments.

And that was that. So much for being legit, one of them said after the bank took the property, we're sticking to the pole from now on.

I see Julian's hotel in the distance, all lit up, and figure I ended up here for a reason, that probably something guided me here. So I keep driving and pull into the hotel parking lot. The rain lets up and I grip the steering wheel. I'm breathing hard and it's hot and muggy in the car and the windows fog up so no one can see in and I can't see out. I open the window and look out to the hotel. There's a few people out front, gazing up at the dark sky, holding their palms out and trying to see if it's still raining. I'm still angry about that ring, still confused. So I get out of the car and take a deep breath, a *courage breath* is what my father used to call it, and walk toward the hotel entrance, all determined like I'm one of those baseball managers stomping across the field to yell at the ump.

Julian stays in the same room every time. He told me once that he likes 1404 'cause it's high up and faces east, toward the ocean, and it's not near the elevator or the noisy ice machine. And also the television is at a perfect angle to the bed and the shower has good water pressure, all of which is true. I strut through the lobby all confident, get in the elevator and press 14. But just as the doors are about to close, a man waves his arm between them and they stop real fast, shudder like they've just got punched, then open right up. In walk two men, and the second I see them I know all I need to know—'cause that's how I am, super-observant and good at sizing up a man in a matter of seconds.

The doors close and I smell the booze, bitter and sick and seeping out of their skin, the same way you can smell when someone's got the flu, and I figure that's God's way of protecting us, our senses telling us when danger and disease are close. The first guy in, the one with the goatee and the yellow tennis sweater draped over his shoulders, he says what floor you going to, like he's being a gentleman and trying to help. I point to the panel, to 14, which is all lit up and I say already got it, thanks. And then the second guy, he's got a sunburned face, a little purple on the tip of his nose, he's wearing chinos and a golf shirt and his phone is clipped to his belt. And this is just not a good look. This guy says to me, get this, he says wanna come over to our room—we got a suite—and watch some porn? He starts laughing as soon as he says it and looks over to his friend all cocky like he's got some game.

Now, I'm a little girl, thin and no more than five four in flats, but I *am* a stripper, and a Latin stripper, and I don't take shit from anyone, especially a couple of middle-aged white guys with golf shirts and khaki pants. So I'm watching the floor panel blink in red numbers—four, five, six—and I step forward between the two guys and I put my finger in the chest of the one who suggested the porn and say . . . I pause to make it more dramatic . . . I say let's do it, boys. How about I take the both of you back to the room and fuck you 'til you can't breathe. Sound like a plan, Romeo?

Well, this is where you separate the men from the boys, and trust me, there aren't many men when a girl like me does something like this. And sure enough, this boy gasps, turns redder than he was before, which I didn't think was possible, and staggers against the elevator wall. He clutches his belt-phone with one hand and his chest with the other and says uh, uh, uh. Ten, eleven, twelve, fourteen. There's no thirteen 'cause of bad luck. The doors open and the two guys part, open up a path for me and I step out of the cab. I walk down the hall toward Julian's room and I can feel their eyes pointed like lasers on my ass.

I stand in front of the room and press my ear against the door, which is cold, and I can hear noises inside. It's Julian's voice on the phone. Yes, a hamburger, please, medium well, with sweet potato fries and a club soda. There's also the sound of a TV, sports I think. Here goes, and I raise my hand and knock all forceful, one time, two times, until I hear the TV go quiet and the squeak of the bed as Julian gets up and the slide of that stupid dangling chain out of the slot. And I wonder how it is that little chain is ever gonna stop someone from kicking the door in. I take a step back, fix my hair and straighten up my shoulders, try to get every inch out of my small frame.

The door opens and Julian stands there in his bathrobe, and he's got a look on his face that says *how the hell did the food get here so fast, 'cause I just hung up the phone*. But when he sees it's me and not room service, he grabs his left hand with his right, covers it up. He looks at me, shrugs his shoulders and says you hungry? I just ordered dinner. He steps to the side and opens the door wide. I walk inside and toss my purse on the dresser right next to his wallet and his gold watch and I say I'm gonna take a shower. And I'll take a burger and those sweet potato fries I love and some ginger ale. Orange slice? he asks, and I nod yes.

The shower has two heads and they're adjustable, so I aim one at my face and one at my chest and it feels so good, not too hard, not too misty, but just right. I'm scrubbing up with the nice body gel they have, seaweed and cucumber it says on the bottle, which seems like a strange combination but turns out that it smells great, and I'm wondering what I'm gonna say to Julian when I get out.

My first thought, option number one, is that I tell him to go to hell, tell him that even though I'm a stripper I have certain rights—rights to be treated with honesty and kindness. And that this isn't working for me. Maybe I say don't you ever come by the club again, 'cause I'd rather dance for some married guy in a bad golf shirt with a ring on his finger, someone who doesn't say anything sweet to me, 'cause at least *that's* an honest man.

My second thought is to not even bring it up, just pretend I didn't see a thing. Turn this back into what it should've been all along, and that's a commercial transaction. Go back to where I dance and he gives me money. Dance, money. Dance, money. No more sleepovers and room service and hot showers, no more free dances or screwing him in the hotel. Dance, money. And leave it at that.

I dry off and put the robe on, wrap a towel around my wet hair so it looks like a turban, white and high like the Sikh from the club. There's a little sign on the sink that tells me I can save the planet by reusing the towel. I wonder why anyone *wouldn't* want a new towel and I figure they really don't care too much about the planet but they're just trying to save some money on cleaning— so I toss the towel on the floor and step out of the bathroom. And I don't feel guilty about it at all, 'cause I got a footprint, a *carbon* footprint as small as a mouse, and I get to have a little fun some- times without worrying about the whole fucking world.

When I come out, Julian's sitting on a chair at the desk and he's reading a book. I can't see what it is, but it's thin and has a soft cover. He closes the book and looks up to me, sort of sad, and he raises his left hand high above his head, still, like he's a real polite kid trying to get the teacher's attention. And he says I guess you want to talk about this, and he points to the ring.

I sit down on the corner of the bed, cross my legs and adjust my towel-turban. Yes, I say, I'd like to know, 'cause I'm a bit confused. Julian takes the ring off his finger and holds it up to the light, rotates it, examines it. He looks at me, but he's having trouble with eye contact, keeps looking down every time our eyes catch. He shrugs his shoulders and places the ring on the desk, on its edge. Then he holds the top with his left index finger and flicks it hard with his right. It spins tight like a top, stays in a small area of the desk, about the size of a dime, and holds its speed right there for a few seconds, maybe five. Then as it starts to lose speed, the spin isn't as tight and the ring covers a bigger area, moving side to side, bigger and bigger, the size of a nickel, then a quarter, going slower and slower, no longer standing up straight, wobbling, wobbling, slower and slower until it falls to the desk. Then there's one last little jump before it goes flat and still. We watch the ring, all quiet on the wood.

I reach for Julian's knee. He pulls back just a little, a flinch like he's afraid. And just then, at that moment—perfect timing—there's a knock on the door and it's room service. I turn away from the ring. I'm thinking here comes our food, and I'm glad for the distraction, relieved that right now I get to stay ignorant. I'm hungry and looking forward to my sweet potato fries and I hope they didn't forget to put an orange slice in my soda. Julian jumps up off the chair and says I'll get the door, you try to find something to watch. And as I'm pointing the remote at the TV, waving it back and forth like a flyswatter 'cause it doesn't seem to be working, it occurs to me that there's option number three, which hadn't even crossed my mind.

Option number three is where things just stay the same.

MANNA

There Frankmann sat, at the age of eighty, staring out his office window to the busy wharf below. He scratched his short beard and wondered, despite his advanced age, what role he might one day play in the world. Such thoughts—fantasies of future greatness—had filled his mind during adolescence, when he wondered if he would be an officer, a Talmudic scholar, a sculptor, a hunter of tigers. But during the intervening decades of his great commercial success, he no longer considered his role in the world, choosing instead to focus on the daily ledger, the profit and loss, the measure of his remarkable ability to make money in every possible circumstance—and it was only on his eightieth birthday, when Frankmann looked at himself in the mirror and saw for the first time an ancient man, that he realized he'd not yet made his mark.

Frankmann peered through the window, searching for the tuna boat that was scheduled to return from the Sea of Japan.

He looked at his watch and noted that the boat was three hours late. As the vessel's *de facto* owner, he was concerned. He worried about the safety of the crew. Frankmann knew their wives and children, and he cared for them—not in an apparent manner, but from a safe, some would say unreachable, distance. And, as he was a man guided by economic rationality, he also worried about his investment: the boat, the gear, the fuel, the fish.

He turned his attention to the far end of the wharf. There, the fat woman Garlova stood in front of a makeshift bar. To her side was a green jug of potato vodka and a wooden barrel filled with fermented horse milk that Frankmann had purchased from a slow Mongolian on advantageous terms. Sailors, fishermen, construction workers, young men from the navy, even a poacher who'd come into town to sell muskrat pelts, lined up with rubles in their hands. Frankmann wondered how much he would make selling booze that day—and how much Garlova would steal from him. He didn't mind if she stole just a little, a few rubles here and there; that was part of the unspoken pact between master and servant in this part of the world. A little theft made things work smoothly, greased the gears of commerce. But with too much, things broke down.

Frankmann's eyes moved to a store on the other side of the bar—the butcher Korsikov who sold fresh meats and poultry and was rumored to have taken recently to gambling, drinking and other forms of dissipation. For the past year, Korsikov had been habitually late with his rent, and Frankmann began to worry that the butcher might default.

The old Jew watched as the butcher and his wife, a devout woman, carried boxes out of the shop; he wondered what they could be doing. After unloading a flank of venison onto the back of a flatbed truck, the butcher looked up to Frankmann's office window. Fearing detection, Frankmann quickly ducked to the side and, unsure if the butcher had seen him, peered out from behind the dusty velvet drapes. Frankmann remained still.

The butcher turned back to his wife and beckoned her to hurry. With a rusted cleaver in her hand, she exited the shop. She locked the front door, turned the knob to ensure that it was secure, and then kneeled before the doormat, placing the cleaver on the ground by her side. She appeared to pray, bobbing her head, making vague motions with her hands and finally clasping them together. Her husband watched respectfully as she removed from her bloody apron an envelope and placed it and a ring of keys under the mat. She lifted the cleaver off the ground and joined her husband, who placed his arm around her shoulders. They stared at the shop, rubbed their eyes as if they had just awoken from a dream. After a few moments, they got in the truck, took one final look around the wharf and drove away— bronze smoke billowing from the tailpipe.

Frankmann called out to his assistant, a young woman from town who had been working by his side for three years. Kira was her name, and she was such a consummate professional that, despite her youth and beauty, she seemed to be wrapped in a protective, asexualizing veneer that demanded respect and eliminated any absurd desire on Frankmann's part. "Kira," he said, "I think the butchers have abandoned us. How much do they owe?"

Kira opened the rent ledger and ran her finger down the page. "Five hundred rubles."

Frankmann stepped out from behind the drapes. "And the deposit we have?"

Kira flipped to another page. "Fifty."

"So we're out four-fifty?"

"That's right, sir. Do you want me to try to collect? I can file the papers."

Frankmann turned his attention to the sea. In the distance, his tuna boat—listing slightly to the starboard side—puttered in from the south. He exhaled in relief. "No, Kira, they're poor and in trouble. There's no sense."

Kira nodded. With a marker, she drew a thick line through the butcher's account. "I will try to find someone else," she said.

"Good, but this time, we need a bigger deposit. And no more butchers."

Kira returned to the ledger, calculating the day's receipts from all of Frankmann's enterprises: the liquor, the tuna boat, the mechanic shop, the wharf rentals, the pelt trade, the boardinghouse. She then subtracted the day's disbursements: the wages, the fuel, the wood and, of course, the massive bribes to numerous Communist Party bureaucrats—bribes that allowed Frankmann to operate a capitalist enterprise so conspicuously, so profitably. At the end of every day, Kira would hand Frankmann a slip of paper on which was written the net amount: usually a profit, but on rare occasion a loss. On this day, Kira's calculations revealed a net profit of two thousand rubles, more than some people in town made in an entire year.

Frankmann eyed the metal box overflowing with cash, then turned his gaze to the butcher's shop. "Do you know where the butcher lives?"

"Just up the road from the old tractor plant," Kira replied.

"In a house?"

"Yes, he and his wife live in a house."

"Any kids?"

Kira grabbed a handful of bills from the box and began to arrange them in order of denomination, placing them in neat stacks. "They're older, moved out years ago, I think."

"Do they live nearby? The kids?"

"I don't think so," she said. "One's in the army, the other off to Moscow."

"How do you know all of this, Kira?"

Kira wrapped a rubber band around a stack of hundred-ruble notes. "From church," she said. "I know them from church."

"Do they still make tractors?"

"Excuse me?"

"The factory. Do they still make tractors?"

"Oh, no," Kira replied, confused that the businessman who knew everything that happened in the area did not know about the factory's demise. "It's been a good twenty years since it closed. And now it's all broken windows, rust, drug addicts."

Frankmann shook his head, his anger apparent. "They should have let me run things around here. I offered, you know."

"I know," Kira replied, placing several stacks of rubles back in the box and securing the lid.

"Things would have been different. For everyone."

Having been both witness to and beneficiary of Frankmann's commercial genius, Kira nodded in agreement. The two segued into a state of motionless silence during which Kira imagined Frankmann as a young man, wondered if she would have loved him, borne his children—and during which Frankmann bemoaned his age and the cruel irony of being born in the wrong place at the wrong time.

"So, sir, do you want me to put the cash in the safe?"

"Not today, Kira."

"Okay," she said, pushing the box across the desk in Frankmann's direction.

"Take it to the butcher and his wife."

Kira was surprised. "The money?"

"Yes."

"All of it?" Frankmann nodded. His order was so uncharacteristic, so commercially illogical, that she wondered what his motives might be. "And what should I tell them?" she asked.

Frankmann turned his back to Kira and looked out over the wharf, over his small empire. "Tell them," he said, "to stop cursing the Jews."

Kira observed the old man's silhouette in the window. "Your generosity might make it worse, you know."

Before Frankmann could respond with a story about his dear aunt Elena, one that would have confirmed Kira's sad thesis, a knock on the door interrupted their conversation. Frankmann was accustomed to carrying large amounts of cash, and he had been robbed several times over the years. Kira knew better than to open the door with so much money left unsecured, so she rose, lifted the metal box, stashed it in the safe and hurriedly closed the heavy metal door. Frankmann opened the top drawer of his desk and surveyed the four pistols. He chose the 1933 Tokarev TT, scuffed matte silver with a black handle—a fine weapon, reliable and powerful, that he had purchased under questionable circumstances from a Red Army officer desperate to rid himself of the gun.

Frankmann peered through the peephole in the door but saw no one. "Who's there?" he called out.

"It is Julian. Julian Pravdin."

"Who?" Frankmann asked, turning to Kira for assistance.

"My name is Julian Pravdin."

"It sounds like a boy, a young boy," whispered Kira.

"Are you a boy, a *young* boy?" Frankmann asked.

"Yes, I am, sir."

"Are you here to rob me?"

Confused, Julian did not immediately respond. "No, sir."

"Then why are you here?"

"My mother sent me. She is dead and said you would help me."

Frankmann wondered who this woman could be. "Who is your mother?" he asked through the door.

"My mother is Maria Pravdina, the wife of Ivan Pravdin."

"Pravdin the hunter?"

"Yes, that was my father." Julian pressed his ear against the door.

"I knew of him," Frankmann said. "He was regarded in this region as a great man. A brutal ending with the tiger, though. But I know nothing of your mother." Frankmann raced through the list of women he had known in his life, a short list for a man of his advanced age. "I'm sorry, but I know no such woman," he said.

Kira walked over to the door. She, too, pressed her ear against the wood so that now both she and Julian were listening through the heavy door. "I think he is crying," she said. "We should let him in."

"No," said Frankmann. "It may be a ruse. It wouldn't be beneath these wretched thieves to employ a street urchin in their treacherous scheme." Kira shrugged her shoulders and returned to the desk.

"Please, sir," Julian called out, stepping away from the door. "My mother said you would help. I have no one."

"Who is your mother?" Frankmann punched the door in frustration. "How would I know her?" the old man demanded.

Again, Julian did not respond quickly. He composed himself, wiped away his tears with the back of his hand. "My mother was a prostitute," he said, "and you were her customer. She treated you very nice, gave you things that you were lucky to have."

Frankmann shivered. He dropped his head, trying to avoid Kira's stunned look. He peered through the peephole one more time and again could see nothing, no one. He released the bolt and turned the knob. Before him stood Julian in his frayed church suit, his face wet, his hair combed, a satchel over his shoulder. "Come in, son," he said to the boy. "We have much work to do."

FOR YOU AND
YOUR GOD

There's an old Colombian who lives across the way from me and my mother in Miami, Old Pepe's his name, and he's got a little cottage with a tin roof and a yard in the back with lots of flowers. There's birds-of-paradise, rosebushes, peonies and lilacs, and boy do I love the smell of those flowers, especially after a hard rain when the sun comes out, the ground is moist and the stems are drooping from the weight of the water.

He's also got dozens of birds, bright-colored parrots from all over the world, but mostly from Latin America. Sometimes they're all together in the little shed and sometimes lined up tight on the branch like the bottles behind the bar at Paris Nights, and sometimes, when he reaches deep into a burlap bag and grabs a fistful of seed, you see them flapping, flying, dancing around in a big cloud of rainbow colors.

If you told me that Pepe's a hundred and fifty I wouldn't be surprised at all, 'cause not only does he look every bit that old, but he's got the smarts of a man who's lived for hundreds of years, seen everything and forgotten nothing. Pepe's an Indian, a Guambiano from the south of Colombia in a state called Cauca, which is in the Andes and it's not far from the border with Ecuador. And the only reason I know that is not 'cause I've been to Colombia, but 'cause I looked it up in an atlas that my dad gave me for one of my birthdays.

Of course I'd love to go to Colombia, especially to Cartagena, 'cause Gabriel García Márquez is my favorite writer and if Cartagena is only half as beautiful as the way he describes it then I must see it, stroll through those plazas and churches and smell the flowers. And maybe even fall in love there, 'cause could there be a more beautiful place to fall in love than Cartagena, a more romantic place in the entire world for a man and a woman to fall in love?

The Guambianos make me laugh, so funny, so short and dark-skinned with broad noses and thick black hair, and the sweetest thing about them is how they dress. They wear these colorful ponchos, bright blue with red-and-white piping, stringy scarves, sometimes white, sometimes red. And then there's the hats! Oh, how I love those hats, old-fashioned black bowler hats, and I've got no idea how they came to wearing them. Indians from the jungle and they wear formal black hats like they're going out to the theater in London a hundred years ago. And that's how Pepe dresses. Doesn't matter if it's hot or cold, cloudy or a lot of sun, rain, wind, he puts on his poncho, his scarf and his bowler hat and tends to his birds.

One time when I'm little I forget my key and get locked out of my house. It's raining and Old Pepe sees me peering through the crack in my back door and trying to wedge open the window by the kitchen. He invites me inside and makes me a cup of tea. He gives me a fashion magazine to read, says you just stay here until your parents get home. So I open the magazine and all the photos have girls, pretty girls, dressed the way my mom dressed when she first met my dad, and I'm confused and look at the date on the cover. Turns out, the magazine's twenty years old and I wonder where he got it and why he keeps it after all these years.

I sit in Pepe's living room, flipping through the magazine, and the pages are all stiff and wrinkly 'cause it's old and the air in Miami is so humid that it turns a magazine like this into a swollen, puffy thing that doesn't lie flat. I sit on the couch, tap my feet on the floor, though I can barely reach. I pray that my parents get home soon. It's a mystery to me, this house, and it's the first time I've ever been inside. I look around, and on the wall not far from where I'm sitting is an old photograph of a man in a military uniform. It's not the type that a general wears, with fancy medals and ribbons, but the kind a regular soldier wears, the uniform of a young man, a boy, who maybe has no idea why he's fighting. Olive-green fatigues and a floppy hat and a hand-rolled cigarette. I look closer at the soldier's face, and I can see that sure enough it's Pepe when he's young. The skin is shinier, the jaw stronger and the hair darker, but the shape of the face, rounded and thick, and the eyes, soft and sweet like he's holding back tears, are the same. In a glass frame next to the photograph is a medal, gold-colored and round, dangling from a red-and-yellow silk ribbon.

I sip my tea and look at the pictures of the pretty girls in their funny clothes and decide that I'm going to take some old dresses from my mom's closet and play dress-up. Just then, Pepe steps out into the rain and picks up a metal mallet. He lifts it real high and hammers away at some rusted metal pipe sticking out of the ground. Bang, bang, bang. Now, I don't have any reason *not* to trust Pepe, but I'm nervous anyway 'cause I'm a little girl alone in this house and I'm afraid my parents will be angry 'cause I lost my key.

Between the rat-a-tat-tat of the rain on the tin roof and Pepe pounding away at the pipe, I'm struggling to listen for the sound of my dad's car, loud and rough from a bad muffler. Finally, after what seems like an hour but is probably only ten minutes, I hear the car coughing in the driveway and my parents walking up the back path. They're yelling at each other, not *bad* yelling but in that funny way that a man and a woman yell at each other when they know they're not hurting any feelings.

I jump right up and run outside and hand the magazine to Old Pepe and say thank you, sir, and he smiles and says anytime. I run across his yard and right up the steps, put my arms around my dad's waist. Inside, he dries me off and doesn't even get mad when I tell him I lost the key. And then I tell him about Pepe and how he brought me inside and gave me tea and a magazine. My dad and my mom look at each other and then at me and say is that all? And I'm confused. What else could there be, I want to know. My parents look relieved when I say that, and only when I'm older do I realize why, and not 'cause they had any concern about Pepe, but 'cause that's a parent's job. That's how they're wired.

I tell my dad about the photo of Pepe dressed as a soldier and the medal in the glass frame, and my dad tells me the rumor is that the old Indian fought for the liberals in the Thousand Day War and that he was a fearless warrior but compassionate and loved by many. The Thousand Day War? I ask, 'cause that is one very long war. And my father says yes, three years or thereabouts, and when he says it like that it doesn't seem so long. When I'm older, in my teens, I learn that this war ended in 1902. And that would make Pepe a hundred and twenty-five, maybe a hundred and thirty years old. Which just can't be possible. But that's the rumor, so who knows.

My father didn't have a college degree, didn't even get past the eighth grade, but he was what they call a self-taught intellectual. Our house was filled with old books, magazines, newspapers, and they were stacked everywhere. There was tons of stuff on history and political science, economics too. My father was a *libertario* who believed in individual freedoms and just wanted the government to stay out of everyone's business, let them achieve what God had planned for them without some bureaucrat screwing it all up. He also loved fiction and had an entire bookcase, floor to ceiling, with the great Spanish-language writers. Gabriel García Márquez, Federico García Lorca, Mario Vargas Llosa, Pablo Neruda. So I've been reading some of the best fiction in the whole world since I'm a little girl.

When my father came to the States, I don't think he knew ten words of English, but he got to be a proud American real fast and set his mind to learning the language as good as a native. And he made sure me and my mother learned too. Now, truth is it's hard to ever catch up a hundred percent, but you can get pretty close if you try. We must've had a dozen dictionaries in the house. English, Spanish, English-to-Spanish, Spanish-to-English, even an old Italian one. And my father would walk around with his reading glasses that he got for two bucks and he'd call out new words, new *English* words. And for every one

I got right, he'd throw a coin in a glass jar, usually a nickel but sometimes a quarter for a big word.

One time, he screamed out *scallywag*. Well, that's a funny word to say, scallywag. I never met a single person who can say scallywag without smiling. And it just so happened that I saw the same word in the dictionary a couple of days earlier. Pure luck. So I yelled back *good-for-nothing!* Well, you should've seen the look on his face, so shocked, and he took a five-dollar bill out of his wallet and dropped it right in the jar. And what a thrill, to make that man happy *and* get paid for it.

Anyway, after that day with the tea and the magazines, I start sneaking into Pepe's yard after school and on weekends, and he's been teaching me about his birds ever since, where they're from, what they eat, when they sleep, who they love. And I'm pretty sure that I know more about parrots than most people who make a living knowing things about parrots. Pepe doesn't have any favorites, he loves them all equal, but I'm partial to a few of them. There's a cockatoo, a galah from Australia— *Eolophus roseicapilla*—and it took me forever to pronounce it and even longer to memorize it. This cockatoo, he's got a pink chest, pink like the sand in Cuba, with gray wings, a white crown on the top of his head and a chipped beak. Rojillo's his name, 'cause that's the name I gave him when I was a little girl and Pepe laughed when he heard the name and sure enough it's stuck after all these years.

Then there's a boy and a girl, a pair of burrowing parrots from Argentina, *Cyanoliseus patagonus* they're called, and they're green with patches of gray and a little turquoise blue near the tail feathers, and what I love about them, what I *really* love about them, is that they're monogamous and that's how they're wired, how their genetics work. Chica and Chico, I named them too, Girl and Boy, and they stick to themselves. They've got their own branch where they sit and clean each other and watch the other birds. And the other birds know they better stay away or else Chico, who's real protective of Chica, will raise his feathers, flap them in a scary way and squawk so loud that I can hear him from my bedroom.

When I'm ten, Pepe gives me Chico and Chica for my birthday. He says I'm giving you these birds, but it's not like a normal gift, where you hold it in your hands and you put it on your shelf or a cage in your room and you can do with it what you want. It's a different sort of gift, he says, and they'll stay right here, not in a cage but right here in their home. And he points to their branch in the mango tree. They won't belong to you or to me but to each other. And I ask, so how's that a gift? If I don't get to keep them? Pepe smiles, the type of smile that a wise old man gives a little girl who doesn't know much—and he removes his black hat and underneath is a thick clump of shiny gray hair, almost white, and he wipes his face with his hand, shields his eyes from the strong Florida sun. And he says not only is it a gift, but it's the best type of gift.

Pepe takes a carrot from his pocket and breaks it in half, hands me both pieces and nods in the direction of Chico and Chica. Slow, he says, and I do just that, holding the carrots in both hands and moving careful toward the branch. Chica is closer to me, and as I get near her, Chico moves behind her, slides across the branch and positions himself between me and her, real chivalrous. I hold out the carrots and the two birds move away together along the branch, sliding their claws real quick. Pepe places his hand on my arm, says hold right there. So

I stand with my arms out and the carrots just a few inches from the birds. Chica looks at Chico, and Chico looks me in the eyes, takes a couple of steps toward me and opens his beak. He sticks his tongue out, which is plump and cracked and looks like a piece of old leather that's been out in the sun for days.

Just when I think he's gonna take the carrot, the two of them shimmy a few inches away so they're at the end of the branch with nowhere to go. I'm so nervous 'cause Chico and Chica are mine now. Pepe just gave them to me—even though they need to be free and I understand that—but I love them and I'm afraid they'll reject me. I turn and look at Pepe, and his hat is on his head now and he pulls the brim down and makes a motion with his hands. Go, girl, go.

Chico gives a little squeak and takes a couple of steps back in my direction, but this time Chica doesn't follow. He opens his beak wide, sticks out his leathery tongue and I place the carrot on it. His beak snaps shut like a mean turtle and he nods, turns to Chica. She opens her beak and looks up to the sun and seems to enjoy the warmth. Slow and careful, Chico places the carrot in Chica's mouth and she clasps it tight and looks straight ahead. Chico turns back to me and opens his beak. I place the other carrot on his tongue, and the two birds crunch away, strong and fast, and in no more than a few seconds the carrots are all gone.

I turn to Pepe, excited and feeling real connected to the birds, to *my* birds, and so happy that they ate my carrots and hoping that they trust me now. Pepe lifts the brim of his hat so he can see me better, so I can get a better look at his face. He puts his hands on my shoulders and looks at me the way a grandfather looks at his granddaughter when he wants to say something important. And then he says you see that? He looks over at the birds then back to me. Remember, lovely Perlita, remember what you just saw. And I shrug 'cause I know I just saw something sweet but I don't know exactly what Pepe means.

Pepe gives a little playful pinch on my shoulder and he says remember, Perlita, when you get older, you look for a man like that, someone who protects you, who feeds you first, who won't take a bite of anything, won't take a single piece of food or clothing or firewood until you've had enough first. Firewood? I ask, 'cause why would I need firewood in Miami, and besides, we have an electric heater that we plug into the wall if it ever gets chilly. Yes, firewood, Old Pepe says, firewood. You promise me, Perlita? Yes, I say.

Pepe picks a feather off my shoulder, a little puff of white like a cotton ball, not the kind of feather that's long and thin and full of colors. He holds it to the sky and says here, Perlita, make a wish. And I close my eyes and turn my face to the sky. I can feel my cheeks roasting in the sun, and I make a wish, the same wish I always make, even to this day. And then I open my eyes and the feather's on his palm. I blow real hard and it bounces across his hand like a tumbleweed, then catches a breeze and floats high, high up over the mango tree where Chico and Chica sit, and they watch it fly too, their heads swinging together like they share one brain, then up over the fence and out east, over the bay and toward the ocean.

I turn to Pepe. Want to know my wish? I ask. Pepe shields his eyes from the sun and watches the feather drift until we can't see it anymore. And then he smiles and shakes his head and says no, Perlita, no. That's for you, just you. And your god.

SCARCITY. NEED. KNOWLEDGE.

In the corner table of a popular restaurant that Frankmann operated, Julian sat with Kira and the old Jew. Kira ordered a feast for the table—fish stew, roasted duck, boiled potatoes, carrots, borscht, broiled venison, hot bread drizzled with butter, and a cola for the boy. Julian was mesmerized by the bustle of the restaurant: the streaks of white-coated waiters, the naval officers dining in their dress uniforms, the Party bureaucrats, the merchants, the variety and amount of food, the deference with which Frankmann and, by extension, Julian and Kira were treated.

"So," Frankmann started, as Julian devoured a piece of delicious bread, "you need two things." He turned to Kira. "Take notes, please." Kira removed from her bag a legal pad and a pen. "You need two things, Julian, and we can work on both of them simultaneously. First, we need a plan to get you to the States." Julian nodded in agreement, as this was consistent with his mother's wishes. "And then you need to develop skills. It's a hornet's nest over there, you know. And your mother wouldn't want you fending for yourself without the right tools. Now, the good news is you've got strong genes, believe it or not. You have your mother's good looks. And crafty as hell, she was. And let's hope you have your father's best traits."

Julian placed the bread on the plate before him. "My father? What were my father's best traits?"

Frankmann bellowed, "Your father? I saw him only once, when he came into town with three tigers—the biggest, most beautiful pelts I had ever seen. He'd taken them down in just one week, and word had already spread throughout our town, our *entire region*, that a hunter had done something remarkable. And because he was one of our own, you can imagine the pride. Hundreds lined the street into town, waiting to get a glimpse of the tigers and the man who had hunted them. It was all so dramatic, like you see in an opera, a *German* opera. Your father standing tall with two rifles strapped to his back, a knife on his belt, a bloody shoulder, working the reins of the troika, three horses up front, trotting shoulder to shoulder, the three of them working together, their hooves in perfect harmony and dancing proud like those Lipizzaner stallions. And in the back of the troika, in the carriage, were these colossal cats, brown and white and a brilliant orange." Frankmann lifted a glass of wine to his lips and drank, not for pleasure, but to lubricate his throat. "Those were tough times around here, still are. The corruption, the poverty, the bureaucrats. The bureaucrats! So cowardly and pathetic, every one of them. And what they did to God . . ." Frankmann paused. He studied the boy's face. "But when your father rode into town, Julian, that was a moment that gave everyone hope, a little inspiration that they could still strive, that they could do something otherworldly."

Julian watched as Frankmann placed the wineglass back down on the table. He cleared his throat. "So, Mr. Frankmann, what were my father's best traits?"

Frankmann looked at Julian pityingly. "I just told you, boy. I just told you." Kira reached over and stroked Julian's hair. "Kira, please, don't baby him. We have work to do." She withdrew her hand and straightened the pad in front of her. "Kira, I want you to go visit Dmitriev at the Family Service Bureau. He's as corrupt as they come, so no calls or letters. Take two thousand out of the safe and put it in a bag for him. Make sure no one is around when you hand it to him and tell him I need adoption and transport papers for an orphan." Frankmann eyed Kira as she took detailed notes. "Burn those when you're finished," he said.

"Of course," replied Kira, having become a master at destroying potentially incriminating documents.

The waiter arrived and covered the table with food. Frankmann and Kira barely looked at their plates, so immersed were they in the execution of the plan. Frankmann's ability to focus on the task at hand to the exclusion of all else had, he believed, been one of the primary contributors to his success. Julian stared at the food before him and wondered what to do—start eating or wait until the adults began. Out of caution, he chose the latter.

Frankmann continued. "I will call a couple I know in America, outside New York somewhere. I made them rich in the sixties and kept the husband out of jail in the seventies. And I always told them that one day I would collect my debt. Well, today's their lucky day, Julian, because you're going to be adopted by an old Petersburg couple. A husband and wife, Americans now with a fancy car and a house and cupboards stocked to the ceilings with food. They are good people, sneaky rascals of course, and they'll protect you, educate you, feed and clothe you until you turn eighteen. How old are you now?"

"Ten."

"Okay, so then you'll have eight years with these people. And then, well, who knows . . ."

"Okay," Julian muttered, trying to hold back his tears, "eight years." Despite the years spent without his parents and the resulting acceleration of his childhood, the thought of his future and permanent emancipation terrified him.

"When will Julian be traveling?" Kira asked.

Frankmann drove a fork into his venison and cut off a large piece. "It's impossible to be kosher in Siberia, you know. In the big cities, it's easier. But out here?"

Puzzled, Julian and Kira stared at the old man, who dropped the meat into his mouth and chewed with great force.

"Sir?" Kira asked. "The travel plans?"

As Frankmann swallowed the chunk of meat, a rivulet of russet grease slid into his beard and mixed with the white bristles. He took a sip of water and cleared his throat. "You a fast learner?" he asked the boy.

"The fastest, sir," Julian responded, straightening his posture in the chair.

"And competitive?"

His confidence rising, Julian nodded and expanded his chest. "Just like my father, sir."

Frankmann cut another piece of meat and observed the boy.

He had spent a long career sizing up people and had, through both success and occasional failure, developed a keen instinct that allowed him to quickly determine the strengths and weaknesses of a human being. He considered Julian's parents, the boy's ability to survive great tragedy, the knock on the office door, the assertiveness with which Julian demanded to be heard. "Two months, Kira. That's all the time I will need with this boy."

"To do what?" Julian asked as he lifted his knife and fork and prepared to cut a piece of duck.

"To teach you how to be rich."

Julian smiled wearily and placed his utensils back on the table. "When do we start, sir?"

"We start now." Frankmann took the pad and pen from Kira and handed them to Julian. With a linen napkin, Frankmann wiped the grease from his beard. "You see that waiter over there, the young man with the glasses? With the feminine features?"

"Yes," said Julian, unsure what it meant for a man to have feminine features.

"Well, he came into town last week from the west, arrived by train, and he's got a valise full of old books. Art books, history, old Russian literature, he had something by Lermontov, beautiful atlases, that sort of thing. He even had a few volumes in English, including a first edition of *Ulysses*, fourth printing. It was pretty clear from looking at the books, in perfect condition with plastic covers on them, that whoever used to own these was a serious collector. So the man pulls into town with the books and asks around, trying to find out who might be interested in buying the lot. Well, given I'm the only man in town with any real money, he ends up in my office. It turns out he's a painter, an artist, and he came here to paint the sea and to capture the light for which we're famous."

Kira and Julian look surprised. "I know," Frankmann continued, "why *anyone* would want to live here is beyond me, but that's a romantic for you. Anyway, the young man wants to paint here for a few months, then go to Moscow with his work and join the Academy of Arts, which they say is the finest institution of its kind. So, this painter is broke, and the only asset he owns is these books that he inherited from an uncle, and he doesn't know much at all about book collecting. So when he comes to me, I've got scarcity, need and knowledge in my favor."

Just then, the painter approached the table with a pitcher of water. In deference to him, Frankmann stopped the story until the young man filled the glasses and moved on to the next table. "Remember these three words, boy. Write them down. *Scarcity. Need. Knowledge.*" As Julian wrote down the words, Frankmann lifted a bottle of wine from the table. "This," he said, "is a 1975 Château Lafite Rothschild. You can buy it from a fine vintner in Moscow for three hundred rubles. In Paris, it might cost the equivalent of two hundred, but in francs, of course." Julian scribbled more notes on the pad. *Wine. 300. 200. 1975.* "So, Julian, what would you say is the value of this wine?"

The boy looked first at Kira and then at the bottle of wine. He reached for the bottle and rotated it one complete revolution, reading the yellowed label with the elegant French cursive. "I think the value would be two to three hundred. Is that right?"

"Yes, boy, that would be the price, the range of prices, for this bottle in Paris or Moscow. I agree. But that is not the *universal value* of the wine." Julian appeared confused. "What if I were to tell you, Julian, that this particular bottle was not being offered for sale in Moscow or Paris, but rather hours from the city, in the countryside, near a dacha owned by a rich industrialist?"

Julian wrote on the pad: *Moscow, Paris, dacha*. "I don't understand, sir."

"In the countryside, hours from the city, there are no stores that sell such a fine wine. It is not so easily available. So the wealthy owner of the dacha does not have the benefit of an alternative supply if he is not happy with the price. In Paris, he can walk into a liquor shop, and if the wine is too expensive, he walks to the next shop and buys it there for a better price. So, in the countryside, in the Russian countryside where there is only one vintner, and this vintner holds in his inventory a very small number of wines, what might be the impact on the price of the wine? Higher or lower?"

"Higher, sir," Julian said. "The wine would be more expensive."

Frankmann smiled. "And would that be an example of price impacted by scarcity or by need?"

"Scarcity, sir."

"Good, boy. Now let's alter the facts." Julian straightened the pad and held the pen an inch above the paper. So focused was he on Frankmann's lesson that he did not eat his food. Frankmann continued. "We agree that the wealthy dacha owner from the countryside wants this bottle of wine. He's hours from the city and has no other way to get it, so he pays more. Maybe instead of three hundred, he pays four hundred. That we agree on. Now, let's make another assumption. Let's assume that not only is this rich landowner a wine aficionado who is willing to pay a few extra rubles for a fine wine, but let's assume that in addition to being wealthy and many hours removed from the city, let's assume that he is also an alcoholic. Let's assume that this rich man is *addicted* to wine."

Julian winced at the reference to addiction. He stopped writing and looked up to the old man. "An alcoholic?" he asked.

"Yes, an alcoholic. And what that means is his need for this bottle of wine . . ." Frankmann tapped the bottle before him for effect. "His *need* for this particular bottle of wine is greater than the need of the average rich dacha owner. Our buyer *has* to have his alcohol. He can't go a night without drinking or he starts to shake, and he gets nasty and kicks his dog."

Julian looked at Frankmann, turned to Kira, and then returned to the old Jew. "Why would he kick his dog, sir?"

Kira was alarmed. "Mr. Frankmann didn't mean that, did he?" she said, eyeing the old man.

Frankmann recognized that his words had frightened the boy, that he had offended Kira's sense of propriety. "I misspoke, boy. He would never kick the dog. He loves the dog. But if he simply cannot go one single night without a bottle of wine, what's he willing to do, boy? What's he willing to do to get that wine?"

"He's willing to pay even more," Julian responded.

"Precisely!" Frankmann roared and slapped his hand on the table. Then he carved a piece of venison and dropped it into his mouth with great satisfaction. The old Jew raised his wineglass and took a luxurious gulp. He lifted the linen napkin from his lap, snapped it in the air, and wiped his lips. "And *why* is he willing to pay even more?"

"Because he *needs* the wine, sir."

Frankmann patted Julian on the top of his head. "Well done. Now let's alter the facts one more time. Let's make this a '73 Lafite instead of a '75. And let's say that this rich alcoholic dacha owner thinks of himself as a real wine expert. But let's also say that his knowledge of fine wines is not as extensive or as accurate as he thinks. He thinks he knows more than he actually knows. He's blinded by his arrogance, which is a common affliction among the wealthy. Myself included. So, the buyer knows that Château Lafite is one of the finest, most famous vineyards in the world and has been for hundreds of years. But what he doesn't know is that there were a few years, 1973 being one of them, that were not up to snuff. Not terrible, but certainly not the caliber of what one would expect from Rothschild." Frankmann paused and took another gulp of wine. "Let's also say that the *seller* of this wine is a true expert. He knows everything there is to know about wine. And he knows that only the most sophisticated connoisseurs will know that '73 was a hard year to make good wine."

Frankmann noticed that Julian had barely touched his food, so he reached across the table and grabbed the pad. "You've written enough," he said to Julian. "Just listen now. Eat, eat." Julian hesitated, then tore the leg off the duck before him. "So," Frankmann continued, "we have a seller who knows something that the buyer doesn't know. We have a transaction in which the buyer thinks the wine is more valuable than it actually is, that the '73 was as good as, say, the '75. And the seller suspects that the buyer might not realize that '73 was a bad year. The seller has more knowledge than the buyer. And when one party has more knowledge than the other, what happens?"

"It changes the price," Julian said, waving the duck leg excitedly.

"Precisely! It creates an imbalance, an inefficiency that the seller can take advantage of. And in this specific case, our rich, unknowledgeable, arrogant, alcoholic dacha owner pays *what* for the wine?"

"He pays even more."

"Yes!" Frankmann raised his glass. "To scarcity, to need, to knowledge," he toasted. Kira and Julian looked at each other and raised their own glasses. Kira tapped the edge of her glass against Julian's, and the sound created by the contact of the fine crystal reminded Julian of a flute—one perfect note from a flute. Kira smiled at the boy. He blushed and wondered if he would one day marry a woman as pretty and as kind as Kira. Frankmann rolled up his napkin and tossed it to the table. He smiled at his dinner companions. "Shall we have some dessert?" he asked. "Yes, yes," he continued without waiting for a response, "let's have some dessert and celebrate."

Frankmann waved his hand and quickly caught the attention of the waiter who had sold the books.

"Gregori," Frankmann yelled, "sweets for my friends!"

Frankmann had a soft spot for artists, so with respect to the painter, he didn't use scarcity, need and knowledge to his advantage. Rather, he paid the young man a full, fair price for the books. Frankmann also provided him with a job and a free room on the wharf with perfect light and unobstructed views of the sea. He gave the man what every painter needs: enough money to eat and a room with a view.

CYCLE OF ABUSE

'm at the club and I'm having a terrible time. And one of the
reasons I'm having a terrible time is 'cause Schultz is out on
disability for a couple of months, hurt his back throwing a guy
out of the club. There's a new bouncer filling in, Slick's his name,
and he's anything but. He's a sick bastard who's always pressur-
ing us girls to give him head for good shifts. Now there's no way
I'm giving a blow job to a guy like Slick, bareback no less, so now
there's no one looking after me when I get a rough customer. On
top of it, work is slow 'cause the season's almost over and the snowbirds are pretty much done and gone back up north. The locals still
come around, but they tip like shit and no way you're ever gonna
get them in the Champagne Room.

The other reason I'm having a terrible time is 'cause I broke
up with a guy yesterday, the first sort-of boyfriend I've had in
two years. I mean, I've gone out on dates here and there and
even slept with a few guys, and except for Julian I always feel

awful the morning after, really awful. But this is the first one I'd say was a steady thing. It's hard, of course, for a girl to have a good relationship with a good guy when she does what I do for a living. Like I said, there's slim pickings at the club 'cause all the guys are either married or real old or beyond creepy, and the rare guys like Julian, even if he wasn't married, the guys who seem to have everything a girl could want, well, even those guys are so complicated that there's just no hope.

You could even say the ones that seem the most desirable are actually the *least* desirable. They have everything going for them, but there's some flaw, some tiny flaw that no one can see, that maybe they don't even know exists, and it's this tiny flaw that's so huge, so unfixable, so powerful that it brings everyone down with the man. Or maybe they know it exists and they use it to their advantage like some secret weapon. The scary thing is that sometimes it's that flaw that makes you want them in the first place, which is something I don't understand about human beings. Why is it that the flaws draw us to a person? You'd think it would be just the opposite.

So when girls who work at law firms, car dealerships or insurance companies are finding their husbands right there in the workplace, that's not going to happen for a stripper, at least not for a stripper like me. This one I was seeing, his name's Derrick and I met him at the car repair. I was there getting a new muffler, which turned into a new muffler and a new clutch and a new transmission and ended up costing me three thousand dollars. And I'm sure they saw a pretty girl and thought here's an easy mark, 'cause I never once just walked into a mechanic looking for one thing and not walked out with three completely different things.

I'm standing there while the mechanic is tapping away on the calculator and there's a customer who pulls his car into the garage. It's a nice car, a clean Toyota without a single scratch on it, and this guy gets out and says he needs an oil change, and how much is it gonna cost? Turns out the mechanic gets a call and goes in the back to take it and this guy walks right over to me. He points to my car—I have a cute Mini, British racing green—and he says those your wheels? Yup, they're mine, and it looks like I'm about to spend a few thousand bucks to get it working again. Well, he holds out his hand and says Derrick, good to meet you. Now, some girls go for a type, a physical type, and other girls don't have a physical type but they got a personality type. And then there's others who don't have a type at all, just take whatever's in front of them. In some ways those girls got it easy, not all hung up on finding perfection, just recognize a relationship for what it is, someone to get through this life with, a companion to help pass the time and share the costs.

I'm the complicated type of girl who's got both a physical type *and* a personality type, which causes me one problem after the next, and Derrick doesn't fit the bill on either count. First off, he's got fair skin and blond hair, short and curly—and blonds, they're just not my type. Probably it's 'cause I'm Latin and every man I grew up with in Cuba had dark hair and dark skin and that's all I ever knew. But then again, I have a Colombian friend and she loves blond guys, says she's sick of the men from her country and that she wants something completely different.

Second thing is I like real smart guys with a certain kind of humor, clever and not too obvious. And I like a guy who makes fun of me but isn't really making fun of me, who's got the confidence to mock the little streak of white hair in the back of my head that's caused by some pigment problem I've had since I was a kid. And what's really weird about it is that dye won't stick to it for long, which a customer once told me has something to do with the thickness of the hair's cuticle. So I just keep it white.

Third time I saw Julian, he puts his fingers around the tuft of white and lifts it up to the lights and says damn girl, my baby looks like a skunk, a smoking hot skunk, but smells like lily of the valley. And that made me smile, made me feel less self-conscious about the streak, made me proud of it actually. So when Derrick points to the mechanic and says to me I'm not sure why they call them grease monkeys 'cause I sure don't see any bananas around here, I know that we're not dealing with a genius.

But I laugh anyway, and I do it by instinct. The fake laugh comes natural to me 'cause that's all I do at the club, make a man feel like he's smart and funny and attractive. And it's real hard for me to turn off the acting when I'm out of the club, getting harder and harder as the months pass, until sometimes it feels like there's no difference between Perla at work and the real Perla. It's like those actors from *Apocalypse Now*—that was my dad's favorite movie—the actors who were playing maniacs on the set and sure enough they become maniacs *off* the set, so much that it didn't take a damn bit of imagination for them to get into character, and no way to get out of it.

Derrick asks for my number and I figure what the hell, it's been months since I've been on a proper date, and I doubt Julian's ever gonna turn into something real, what with him being *married* and all. Derrick seems like a real nice guy at first, picking me up for dinner, opening doors and buying me perfume and sweet little gifts. Now, I've seen this sort of thing before and sometimes it keeps going 'cause what you've got is a real nice guy, a gentleman who really cares about you. But other times it's really a guy who's insecure and afraid you're going to leave him—and this is his way of feeling safe, like he's got you under control. I keep on the lookout for that type of guy, and sure enough that's exactly what happens with Derrick.

He starts out real nice, and him being so nice is the only thing that gets me over the fact that he's not as dark and as smart as I like them. After a few weeks I start seeing the signs, and the behavior's so predictable it would make you laugh if it weren't so scary. It always starts out with something small, like your car's a bit messy today baby—and maybe he runs his finger across the hood, looks at his dirty finger, waves it in the air all disapproving. Then maybe one night he says you sure you want to wear that color lipstick? I don't think it complements your eyes, baby. Shrugs his shoulders, all innocent, and says just trying to help.

Then one night he picks me up for dinner and I'm feeling extra-sexy, lost three pounds and just got over my period so I'm not feeling bloated anymore, and I put on a real short skirt and a little top with spaghetti straps and high heels, not the fuck-me pumps I wear at the club, but pretty damn close. And when I open the door, expecting him to give me a big hug and a kiss, he gives me a scowl instead and says get back inside and put on something decent, something so you don't look like a cheap slut.

Well, I'm an expert on the cycle of abuse, which is nothing to be proud of, and I can write a paper on it. There's the setup phase, which is where they're causing little conflicts, chipping away at your self-esteem, and that's exactly what this comment about my outfit is doing, trying to make me feel cheap. Then there's the abuse phase, that's when you get slapped across the face or they pull your hair or they fuck you when you don't want to be fucked. Then the reconciliation phase, when they tell you they're sorry, that it's never gonna happen again, and they're showering you with gifts like you're on a honeymoon. Then the setup starts again. Maybe they say your new haircut looks terrible or you got thick ankles, which I don't but they say it anyway. And the cycle repeats as many times as you let it.

Like I said, I'm an expert on abuse, but I'm a slow learner. I had to go through this three or four times before I started recognizing the patterns, before I realized that while the guys were bad and abusive, I had to take some responsibility, 'cause what was I doing always getting involved with men who act like this and what was I doing waiting so long to get out. So as soon as Derrick tells me to go inside and change, I go inside like he says and lock the door. I yell through the door to Derrick. I scream we're over, now please leave. But instead of leaving, Derrick pounds on the door, starts kicking it, screams let me in you fucking whore, you let me in or I will cut you the fuck up.

Now, I've been in this situation too many times already, the wrong side of this door so many times that I'm starting to feel tired, exhausted way down deep, and wondering more and more about my choices. Most of the time I don't think this had anything to do with my dad's death. I like to think that everything would be exactly the same, the same crappy boyfriends and the same crappy job, 'cause it's hard enough for me to deal with the loss, but I couldn't bear it if his death made this happen. If there's that kind of cause and effect, then it means I dishonor him every day. And that's too much shame for me. But if I'm real honest with myself, and that's not something I like to do, then I've got to admit that everything started going downhill the day he died.

Derrick kicks the door. Open the door, whore! My mother's not home, so I pick up the phone and call Dino, that's Carolina's Dominican boyfriend, and he's messed up. I say Dino, there's a man on my front steps with blond hair and a bad sense of humor, and he's threatening to kill me. Well, that's all Dino needs to hear, 'cause he has too much rage, from the steroids and from something that happened to him when he was a kid, and he's always looking for an outlet, and the more righteous the better. He's over at my place in five minutes, and I look through the hole and watch him get out of his car and walk toward the house all pissed off and focused. It doesn't take more than a few seconds before Dino comes up fast behind Derrick. Dino grabs him, slaps Derrick across the neck so the guy can't breathe. And the beating begins. After a few punches, Dino takes a quick break and smiles at the door like he knows I'm watching. He throws me a kiss. Through the door, he says I got it under control, baby. Best not to watch.

I take a seat on my couch, flip through a gossip magazine and try not to listen, try not to get up and look through that peephole.

So that's why I'm feeling terrible today. That and I've been missing Julian, which I've got no business doing.

SAINT ANNA
OF KASHIN

Julian sat in the plane, his eyes open, his cheek pressed hard against the cold window. On the boy's lap, its lid lifted, was the box that held his few precious possessions: the photograph of his parents, a yellowed newspaper article with a picture of a boot in the bloodied snow, the immigration papers purchased by Frankmann, a photo of the adoptive parents he would soon meet, a copper cross, his toy tank. And at the bottom of the box, clipped together, were his mother's birth and death certificates—the beginning of a life and the end of a life separated only by one holy card.

The boy looked down to the box and withdrew the card, revealing the image of Saint Anna of Kashin. Nervously, he flicked at the corner of the card. He recalled his mother's funeral: the frozen earth, the metal blade of a shovel snapping in half, the gravedigger pouring buckets of hot water over the ground, the bearded priest in a black *skufia*—flakes of dandruff on his dark cassock—handing the holy card to Julian.

Julian ran the edge of the card under his left thumbnail and examined the icon, focusing on Saint Anna's face. There she was, standing by a still river, a tree, a castle, Jesus Christ in an amber cloud above, unfathomable loss apparent in her eyes, her gaze to Christ projecting rage, mistrust and yet, Julian sensed, some willingness to believe in Him, to believe that there was, despite the death of every person she had ever loved, some divine and glorious plan.

The plane hugged the Long Island shoreline, then swerved downward and to the right in such a jerky manner that Julian dropped the holy card into the box and snapped the lid shut. The old woman in the next seat, a stranger to Julian, noticed the young boy's anxiety. She reached over and placed her hand over his. Julian was startled, surprised by the unexpected warmth of her corrugated skin with its wormlike veins, and he could not decide if she sought to comfort or to be comforted. But rather than withdraw his hand—his natural instinct—he permitted the contact, pleasurable and reassuring. He braced himself as the plane continued its steep decline and then flattened out for the final approach to the airport.

These maneuvers—the dip and the leveling off—revealed a new line of sight to the west, and it was then that Julian for the first time saw New York City: pointed tips, impossibly high, piercing the umber, summer smog; a trio of freighters making their way upriver past Gravesend; a flash of sunlight, like the white blast of a firecracker, off the surface of Jamaica Bay below. He withdrew his hand from the woman's and pressed his forehead against the window. Considering the image before her, recalling with a painful throb her own child at this same age, the woman waited for a moment and then repositioned her hand so that it rested on Julian's shoulder.

"Is this it? The United States?" he asked in Russian, without turning around. The woman, a German, did not understand and thus could not answer. Instead, she squeezed the boy's shoulder.

The touchdown was so smooth that Julian was unaware the plane had landed, and only after he noticed a truck keeping pace on the tarmac did he realize that he was no longer in the air. The plane approached the gate and made a series of short lunges that, in what resembled some odd communal ritual, propelled the passengers forward, back, forward, back, forward, back. Julian exited the plane with his box and his satchel, the German woman sticking protectively close. Outside the gate, they were greeted by an immigration officer who escorted the boy—and the concerned woman—through customs and out into the hall where welcoming families and friends awaited.

Julian held up the photograph of his adoptive parents and showed it to the woman and the officer. As Julian searched the crowd, he wondered if he would always need a picture to identify the most important people in his life. The woman pointed to an elderly couple, somewhat older than the photograph suggested. They resembled the couple in the picture—both short, narrow-shouldered and wide in the waist—and were dressed in unremarkable clothes: the man in a well-worn gray suit, shiny in the elbows and the knees, and the woman in an unflattering floral dress that was too loose even for her pudgy physique. This woman, too, held a photograph. And when she saw Julian, she pointed to the picture and raised her hands as if she were a surrendering soldier.

The German woman and the officer guided Julian to the couple. Frightened by everything—new people, a new country, a strange language—the boy stood before them. He extended his hand in their direction. "I am Julian Pravdin," he declared in Russian.

The woman stepped forward, leaving her husband behind. Rather than shake the boy's hand, Irina leaned down and wrapped her arms around him in a slow, deliberate manner. "We're happy to have you," Irina whispered. "Frankmann has sent me another gift." She withdrew and turned to her husband, who looked unsure, trepid, as if it were the first time he had ever come so close to a child. Their own children—two daughters now in their late forties—had left home nearly thirty years ago, and it had been decades since they'd lived with a child of Julian's age. Irina grabbed Oleg's elbow and pushed him toward the boy.

"Pleasure to meet you, sir," Julian said with a formality he had perfected at the orphanage.

Oleg sighed at the sight of his new responsibility—and he wondered if his debt to Frankmann would ever be repaid. "Pleasure to meet you, too," he said, stiffly shaking Julian's hand.

After the official completed the required paperwork, the German woman gave the boy a kiss on the cheek and moved to her awaiting family. Julian watched her leave, watched with longing as her children and grandchildren embraced her. He turned back to Oleg and Irina, who walked him to a large American sedan in the parking garage. Julian marveled at the car, with its soft cushions and an illuminated dashboard that was unlike the small, austere Moskvitch and Zhiguli so common in Siberia. Oleg drove and, except for the occasional gasp when her husband glided out of the lane and then jerked the car back into its proper place, Irina sat silently in the passenger seat. The route to northern New Jersey took them through Queens and its endless landscape of semi-detached homes, down through the

Midtown Tunnel, under the East River, then ascending to the eastern edge of Manhattan.

Unaccustomed to driving in the city, Oleg made a series of unwise and strange decisions that took them on a route so circuitous that it resembled the winding nonsense of a child's Krazy Straw: up Third Avenue to Seventy-second Street, east along Seventy-second, down Second Avenue, west along Sixty-sixth Street to a transverse that cut through Central Park and then south on Columbus Avenue. But rather than continue straight down Columbus, then Ninth Avenue—a clear path to the Lincoln Tunnel and, on the other side of it, New Jersey—Oleg veered left onto Broadway, toward Times Square.

Irina turned to her husband. "Wrong turn," she said, unable to contain her frustration any longer. "Again."

Oleg gripped the wheel. "This one was on purpose," he said.

"On purpose? Now we're stuck. Why would you get on Broadway?"

Oleg lifted his right hand and, with his thick thumb, pointed to Julian in the backseat. "To show him the lights. After everything, the boy deserves to see the lights."

TRIGGER FINGER

Julian's new home sat at the end of a tree-lined cul-de-sac about a half hour west of New York City. It was a sturdy Tudor built in the 1920s, with a manicured lawn that had clean, clipped edges and a row of rosebushes bearing the signs of fastidious attention: ample and precise spacing, healthy blossoms, the stalks pruned with forty-five-degree cuts, leaves free of spots and mildew, a base clear of weeds.

When Julian first arrived in the suburbs of northern New Jersey, he was enrolled in a local public school that was poorly equipped to ease the boy's difficult transition. So when he appeared for the first day of the academic year dressed in new clothes that were too formal for this casual—some would say sloppy—school, he was met by two brothers who bore not even the slightest resemblance to each other. The older of the two—by ten months—was wide in the shoulders, with cropped hair, a pug nose and protruding ears. The younger boy had a slight build, with dangling curls, droopy eyes and a nose that was so long and so impossibly thin that, when viewed from the side, it resembled the beak of a puffin and, when viewed from the front, appeared as if there were no nose at all—just two pinpricks for nostrils. Yet despite their physical differences, the brothers were identical in their provincialism and xenophobia.

Within minutes of the opening assembly, they seized upon Julian's newness, his separation from the herd, and they mocked his clothing and his strange accent. Julian tried to avoid the brothers—slipping behind a door, sticking close to a teacher—but despite his best efforts, he was not able to escape their pursuit. They followed Julian down the halls, flicking at his ears, yelling *commie, commie!* Please, Julian begged in his accented English, terrified and desperate to avoid conflict; please, he cried, one of the few new words he had learned in the weeks since his arrival. But the brothers were unrelenting, and Julian soon found himself cornered, with a gathering crowd of bloodlusters cheering wildly.

As the brothers closed in, Julian thought about his father's courage and his mother's deathbed instruction. Intent on extending his brave lineage, Julian sized up the boys. He decided first to attack the larger and presumably more menacing of the two, and then turn his attention to the thin one with the droopy eyes and the peculiar nose. Commie, they yelled. Anything but, Julian thought, proud of the lessons in commerce he had learned from Frankmann.

The boys drew closer. And then, just as Julian prepared to throw the first punch, he took his eye off the smaller of the two boys. And in that moment, the less menacing one—in appearance only—leaped forward, like a bullfrog vaulting off a log, and nailed Julian with a clean shot to the jaw that knocked him to the ground. The other brother then delivered four quick kicks to Julian's gut and ribs before a teacher, noticing the raucous crowd, ran over and intervened.

"Your first day?" Irina cried from a seat in the kitchen that was stocked with appliances Julian had never seen in Siberia: a dishwasher, a microwave oven, a refrigerator with an ice dispenser in the door, a shiny copper and brass espresso machine. "A fight on your very first day of school, Julian! How could you do such a thing? And a suspension on top of it." She looked forlornly over to her husband. "Our girls never got into trouble. Did they, Oleg?"

Embarrassed by both the suspension and the outcome of the fight, Julian dropped his head. With his right hand, he held his aching ribs. Oleg had been in dozens of fights as a young boy, and he understood a schoolboy's shame. He held his hand up to his wife. "Calm down, Irina, please," he said as he sipped cappuccino his favorite—from a porcelain cup. "They called you a commie?" he asked Julian.

"Yes, sir."

"And they mocked those handsome clothes Irina bought you?"

"Yes, sir."

"And you come back from your first day with your brand-new shirt torn up?"

Julian rubbed his eyes. "Yes, sir," he said, frightened of what punishment awaited him.

Oleg placed the cappuccino on the kitchen table, crossed his hands over his chest and smiled. "So, let me get this straight, boy. You can kill a man with your own hands but you can't hold off a couple of little punks from Jersey?"

Julian blushed at the reference to Krepuchkin—a man and

an event that Julian wished to strike from his memory. "Frankmann told you that? He told you I did that?"

"Frankmann told us everything, boy. That's why my wife was so happy to have you." Julian looked over to Irina, who was fingering a strand of beads. Oleg stood in front of the espresso machine and steamed more milk. "It's always the little ones who have the trigger fingers," he said, pouring the hot milk into his cup.

"Excuse me, sir?" Julian asked, distracted by the beauty of the glistening machine: its levers, its tubes, a shiny eagle on top, the locomotive hissing sounds.

"The little ones, boy. Always hit the little ones first. And remember, anything goes. The throat, the eyes, the ears." Oleg paused and looked at the boy, recalling his own difficult childhood in a Saint Petersburg ghetto and the horrors he endured. "And the groin," he said to the boy, "don't forget the groin."

Julian looked down to his own waist. "The groin?" he asked.

"Of course, Julian, anything goes. They don't follow Olympic boxing rules in the schoolyard."

Oleg returned to the machine and steamed even more milk. He pulled a cup from the cabinet and dropped in several spoonfuls of cocoa. After giving the milk one more prolonged blast of steam that created a fluffy froth on top, he poured the milk over the cocoa and placed the cup on the table before Julian. The boy looked at the hot cocoa, leaned over the cloud of steam, inhaled the sweetness—but did not touch the cup.

"Go ahead, boy," Oleg directed. "If you were expecting a punishment, that's not going to happen around here. We're not your parents, more like grandparents. And grandparents aren't in the punishment business, you know." Comforted, Julian reached for the cup, held it with both hands, felt its warmth.

"And besides, Frankmann said that you're a child who needs his space, that you're not the type of boy who responds well to authority. That with you it's just the opposite. And the last thing I want," he said, chuckling with admiration for the boy's gallantry, "is my skull split wide open."

Julian blushed again. Noticing the boy's discomfort, Irina cast a disapproving glance at Oleg and pulled Julian's chair close. "I tell you, boy, it's a blessing that you're here," she said. "A gift from God."

Rather than consoling him, Irina's expression of kindness evoked in Julian deep shame; for Julian, being valued invariably preceded great loss. He drank the hot cocoa and looked around the kitchen, careful to avoid the woman's gaze. "Don't worry," she said, "you will get used to this new world. It was a big adjustment for me and Oleg, but now life is easy for us." She picked up the beads and rubbed them with her thumb and forefinger. "The biggest barrier," Irina continued in Russian, "will be your English. So tomorrow you will start with a tutor, a professor from the university in Petersburg who now lives in New York. We were on faculty together in Russia, he's a member of the intelligentsia like me, and a master in Russian, English, French, Dostoevsky, Tolstoy, Shakespeare, all the greats. He will come here twice a week to teach you. It will take time and much effort, but in three, four years' time, your English will be better than the philistines' around here." Irina noticed a speck of blood in the corner of Julian's mouth. After placing the beads back down on the table, she licked the pad of her thumb and wiped the blood away.

That night, Julian lay in his bed, sobbing, replaying in his mind every moment of the lost fight. He longed for Petrov and Volokh, and he mentally revised the confrontation by inserting his friends into the scene. There they were, in the school with him, by his side, ready to fight. Julian imagined Petrov blocking the punch of the thin boy with the odd nose. He pictured Volokh delivering a straight right to the jaw of the older brother with the crew cut. He fantasized about pummeling the brothers into submission, being celebrated by the encircling crowd, hugging his friends from the orphanage. Julian came out of his fantasy and wondered what Petrov and Volokh were doing at that very moment, if they had enough food, if they too had been adopted— or if another boy had joined them in the drafty room with the bulging mattress. Julian wondered if he had been replaced.

Julian returned to an image of the fight, to the altered, nourishing version in which he emerged victorious. His father now joined him in this fantasy, and he thus imagined himself returning home at the end of the school day and boasting about the bullies he had defeated. His father beamed, praising his only child's courage, his victory in battle. This imagined validation soothed Julian, brought an end to his tears.

And then Julian thought of his mother—whose participation in this fantasy was essential. Julian imagined her entering the flat in the boardinghouse with dinner for the two of them: cured meat, potatoes and a slice of berry pie. He saw his wounds, his bruised lip, how his mother licked the pad of her thumb and wiped away a speck of blood from the corner of his mouth.

"Tell me," she said to Julian in his imagination—or was it now a dream? "Tell me again how these monsters threatened you, how you were outnumbered, how you prevailed. Tell me, dear Julian, how you refused to submit."

TO THE DOGWOOD
HE POINTS

The first time Julian and Sophie ever spoke—years before they became lovers, years before they married—was in a writing class, senior year in high school. Julian was a handsome young man, not conventional or perfectly symmetrical, but beautiful in an atypical way, what with his crooked nose and a pale scar across the right cheekbone, the chipped incisor. There was the tar-black hair and the dark eyes. And then there was his physicality, the twitching litheness in his body, a restlessness deep within. Julian was not large, but strong and sinewy, smooth in his movement—feline, powerful, agitated.

There were some tough guys in the school, but none wanted any part of Julian—for with Julian there was the tacit threat of disproportionate response, a disregard for civilized combat. It was as if, in response to a light slap, Julian might tear off a boy's ear or gouge out his eyes. The only fight Julian ever lost, his very first fight, was in sixth grade. A month after that defeat, he approached the two brothers who had beaten him; he took out the little one first with a knee to the groin, then he punched the big one in the throat, smashed his face into a locker. After that, Julian's reputation was sealed.

Despite his physical appeal, despite the giggles of the girls behind the locker doors and the notes passed to his unwilling hands, Julian seemed oddly disinterested in the local girls. During his senior year, a rumor spread that Julian preferred older girls, *women*, in college or out of school, and that he preferred them from the city. At different times, he was said to be dating a freshman from NYU; an actress with tattoos and a Mohawk who lived in the East Village; even a single mom, a waitress, who had a railroad apartment in Hell's Kitchen. Some of the boys speculated that Julian's reluctance to date girls from school was really a cover for a hidden homosexuality, but none had the courage to confront him with this accusation. Not that he would have minded. In fact, he would have found it entertaining. He was self-contained, autonomous, *sui generis*.

Sophie and Julian sat next to each other in the writing class taught by Margaret Bristol, a middle-aged woman who at first glance appeared dowdy and sheltered. But for those with sharp powers of observation, there were signs that suggested otherwise, signs that suggested Bristol nurtured a fading inner wildness and that, in her youth, her insides and her outsides were aligned. And it was only when she aged and got puffy, when her hair thinned and became brittle, that her physical appearance diverged from her inner life.

Sophie was intrigued by Bristol, and she searched for clues to the teacher's past. There was the sloppy tattoo of a serpent on her right ankle that had been rendered hazy and vague from years of sun and migrating skin cells. There was the tiny dot on her left nostril—an indented freckle that Sophie imagined might be the remnant of a nose ring. When Bristol readied herself at the end of each day, she put on round retro sunglasses with blue lenses.

There was not what one would consider a sexual chemistry between Bristol and Julian, nothing to suggest a teacher's improper romantic interest in a student and that student's misguided reciprocity. But what existed between them was a silent understanding that they would be lovers if only Bristol were forty years younger (but not if Julian were forty years older). Bristol, as beautiful and as enigmatic in her youth as Julian was now, knew from personal experience that there were layers of pain beneath his sangfroid. She understood Julian innately, for she too once kept people at a safe distance through similar conventions: aloofness, physical beauty, an internal algorithm that allowed her to quickly distinguish friend from foe and, for the unfortunate one identified as foe, the threat of a brutal and disproportionate response.

Bristol's assignments were designed not only to improve the writing skills of her students, but to provoke self-examination, to coax from her students the mysterious secrets and conflicts that formed their characters—further enhancing their craft in the process. Often, students participated in this exploration with little understanding of their own involvement; they wrote, only to realize after the fact that something unintended and therapeutic had occurred.

But Julian was keenly aware of Bristol's intentions—and because he saw in her something daring and protective, not unlike his mother, a deep trust developed within him. So when

Bristol asked the students to write about a *thing*, to describe an object in careful detail, Julian bravely chose a tiger's paw (wide as a dinner plate, claws curled like the tip of a witch's boot, leathery pads painted with strips of wet grass); when asked to describe a smell, Julian chose the odor of encroaching death (bitter, acrid, as if milk had curdled and spoiled, but also sweet, like a pot of sunflower honey in the Siberian sun).

The most challenging assignment coincided with the nearing end of the school year, when Bristol asked her students to describe a *fundamental disconnect*—where one's unwavering convictions were at odds with reality, where what one sees and believes and what others see and believe diverge to such a degree that they are irreconcilable. One student described her color-blindness, how she could not distinguish between navy blue and black, and the fashion failures that ensued.

One boy wrote about being raised in a devout Presbyterian home, only to discover that his mother was born Jewish and that, either by design or lack of interest, she didn't convert as planned upon her marriage. The boy described his surprise when he learned that under Judaic law he was indeed Jewish, that he was—at least in someone's eyes—something different from what he thought.

At first, you're shocked, questioning who you are. But then you realize it's just other people making up the rules, the classifications. The mother's side, the father's side? What if the Jews say it's a maternal lineage and some other religion say it's paternal, then what happens? Or what if they both say it's maternal? Or both paternal? Can you be both? Can you be neither? And once you realize that it's someone you never met trying

to tell you what you are and how you should view your-
self, present yourself to the world, then what does it
really matter? That's when you realize how absurd it is.
That's when you realize that the disconnect isn't being
something different than what you thought you were;
the disconnect is even thinking that you were something
in the first place.

Bristol stood before the class and fanned herself with a piece of paper. "Here's one that I'd like to read," she said, moistening her lips. "It's something Julian wrote." And as the students awaited the rare chance to learn something about their guarded classmate, Julian braced himself.

I am ashamed—ashamed to admit that I am so unat-
tractive that I have never kissed a girl. That's not true. I
did once, when I was eight, before the girls knew what
ugly was. That was a bright-life moment. But soon the
fist of hierarchy squeezed tight and rammed me to the
underworld.

My great loves have been unilateral and unknown to
all but me. That is why I write, to create voices, back and
forth, with Her, where only a muffled soliloquy once
existed—a maddening, tortured, silent scream.

Sometimes I dream about a blind girl, but fear that
her sighted friend—the one she's known since third
grade—would tell her she'd made a terrible mistake.
He's hideous, she might whisper, just hideous. Or maybe
the friend would have mercy on me. Do you think she
would? Have mercy?

I once asked a man, my father, if mercy exists. Yes, he said, mercy abounds. And he gave me a tap on the top of my head, a loving yet hollow tap that foretold both the tragedy of a child and the powerlessness of a father, the awful soul-sickening impotence of Our Father. Yes, He repeated, mercy abounds.

But I'm not so sure. I was born in Mercy General, says it right here, right on this piece of paper. But that's as close as I get.

When Bristol finished reading, a restless silence ensued, followed by secretive whispers, the rustling of paper, soles brushing the floor. And once the students had digested Julian's words, had repeated a memorable phrase or two in their minds, their reaction was vocal, animated—and divided mostly along gender lines. The girls giggled, were drawn in by Julian's sensitivity, an inner pain that for them was identifiable and that humanized him, made him more accessible to them. They appreciated the absurdity of this *disconnect*, how a man so beautiful could feel so unworthy—and they thus desired him even more. The boys, confused and even threatened, offended by what they perceived to be either an admission of weakness or a mocking, dishonest taunt, snickered and rolled their eyes.

His mind already on to other matters, it seemed, Julian merely shrugged his shoulders and doodled in his notebook. He appeared unconcerned with the attention thrust upon him, remaining distant and introverted. It was this distance that defined Julian, and it was as if his detachment fueled the mystery surrounding him, brought him increased and undesired attention.

Weeks after Bristol read Julian's piece aloud, rumors circulated through the school: that Julian was an orphan, that his mother was a prostitute, that he was sexually abused in the orphanage, that he had savagely murdered a gentle, elderly man. Sophie heard the rumors and wondered who had started them, if they were true or false; she wondered what impact they would have on Julian. She was astonished that someone could have betrayed him in such a manner. It must have been a woman, Sophie thought, someone in whom he had confided and who, her heart wounded, had violated his trust. Sophie wondered if the rumors would diminish him, destroy him. Or would they embolden him? Would they intensify his strength, the fear that he evoked in men? Would the rumors make him even more mysterious, more complex, more attractive to women?

From a safe distance, Sophie watched Julian. She observed her classmates' whispers and curious glances. She studied Julian's reaction or, rather, his *in*action. He remained chivalrous and polite with the girls: opening doors, guiding chairs, offering an umbrella in the rain. To the boys, he remained detached, neither polite nor rude, but enforcing a conscious separation with the implied threat of violence. Still, there were foolish souls who taunted Julian—anonymously, of course. Once, he sat down at his desk and found a copy of *Oliver Twist*. He lifted the book. He saw that *Oliver* had been crossed out with a marker, and *Julian* written in block letters above it. He flipped through a few pages of the book and grimaced, noting with simmering rage the intended reference.

Bristol assigned writing partners for a poetry project, and Julian found himself sitting next to Sophie. And although they had shared classes for years, Julian observed Sophie closely for the first time. He noticed her awkwardness, an unsteadiness in hand and in gaze for which she had become known. But Julian looked beyond the easily apparent, past her precocious height, past her poor posture, her blemished skin and eclectic style. When Julian looked into the mature distance, when he looked past the misleading present, he saw in Sophie the inevitability of spectacular beauty.

"What should we write about?" she asked, tapping a pencil on the desk in crisp couplets.

Julian leaned back in his seat to get a better look at Sophie. He noticed her ragged fingernails, her torn cuticles, a tiny flap of bloody skin on her left thumb. Sophie looked at Julian and, following his eyes, sensing that he had noticed her gnawed hands, dropped the pencil to the desk. Self-conscious, she made two tight fists—knuckles up and her thumbs inserted, so the markers of her distress were hidden.

Julian touched his fingertips to Sophie's forearm. "You okay?" he asked.

The sensation of Julian's skin on her own caused Sophie to blush. "I think so," she said.

"You seem upset." Julian nodded at Sophie's hands, prompting her to tighten her fists.

"It's just that, it's just I heard the rumors, and I . . ."

Julian thought about the girl who had betrayed him—her face so earnest, her tickling toes, the exuded trust that had prompted his imprudent disclosure. "It's nothing," he said. "In the end, it's really nothing at all."

Sophie shifted in her seat. "It's not nothing," she responded. "It's *something*. Fact is, the same thing happened to me. My uncle did it to me when I was little." Sophie released her fists. She placed her palms flat on the desk and spread her fingers.

Julian's jaw tightened. He looked around the room, then back to Sophie. He considered revealing to her the falsity of this particular rumor, how it was one of several about him that was untrue, but he feared that a denial at this moment would magnify Sophie's shame and sense of isolation. "Your *uncle?*" he asked.

"Yes. When I was little, maybe around six, seven years old."

"Did you tell anyone?"

"I told my mom, that's her brother. But she wouldn't hear of it, said I must be confused. And that was that."

"What ever happened to him?" Julian asked. His thoughts turned to Petrov, how his friend had been violated by the cook who smelled of rancid oil, how, after the incident, Petrov had returned to their small room, his eyes cast downward, and fell mutely to the mattress. That night, Julian and Volokh slept on either side of Petrov and, with power that was more imagined than real, protected their friend from further harm. "Your uncle?" he asked, furious with himself for not having avenged the harm done to Petrov. "What happened to him?"

Sophie paused, hesitant to reveal any more. But after Julian placed his hand on hers and nodded encouragingly, she continued. "Nothing happened. I just let it go. And he's gone on with his life like nothing happened, not a care in the world. Wife, kids, a good job. He's the fire chief at station eight, down by the church. He's sort of a celebrity around these parts, a *local* celebrity." Ashamed of the abuse, ashamed of her confession, Sophie paused again and examined her raw fingers.

As Bristol walked the aisles of the classroom, she noticed that Julian and Sophie were more engaged in their conversation than in the writing assignment, and she approached them. "How's it going?" she asked, tapping the blank paper on the desk. "Making any progress?"

"Tons," Julian responded with a wink—one that weakened Bristol and forced her to admit that she could not keep pace with the velocity of her own life. Fearful of authority, even compassionate authority, Sophie leaned over the desk—head down— and began to write. Julian, though, stood up. "I need a break," he said to Bristol. And before she could ask why, Julian walked out of the room, purposeful in his stride. Bristol had seen so many men walk out of so many rooms that she knew when you could convince a man to stay and when you had to let him leave—and she thus returned to her students.

Julian marched out of the school and across the front lawn. He crossed the parking lot, taking a shortcut behind a row of parked buses, and made his way out to the main road. From there, it was a half-mile walk down to the station. Julian entered the firehouse and was met with the suspicious glances of a half-dozen idle firefighters. Next to one truck, he saw a man in a white uniform that was more formal and ceremonial than the blue work clothes worn by the others. He approached the chief.

"Can I help you?" the man asked, wiping the shiny truck with a chamois.

"I'm in class with your niece," Julian said.

The man tossed the rag to the floor and approached Julian with menace in his step. "Sophie?" he asked.

"Sophie."

"And?"

"And you know why I'm here."

The chief squinted, attempting to read the intentions of the young man. "I have no idea why you're here."

"I think you do," said Julian grimly as he moved closer to the man, so close that they were now separated by no more than two feet.

The chief took a short step forward and further closed the distance. "I think I don't, and if you don't get out of my station, I'm going to throw you the fuck out."

Julian released a sigh of predetermination. He imagined the gnarled oak, the wind whipping through the courtyard, Krepuchkin's hand on his mother's shoulder. He recalled the high of braining the old man, the euphoria of restoring a natural, harmonious order. And then there was Petrov's anguish—so great, so negating, that the boy would forever reject even the *possibility* that a benevolent god might exist. Julian cocked his head. He drew it back and held it with the still force of a cobra. Then he drove his skull, his forehead, through the bridge of the chief's nose, a thunderous crack that shattered the man's face and propelled him backward into the truck's wheel. The chief looked up, barely conscious, blood drenching his crisp white shirt.

"You know why I'm here?" Julian asked.

Yes, the man nodded.

"So we're done?"

Yes, the man nodded again, waving off his approaching colleagues.

Julian returned to school later in the day, a red scuff on his brow. By that time, news of the attack had already spread through school, further magnifying Julian's mystique. In the cafeteria, Julian encountered Sophie. He approached her, fearful that he might be rebuked, afraid that he had crossed a line that Sophie did not want crossed. Sophie blushed. From her pocket, she removed a piece of paper. "For you," she said. Sophie watched as Julian unfolded the paper, as he looked around before reading, his lips mouthing her words, the weary smile, the moisture in his eye.

> *Today I wilt,*
> *in the air-sucking heat*
> *of my failure.*
>
> *Or is it?*
> *Mine,*
> *or a failure.*
>
> *A friend,*
> *he surrounds me.*
> *A cool, draping mist.*
>
> *Picks an eyelash from my cheek,*
> *lint from my sleeve,*
> *a shard from within.*
>
> *And it is no longer mine—this failure.*
> *It is his too,*
> *his to chew and swallow—and digest.*
>
> *To the dogwood he points.*
> *If the trees can do it,*
> *so can you.*

In deference, in gratitude, Julian nodded to Sophie. And then he bowed, dramatic and ceremonial—like Svetlanov after the final note.

HOLDOUT

At the age of twenty-six—yet another young man in New York City struggling to translate his considerable talents into commensurate results—Julian stood in his studio apartment: a small, barren room reminiscent of the one in the orphanage that he had shared with Petrov and Volokh. His apartment on the Lower East Side, too, had a broken window, courtesy of a real estate developer who owned the properties on either side of the decaying tenement. Julian placed his hand over the newly formed hole and cupped the harsh winter air. He peered through the open space, out to the street below, and then stuffed a ball of rags into the hole—a maneuver that only partially prevented the cold from entering.

As Julian watched a taxi spin its wheels in a hump of dirty snow, his thoughts turned to the speed with which four years had passed since his graduation from college—and how little he had accomplished. He thought about his time at Columbia, how, near the end of his freshman year, his adoptive parents had died within six months of each other. Oleg had hoped that his wife would pass first—not because he wished to have time alone at the end of his life or because he wanted Irina to suffer a punishment for some imaginary sin, but because he understood how fragile Irina had become in her old age, how terrified she was of solitude.

So, when Oleg imagined the sequencing of their deaths—who went first, who carried on—he pictured Irina alone at their home: gloveless, pricking her finger on the pointed thorn of his prized floribunda bush, scalding her hand in the hot steam of the espresso machine, the maniacal rubbing of the beads. And with those troubling images in mind, he concluded that he, not Irina, was better suited to outlive, and that it would be a blessing if Irina died first. But as he lay in the hospice, Irina pacing at the foot of the bed, he conceded that God had other plans.

Oleg and Irina left Julian with just enough money to complete his undergraduate studies, and he did so with a major in economics and a minor in English literature. After graduation, he joined a think tank that conducted what was described vaguely as "nonpartisan research on international economic issues for the betterment of the global community." There, he joined a team of intellectuals from various disciplines: economics, law, public policy, international relations. Julian's love for business had been instilled in him at a young age by Frankmann and cultivated in college by his professors. So, when he first entered the institute's Beaux-Arts mansion on the Upper East Side, he thought he had discovered an exciting entry point into the world of commerce.

But Julian's excitement was short-lived. He soon realized that the institute's work was too academic, too abstract for his liking, and that what he craved was the buzz of Frankmann's horse trading, the quick-twitch negotiations with colorful characters like the barmaid Garlova and the dimwitted Mongolian with the fermented horse milk. Julian dreamed of being in the middle of the fray. When he concluded that he had erred, that he was far too spirited for policy work, he resigned apologetically and took a job at a downtown brokerage house that he hoped would better suit his personality. There, in the boisterous, electric setting of the trading floor, he would buy and sell arcane financial derivatives. He loved the bustle of the floor, the frequency and speed of the transactions, the ability—like Frankmann—to quantify the profit and loss at the end of every day.

Yet, as the most junior broker on the desk, he was subjected to a ritual hazing that had been ingrained in this culture for decades. At first, the senior brokers required Julian to fetch coffee, cigarettes, sandwiches: tasks that were irritating but tolerable. But then his supervisor named him *board boy*—a demeaning role that required him to stand before two hundred brokers and update the latest prices on a towering white board. When the prices on the top row needed to be changed, Julian would climb a ladder—a wooden, wheeled type that might be found in an old English library—and glide from one end of the board to the other with marker in hand.

And it was here, atop this ladder, that an exhausted Julian mistakenly transposed two numbers—and a broker who drank too early and too much, with a map of magenta veins on his sprawling nose, noticed the error. At the age of fifty-two, ancient in this field, the broker screamed at Julian. Hey, board boy, you fucking suck! And then he grabbed an orange from his desk and threw it across the room, striking Julian in the back of the head. To the great delight of many, Julian lost his balance, fell off the top step of the ladder and crashed to the floor.

But rather than accept this humiliation as a necessary rite of passage—for every young broker took at least one demeaning turn as board boy—Julian rose from the floor and, orange in hand, walked over to the broker. He stood over the man and considered a backhand slap across the offender's face, an antiquated battery designed to debase rather than to injure. Julian looked at him: the gin blossom in full bloom, the shaking of the hands, the gray hair dyed a sad orange-black, his sandwich cut in quarters, his full name written on the side of a brown paper bag.

There was an uneasy feeling in Julian's chest, as if his heart itched. He looked at the rows of brokers lined up in front of their monitors—many laughing, some heckling, a small number unaware of this incipient conflict and focused on more important things. He squeezed the orange, crushed it so that the juice drenched his hand and dripped onto his polished shoe. Wondering if his inability to submit to another man was a blessing or a curse, he dropped the ruptured orange in the man's lap, glanced around the office for the final time and walked out.

Months later, Julian watched from his apartment as the taxi made it up over the peak of the snowy mound, caught its rear wheels on the pavement, and shot east toward Ludlow. He repositioned the rags to better fill the hole in the window, but as he twisted the cloth, his right thumb grazed the sharp glass and sliced the skin over his top knuckle. He shook his hand, sucked the blood from the wound, examined it, confirmed its superficiality. Then he cursed Austerlitz—the shadowy and private figure who had paid many millions to assemble the surrounding properties and who, Julian surmised, was responsible for the broken window.

According to neighborhood gossip, the developer intended to demolish the entire block and erect a hotel, a high-rise and a row of retail shops. However, Julian's landlord, a prideful Greek who refused to sell the tenement, was frustrating Austerlitz's plans. "I'm a holdout, a principled and irksome holdout," Fotopoulos would announce to the dwindling universe of people who would listen to him, to his tale of futile resistance.

The tenement stood dead center in the middle of the street and blocked the construction of the new building. Austerlitz had offered Fotopoulos an amount that was only a small fraction of its inherent value and an even smaller fraction of its market value, given its importance to the development. But when Fotopoulos stood firm, demanding a higher price, the developer resorted to acts that were devious and illegal, yet difficult to prove. First, the power lines to the building were cut, leaving the tenants in darkness for several days. Then the underground pipes were mysteriously severed, causing floods and leaving the tenement without running water. These inconveniences, life-threatening to some, caused an exodus among the tenants; only Julian and the landlord remained.

As Julian applied a sheet of tape over the rags, Fotopoulos knocked on the door. The landlord looked agitated, unstable. He held a cigarette in one hand, burned low against the filter. In his other hand he waved a document that had been rolled into a thin tube.

"We're at the end. . . . *I'm* at the end," Fotopoulos fumed. "No tenants, no rent. I haven't paid the mortgage in months." Fotopoulos tossed the roll of paper to the table and pointed. "There, a foreclosure. And then this bastard will get his wish."

Julian picked up the paper, unrolled it. He trembled at the injustice, enraged not only by the depravity of Austerlitz, but also by his own powerlessness. "Maybe I can pay you a few months' rent in advance," Julian offered. "I don't have much, you know, but it might help you hold on for a bit."

Fotopoulos grimaced and shook his head. "That would be very kind, but I couldn't. It would be money wasted. Even worse than wasted, if there's such a thing." The landlord snatched the foreclosure notice from Julian's hand and tore it to pieces. He stuffed the shredded paper into his coat pocket, waved farewell dramatically and descended the buckled stairs to his first-floor apartment.

Julian checked his watch, remembering that he had early dinner plans with Sophie. His wallet emptied of cash, he put on his coat and headed around the corner to the bank, where he withdrew money from the machine. He removed the receipt and, expecting once again to see irrefutable proof of his struggle, looked at the account balance. But Julian was shocked by what he saw, and he carefully examined the balance several times until he was satisfied that he was reading the numbers correctly.

Classic, fucking classic, Julian muttered with a mixture of dismay and regard—for it was at this moment that he first learned of Frankmann's death. There was no telephone call from Kira, no letter from a rabbi, no legal notice from a Russian probate lawyer. Rather, Julian learned of his mentor's demise when he checked the bank receipt and, expecting to find a balance of several thousand dollars, instead discovered that his net worth had ballooned to just over one million.

Julian knew that only one person could give him so much money—*would* give him so much money—and he smiled at the crafty manner with which Frankmann had announced his own death. He recalled the beloved iconoclast's gruff affection after his mother died, the months that he slept on Kira's sofa, played with her nieces, even kissed the one with the blonde hair and the scabby knees—how he stuck close to Frankmann's side, absorbing as much of the old man's business cunning as he could.

With the receipt in his hand, Julian walked out to the street and imagined what he might do with this windfall: a bright apartment uptown, a cottage in the country, maybe a car. He wondered if he should finally propose to Sophie. Walking up Avenue A toward Sophie's apartment, he approached the antiquarian bookstore that he loved. In addition to books and old autographs, the aromatic shop sold loose tea and pipe tobacco in enormous glass apothecary jars. The store was closed, but he stopped for a moment to look in the window. There was a stuffed fox baring its sharp teeth; a misshapen globe with the sprawling splash of the Soviet Union in red; several leather-bound volumes of indeterminate authorship; and there, leaning against a shelf draped in gold velvet, was an English edition of Turgenev's *Fathers and Sons*.

The book's plastic cover glistened in the streetlight, and Julian was reminded of the painter with the feminine features and his collection of fine books. Recalling with specificity Frankmann's lesson on scarcity, need and knowledge, he looked again at the receipt—at the million-dollar balance—and considered again what he might do with the money. This bequest was, Julian concluded, Frankmann's final lesson, his final challenge. The old man had guided Julian to the States years earlier, and now, with this ultimate act, he was leading the boy—the man—toward abundance.

He imagined what the old Jew might say to him at this instant. *Remember your wiring, Julian, the greatness of your lineage. Remember your mother's beauty, her faith. Her guidance. Submit to no man. And remember your father's courage, his quiet power. Go, boy, go. Just like I taught you. And don't screw it up.*

As he recalled Frankmann's preternatural ability to make money—to identify some quiet inefficiency in the marketplace that was invisible to others—Julian dismissed the idea of a cottage and a car, and this impulsive longing for immediate comfort was replaced by a hunger to turn this million into many more. Without intention or effort, his gait increased in speed and length, a reactive response of the nervous system that propelled him into a full sprint—an indication that his brain had transmitted a command to his body but had not yet revealed to him the reason for this command. A half block from home, still in full stride, a signal from deep within penetrated the lustrous membrane that separates unconsciousness from sentience, and an idea began to crystallize.

Julian considered the scarcity of the building and the land beneath it, how, given its singularity, it could not be more scarce; he thought of Austerlitz's need to own the property, its critical importance to the massive project; he estimated the many years and many millions that the developer had spent to assemble the surrounding properties and how those investments would naturally inflate the value of the tenement.

Julian pounded on the door of the landlord's apartment. After a few moments, Fotopoulos answered—holding yet another cigarette burned down to the filter. "No, boy, I cannot take your money," he said, closing the door.

Julian jabbed his foot into the doorway before the lock could engage. "Even if it's more than just a few months' rent?"

"Two, three, four . . . It doesn't matter, he wins."

Julian smiled. "He's not going to win."

The landlord dropped the cigarette into a bucket of sand on the floor. "How do you figure?" he asked.

Julian waved the bank receipt in the air. "What I have in mind is this. Through good luck, bad luck, some of both, I now have enough money to make your mortgage payments. And if necessary, I can hire some people who are as smart and nasty as Austerlitz. I put up the money, I join the fight, and we go from hunted to hunter. And after I get my money back, we split the profit fifty-fifty." Julian paused to let Fotopoulos consider the offer. "What do you think?"

Fotopoulos extended his hand. "Deal."

That night, flush with both cash and optimism, Julian took Sophie not to the cheap bar on Stanton with the great burgers but out for a grand dinner in the West Village. They settled into a cozy banquette; seated side by side, their shoulders touching, supporting each other, they reveled in the pop of the wood in the fireplace, the smells of pizza and cedar-plank salmon escaping from the wood-burning oven, the beautiful, prosperous people. Julian recalled the magical dinner with Frankmann and Kira, and he wondered what ever became of the young painter. He considered the series of unrewarding jobs he had held since college. And as he reached for Sophie's hand, he—like Frankmann at the age of eighty—wondered what role he might one day play in the world.

The ability of Fotopoulos to avert foreclosure with Julian's money—with *Frankmann's* money—first surprised and then infuriated the developer. When Austerlitz learned that Julian was bankrolling the landlord, that minor intimidation would not expel them from the building, he increased the pressure. Hardened by decades of competition in the city's vicious real estate market, Austerlitz knew every trick and was willing to resort to most of them. The developer hired a retired detective who was crooked enough to imply violence but, given his age and comfortable pension, disinclined to resort to it. The man showed up, unarmed, at Julian's apartment one evening, intending to bribe him with a knapsack full of cash. "A down payment on a new apartment," he said, raising the bag.

When Julian responded with nothing but a shake of the head, the man opened the top of the knapsack and turned it sideways, revealing stacks of hundred dollar bills. He pushed the bag toward Julian. When Julian again shook his head, the man refastened the bag and placed it on the hallway floor. He made a circular gesture with his folded right arm, a loosening up of the shoulder joint that was not a precursor to violence but a test of the young man's resolve. The detective looked for signs of panic that might indicate some willingness to compromise, a timorous reaction that he had elicited so often during his years on the force.

Julian, though, remained composed, leaving the detective to wonder if the young man's poise was the result of an exceptional confidence or if Julian's mind was so dull that he could not process the implications of his disobedience. And then, with a shiver, the detective considered another possibility; he wondered if his inability to instill fear was caused instead by his sagging pink skin, his tight-fitting suit, the osteoarthritic difficulty with which he had rotated his arm—if he had crossed into that age where a man can evoke fear only with a gun or the power to sign a paycheck.

Austerlitz was the most rational of economic animals, and when he heard the detective's report he understood that he had little choice but to raise his bid for the tenement. Resigned to an additional expense, he arranged to meet with Julian and Fotopoulos.

"How much do you want?" the developer asked, pointing to the building.

Fotopoulos looked at Julian, who nodded his encouragement. "Three times your last offer," the landlord said. The price was millions more than the previous bid, but still within the high end of the range that Austerlitz deemed acceptable. Cursing the added cost, Austerlitz extended his hand in agreement. But before Fotopoulos could shake it, Julian cleared his throat, nodded again and held up four fingers. Fotopoulos smiled. "Four times," he said with a wild grin. "Make it four."

Austerlitz withdrew his hand and considered the price. He stared at Julian, assessing his character. He saw in the young man's eyes not the denseness about which the detective had speculated, but a fierce yet quiet resolve, a determination that could not be shaken by another man; it was a look that he admired—calm and purposeful.

"Fine," Austerlitz said. "You'll have the money by the end of the week."

The next time Julian pulled a receipt from an ATM and checked his bank balance, he confirmed that he was worth several million dollars. This big score was not a terminal event that sated his desire for financial success; instead, his sudden wealth had an energizing effect—for after translating Frankmann's commercial theory into practice and finally eliminating the disconnect between his talents and his accomplishments, Julian was just getting started.

THE NIGHT

Julian would later recall that the beginning of *the night* was as perfect as a night could be—the opalescent twilight that seduced Pollock and Rothko and de Kooning, a light that sliced through the sky at seemingly incongruous angles, as if several suns of varying intensity hovered on different planes above, a light that blistered off the waves of the sea, yet softened to the north and tickled the textured bay.

Julian directed the car down Further Lane and pulled over to the side of the road, a hundred feet from the party. He stepped out of the vintage Porsche Speedster, a silver beauty from the late 1950s that he had obsessively restored. Julian and Sophie inhaled the air, sweet and saline, that blew in from the south, from the sea. Julian marveled at his good fortune, at the remarkable way that a life can, out of nowhere, change for better or for worse—the randomness, the violence of the swings, the transience of people, of things, of money, of states of being, the delusion of security and constancy to which a person reflexively clings.

Julian walked around the front of the car, opened the passenger-side door and extended a hand to his wife. As Sophie stood, he noticed the curve of her lower back, revealed by the tantalizing aperture in her dress. He guided her under a birch pergola, beneath drapes of pungent purple wisteria. They stopped to admire the house, a grand, weathered Georgian mansion with arachnoid fractures in the façade and a dead branch of ivy that wrapped, denuded, around a first-floor window. The cracks and the lifeless bough triggered in Julian a recollection of the orphanage, of the decay and debasement of his childhood. He wondered how it was that the neglect of a mansion, the indolent disinterest in its upkeep, could actually suggest even more confident wealth than a well-maintained home—while the same flaw in an orphanage, a crack running from the roof's edge down to the front door, merely magnified the wretchedness of the place.

The party was not atypical for a party in this particular town during the summer season. In attendance were several prominent bankers, men whose sartorial ease (a frayed collar, a carefully placed abrasion on the khakis, a scuffed loafer, a braided string bracelet) didn't so much hint at fiscal sobriety as it howled an insincere *aw-shucks*, as if their purposeful sloppiness could mask their great prosperity, a false modesty that, in light of his own impoverished upbringing, Julian found distasteful.

There was a cluster of those with inherited wealth who, comforted by proximity to their similarly situated peers, stuck closely together; it was this group with which Julian felt most comfortable, because even though their birthright was the opposite of his own, he related to the absurdity of being born into such an extreme, to a person's being defined by something that he had no role in creating. For Julian, having been both poor and then rich, there was little difference between the outliers of poverty and wealth; for those who were born into money, every accomplishment was—in the eyes of others and sometimes even themselves—unfairly diminished, explained only by their good fortune and the advantages that accompanied their legacy. For those born impoverished, those same great accomplishments were too unfairly diminished, but in that case by the cynical suspicion that any such accomplishment could only be achieved through either extraordinary luck or the commission of a crime.

Julian and Sophie were not big drinkers: a couple of glasses of wine at dinner, a beer or two at a ball game, the occasional cocktail after work. When Sophie went out with her girlfriends, she might splurge; she might have one or two martinis, feel the hot flush in her cheeks, a numb buzz, then back home not to make love with Julian, but to fuck him in a collegiate stupor, evoking the rebellious, sloppy sexuality of her youth.

At the party, Julian and Sophie drank more than usual. They reached for flutes of champagne that, with bizarre frequency, danced by on tarnished trays. To save their appetites for the meal, they nibbled on frugal hors d'oeuvres, but realized an hour into the party that dinner would not be served, that their hosts' intention, consistent with the maintenance of the home, was to offer only drinks and sparse snacks with an early end to the evening. Dehydrated from a day at the beach, their stomachs not adequately filled to counteract the carbonated alcohol, Julian and Sophie experienced a simultaneous wooziness.

A rivulet of perspiration sluiced down the channel in Sophie's lower back. She reached for Julian's elbow and steadied herself. "Let's go," she said.

Julian nodded. "Agreed, but I don't think I can drive. I'm a little buzzed."

"Come on, babe, it's only a half mile," Sophie said, playfully pushing Julian toward the car.

"Let's just walk," Julian countered, as he slipped from Sophie's grasp. "It's a nice night, and we can get the car in the morning."

Sophie extended her hand. "Give me the keys. I'll drive."

Julian held the keys behind his back. "Come on, Sophie, it's only a fifteen-minute walk."

"I'm tired, don't want to walk. We'll be home in two minutes. Please, my feet are killing me."

Julian thought about the short ride home, about his desire to please Sophie—and he capitulated. He guided her to the car. He opened the passenger door, got her settled in the low bucket seat, and waited until her right foot rested on the floorboard. He walked around the front of the car, pausing to place his fingertips on the hood for balance. Julian opened the door, settled in behind the wheel and ignited the engine.

The last words he said to Sophie before the deer jumped out from behind a hedge on Georgica Road, before he overcompensated, turning the wheel violently to the left, before the car crashed into a utility pole, before Sophie went through the windshield . . . before all that, Julian's last words to Sophie—words that he would forever regret—were *fine, I'll drive, but if anything happens, it's your fault.*

ZENO'S PARADOX

'm in the club, it's the middle of the afternoon and real slow
again. I'm sitting at the bar and it's just a few regulars, the fat
guy who's here so often I'm beginning to think he either lives
here or he's a narc, and the smelly lawyer who's been coming
around a lot since he lost his license. I'm chewing on a piece of
ice, wondering about big stuff, what I'm gonna do with my life
or if this is it. Jade walks by and gives me a wink and says hang
in there, sweetheart, 'cause she knows I've been down lately and
I told her how I'm thinking about quitting, maybe working in
the diner with my mom.

The front door swings open and in comes the sun, big and bright
and throbbing like it's got a life of its own. It lights up the dark bar
for a few seconds, shows all the scuffs on the walls, the stains on the
seats, the pimples and wrinkles on the girls' faces. And while the
door's open, while we're getting a big reminder that things aren't
what they seem, everything freezes and we all stand still. The bar-

tender has a rag in his hand, holds it there, Lopez is frozen to the pole, and we hold our breath and wait for the darkness to come back, for the fantasy to return. In steps a small man with glasses and thinning hair, late thirties is my best guess. He's not a handsome man but sweet-looking, and he's got a limp that's real noticeable. And from a distance I can see he's got one normal shoe and one shoe with a real thick sole to give his leg a few extra inches.

I see him talking to Schultz, who's back from medical leave. The small man raises his hand to shoulder height, looks around the bar and squints in the dark—which, best I can tell, is the opposite of what you should be doing in a dark room. Schultz nods and points over in my direction. The man looks at me from across the room, stands there for a bit like he's trying to figure out if he really wants to do this, then limps toward me. I'm thinking maybe I'm gonna get my first dance of the day, make a bit of money, so I straighten up real fast, lip gloss and a toss of the hair, a mint in my mouth and straighten out my skirt. The man approaches me, stops a couple of feet away and in a real soft voice, shaky and nervous, he says sorry to bother you, but you wouldn't be Perla, would you?

I look him in the eye, try to size him up. I can't make him out, good or bad, so I say no bother, and yes, I *would* be Perla. The guy puts out his hand, shakes mine, and says pleasure to meet you, my name's Roger. Well, Roger, why don't you have a seat. And I tap the chair next to me, cross my legs real proper and wave to Jade. She comes over and I say Roger, it's your lucky day, 'cause I'm buying *you* a drink, so what's it going to be? Roger orders a bottle of beer and I get a ginger ale, even though it's not feeling like much of a treat today. I make eye contact with Jade and glance in the direction of his thick shoe and that's my cue to Jade not to play the hundred-dollar joke, 'cause what we've got here is a man who's seriously disabled and the least we can do is have a bit of compassion for the man. Now, Roger could be a total prick for all I know and doesn't deserve one ounce of compassion, but I believe in karma and for now I'm playing it safe and gonna treat the guy real nice. And no matter what, life's got to be harder for him than it is for the same exact guy who's got two good feet.

I start off asking Roger the usual questions. Where you from? How long you in town? Turns out he's from up north, New York area, and just down for a few days. Jade comes over with the drinks and Roger reaches for his wallet before I can even open my purse, says it's on me. Jade gives me a wink, thank God, that says don't worry, I'm not playing the joke, and then she tells him it's fifteen bucks. Roger pays the tab with a nice tip on top and looks around in wonder at the girls and the lights. I put my hand on his thigh and say you want a dance, baby? Right here for twenty or over in one of those private rooms, and I point to the VIP Room and the Champagne Room.

Roger takes a sip of his beer and says no, thanks, you're real pretty and nice but I'm not here for a dance. I'm a friend of Julian's, you see, and it just wouldn't be appropriate. Julian, I mumble, and I'm trying to process what I just heard 'cause it's been a couple of months since I saw him and there's been no news from him since then. And it's pretty painful to share so much with a man and even though he's married and I'm just a stripper, and I really don't have a right to any expectations, to have him just disappear on you is real hard.

I straighten up and cross my legs real tight. You a friend of Julian? Julian from New York? *Married* Julian, who hasn't called me in forever? And Roger nods, yup, *that* Julian. I'm a little confused and a lot angry. I down my ginger ale to make it look real dramatic, but it's not as big a gesture as it would be if I had vodka or scotch or something alcoholic. Then the orange slice somehow gets stuck on my lip, dangles there for a sec, falls in my lap, and I feel like a big fool.

Roger smiles, puts his hand on my wrist, real soft, and says please hear me out, Perla. Julian's my closest friend, I work for him too, the guy I'm most loyal to in the entire world. Julian sat down with me last week, said Roger, I met someone down in Florida. She's beautiful and kind and doing a difficult job with dignity, grace, professionalism. That's the thing about Julian, he appreciates mastery and commitment, doesn't care if you're a brain surgeon or a bank robber. Or if you're painting a bathroom or the Sistine Chapel. Roger gets flushed in the face, says the Sistine Chapel's in the Vatican City, in Rome. And I laugh and say really, Roger? I had no idea. Just 'cause I'm a stripper doesn't mean I don't read. I give him a little poke in the chest and tell him, you know, Roger, I don't have a formal education, but I had a father who knew more about the world than most people with a degree. So one more condescending comment from you and I'm sending you back to Julian in a body bag, your entrails in a separate bag. *Entrails*. See, that's a big word. Not long, but big.

Roger lifts his hand from my wrist and takes a quick sip of beer to wet his throat, wipes his lips with the back of his hand and apologizes. I'm so sorry, it's just that I get nervous around pretty girls. And he looks down at his foot, winces and bends over and rubs his right calf. I'm just awkward when it comes to girls and I'm always saying stupid stuff, so nothing personal and no reflection on you. I'm looking at the man, all thin and hobbled and bumbling through a conversation, and it occurs to me that this Roger is a tender man. And I think of my dad, and how he used to cry so easy, like when he saw a three-legged dog limping down the street once in Plantation or the little boy at the mall in Hialeah who couldn't find his parents.

Roger downs his beer and you can tell from the way his face twists that he's not used to drinking booze. The reason I came down here, he says, is because Julian can't come down for a while, he's got stuff going on in his personal life and some business things too, and he wanted you taken care of. Roger pulls an envelope from his back pocket and hands it to me. There's ten thousand in here, he says, and shrugs his shoulders 'cause it's a little weird to just hand a girl ten grand for nothing. Now, never in my life did I have ten thousand dollars to my name, let alone in my hand, and I'm feeling so giddy and excited that I can hardly hold on to the bar stool. And I'm thinking how happy my mother is gonna be and how we can pay the rent on time, pay off some credit cards and maybe buy myself a pair of sandals that I saw in Coral Gables.

I open the envelope and look at the bills, all brand-new and lined up perfect like they just got printed at the bank. I put my nose close, breathe in deep and sure enough there's the smell of fresh cash. But then I feel some nausea in my stomach, 'cause something about getting all this cash for doing nothing, something about getting all this cash from someone you have feelings for, something about it feels a little cheap and demeaning to me. It makes me feel bad, worse than getting twenty bucks for a dance, 'cause at least there's an equal exchange when I'm stripping. Dance, money. Dance, money. Here, it's just money with nothing in return. There's no *quid pro quo*. I know that, too, a bit of Latin.

But I get over the bad feelings fast, real fast, 'cause at the end of the day I'm a practical girl and all this cash is a huge deal. Thanks, I say, and try to jam the thick envelope inside my clutch, a tiny silver bag that I've been using ever since one of the girls got her keys and phone and ID stolen out of a locker. I look at Roger's face real careful, at his old dress shirt, at his cheap, plastic watch. I wonder how it is that Roger and Julian are friends, how two people with such different looks, such different styles, could be good friends. Looks to me like they come from different worlds.

I flag Jade and give her the 'nother round motion, a circle in the air with my index finger. You flew down here, all the way from New York, just to give me this envelope? Roger nods yes. And Julian asked you to get on a plane, give me this envelope, and then go back home? Yes, again. And you got no other business down here but bringing me this money? That's right, no other business. And you don't mind doing that, spending all this time traveling just for one errand? Roger looks at me all confused, seriously confused, like he really doesn't understand the question, like I spoke in a strange language, maybe one that's not even invented yet. Do I mind? Do I mind? Not only do I not mind, but it's an honor to do something like this for Julian. An honor, I ask, why would it be an honor? I want to know, 'cause it seems more like a big old burden to me.

Jade places the drinks on the bar. I pull a hundred out of the envelope and hold it up to her. This one's on me, I say. Jade snatches the bill from my hand and flashes it under the light, front then back, and asks this real or you just print it yourself? I say it's real as they get and Roger here gave it to me. So Jade leans over, gives Roger a big wet kiss on the lips and struts off. Now, Roger looks like he just got licked by a bulldog and wipes his lips with the back of his hand. Then he knocks down half the bottle in a few gulps, clears his throat, says I'm going to tell you a story, a story about Julian. And maybe when I'm through, you'll understand why I get on a plane for Julian, why I'm grateful to have the chance to get on that plane, why there's nothing I'd rather do than get on that plane and fly down here for that man and hand a girl like you an envelope full of cash.

You may have seen that I've got a bum leg, he says, and points to his funny-shaped shoe. It's shorter than the other by three and a half inches, and the foot's deformed. It's thick and rounded and I have three toes that are fused together, like one big toe. My father has the same thing. My granddad, too. It's a genetic deformity. And that's one of the things I love most about my mother, because she knew when she married my dad, when she decided to have a child with the man, that there was a high likelihood she'd have a kid with a deformed foot. But she loved him so much, and how couldn't you, that she did it anyway. Ignored her parents' advice, even a doctor who said it would be foolish to go into it knowing damn well what was going to happen. But she was crazy about the man.

Anyway, I loved to play sports when I was young, but the foot made it impossible to compete. I mean, I could limp around the schoolyard a bit, but competitive games, organized sports, were off-limits for me. Football was my favorite, but hard to play for a boy with my sort of problem. Still, the coach was fond of me and the other kids on the team had some compassion and they voted me on the team, said I could be the scorekeeper, keep the stats, and even though I couldn't play, they'd give me an honorary spot on defense. They even got me a uniform with my name on the back, put me in the team photo. On game day, I got to stand on the sidelines in my uniform and support the guys. It was a great season for me. My parents came to every game, and even though they knew I would never play, they rooted like I was a starter. How many times did my father introduce me to his friends as *my son, the football star*.

We had a terrific team that year, led by Julian. He wasn't the

biggest guy on the team, but always the most intense, competitive guy on the field, wiry and fast and a threshold for pain that
most of us really couldn't comprehend. He was also smarter, it
seemed, than our coaches, and he would always be huddling
with them, drawing up new plays, different defenses, whatever
could give our team an advantage. Sometimes it almost felt like
he was the real coach.

Julian was a mysterious guy intelligent, handsome, but
very distant from almost everyone in school. Rumor was he was
born in Russia, Siberia they said, and that he lived in an orphanage. They said he came to the States when he was ten or eleven,
and maybe that's the reason why he was a bit withdrawn, aloof.
It's not that he wasn't friendly, just remote and cool, like he was
years ahead of the rest of us, like he was on to bigger things.
They named him prom king, but he declined, didn't even show
up. He was salutatorian, too, but refused to give a speech.

Salutatorian, Roger says with a smile 'cause he knows what's
coming, that's second in the class. Fuck you very much, I say like a
lady. Now, that's a word I never did hear before, and I make a mental note to look that up when I get home. Roger takes another swig
of beer and looks around the room for Jade. She sees him, nods and
struts on over to the bar to get us another round. Fortysomething
years old, and the girl's still got a little shake in her booty.

We were undefeated during the regular season, Roger says,
tops in the county and one of the best in the state. Julian was the
only one on our team who played offense and defense, wide
receiver *and* safety. So we were in the county championship
against Livingston, and we were winning by one point with a
minute left in the game. It was a tough one for us. We'd already
lost five players to injuries, all on defense, one guy starts throwing

up and he was on the sideline, too. Then one of our guys, Clarke was his name, and he had all sorts of mental problems, he gets thrown out of the game for fighting. So, Livingston is on its own ten-yard line, down by a point with a minute left in the game. We keep them off the scoreboard and we win. Simple as that. Julian gathers everyone in the huddle and spells out the defense, tells the guys to stick to their assignments, no free-lancing. Sure enough, the first play of the drive, our cornerback gets hurt, and with all the other injuries, we don't have any more defenders who can play.

The coach looks around and points to one of our offensive play-ers, a tight end, and tells him to go fill in for the player who just got hurt. The tight end is huge and not too fast, and he says coach, I never played corner in my life. That's when Julian steps in, says coach, let's put Roger in. Now, I'm standing right next to the coach with my clipboard and my pencil, keeping the stats, and I'm think-ing this has to be some sort of cruel joke or maybe Julian got the name wrong, but Julian's not the type of guy to make cruel jokes and he's certainly not the type of guy to mix up a name.

The coach looks at Julian like he's nuts, which in a weird, con-trolled way he is, and says *Roger?* You want me to put *Roger* in? And Julian says yes, I want you to put Roger in. Just like that, real matter-of-fact. The coach looks at me and back to Julian and back to me, then pauses for a few seconds and says Roger you're in. Julian's got a way about him, you know. People tend to do what he says. And not because he's threatening, but because he's, well . . . Anyway, I'm so excited I can barely find my helmet. I run out on the field and the first thing I've got to do is cover Livingston's wide receiver, who's all-county and runs like a goddamn greyhound.

Their quarterback, a colossal prick named Ferrara, sees me

limp out onto the field and he yells, real loud for everyone to hear, not just everyone on the field but everyone in the stands too, my parents included. He screams we got gimpy on the right, we're going at gimpy. And sure enough, the first pass he throws is in my direction. I read the play correctly, because that's all I do is study offenses and learn how our defense works, but there's no way I can stay with their receiver. He blows right by me and picks up thirty yards on the first play. Now, no one is feeling worse than me, and in the huddle, I say to Julian that maybe I should get out, bring in one of the other guys. I'm afraid I'm going to lose it for us, but Julian looks at me and says don't worry. Don't worry? I ask. How *can't* I worry?

Sure enough, the next play they go after me again. And it's even worse this time because Ferrara names a play after me, and at the line he calls out *gimpy forty-five, gimpy forty-five.* And he screams so loud that I know my parents can hear. I cringe, try not to look up into the stands. So they beat me over and over, pass after pass, until they're on our eight-yard line with five seconds left, and by this time I'm crying so hard I can barely breathe. Livingston lines up for a field goal, a little chip shot to win the game. We're in the huddle and I'm sobbing, apologizing to my teammates. I can't bear to look in the stands and see my parents, the pain on their faces. Just then, Julian puts his hand on top of my helmet, looks around at all of us and says don't worry, it's their time to suffer now. Julian looks at our nose tackle, the position right across from their center, and says I'll take your guy.

So we line up, Julian right across from the center who is going to snap the ball. We all know what's about to happen. The center is going to snap the ball. The holder will place the ball. The kicker will kick the ball and we will lose the championship.

From this distance, it's a gimme. But Julian apparently has another outcome in mind, and before the center can snap the ball, Julian smacks it out of his hands. Well, that's a penalty, and the ref marches off four yards, half the distance to the goal line. That's the rule. When you have a penalty that close, they walk off half the distance. Now it's an even closer field goal, a chip shot, and we're all figuring that Julian is just blowing off some steam, venting his frustration. The Livingston coach is furious, half the crowd starts booing and I just want the game to end so I can get the hell off the field and hide somewhere.

The center gets down in position and puts his hands on the ball, ready to snap it. And then Julian does it again! Smacks the ball out of the center's hands. Now the booing is even louder, and the Livingston guys are calling him a sore loser and an asshole. Another penalty, half the distance to the goal line and now they're at the two. Then he does it again. A penalty and now to the one. And again and again and again and again; the half-yard line, quarter yard, eighth of a yard, sixteenth, and the ref is having a harder and harder time trying to spot the ball. Finally, after about the tenth penalty, the ref places the ball on the grass and the tip touches the goal line. Touchdown! the ref yells, and the game is over.

No one on the field feels worse than I do, because I'm the one who lost the game for us. I'm crying and I look up in the stands and see my parents standing there in the front row. My mom has her hand over her chest and I can tell she's having trouble breathing. My dad is standing up straight, stiff and proud. He grinds his teeth, which is what he always does when he feels powerless. It's also his way of holding back tears.

I walk off the field, trying my hardest not to limp, trying not to be noticed. And then something magical happens. Julian walks over to the ref. He puts his arm around the ref's shoulder and says it's not a touchdown. And the ref says it sure is a touchdown, the ball's touching the goal line. Julian shakes his head, smiles, says it can't be, because what we've got here is Zeno's Paradox. Zeno's what? the ref wants to know. Zeno's Paradox. Zeno was a Greek philosopher, Julian explains, said if you keep moving half the distance toward a fixed end point, you can never get there. The ref looks confused. Think about it, Julian says, there's always a smaller amount of distance that can be covered. You might need a damn microscope to calculate the distance, but you can never get to the end point. The ref is pulling at his chin with his thumb and index finger, starts nodding his head up and down, and says yes, yes, I think I see what you mean. And then he waves his hands wildly and declares no touchdown, the ball will be placed at the one-centimeter line. Zeno's Paradox, the ref yells.

Well, the Livingston players go nuts and their coach starts screaming who the fuck is Zeno? And the ref says he's a Greek philosopher, and the coach responds, well, what the hell does a Greek know about American football? And the ref says Alex Karras was Greek, and he played pro for the Lions and knew a hell of a lot about football. Then the coach screams at the ref, says Ref, your mother must have been a mongoloid, and the ref understandably calls an unsportsmanlike conduct penalty, because who uses a word like that, *mongoloid*, that's just terrible and bizarre, and the ref sets Livingston back fifteen yards. Next thing, one of their players sticks his finger in the ref's chest and says Zeno was a mongoloid *and* a homosexual, and damned if anyone has any idea what that even means, but the ref gives Livingston another fifteen-yard penalty, and now they're backed up to the thirty-yard line. Plus a centimeter. It takes a few minutes for them to calm down, and they finally get lined up again for the field goal. But because they're so far out now, the kicker has to change the trajectory of the ball, has to hit it lower to get the distance.

The center snaps the ball and the kicker takes his shot, but hits it so low that Julian blocks it and the ball hits the ground. It bounces right in front of Julian, and all he has to do to end the game— there's only a couple of seconds left at this point—all he has to do is to fall on the ball. But instead he picks it up and he grabs me by the jersey and says you're coming with me. And before I can say no, he hands me the ball and pushes me forward, toward Livingston's end zone. Everyone is so dazed by what happened that I'm halfway down the field before anyone notices. Julian is running by my side, keeping his eye on the Livingston players, blocking for me.

I'm fifteen yards from the end zone and I glance up to the stands and there's my parents, clapping like circus seals and my dad is crying, he's so happy. Ferrara, the prick who called gimpy forty-five, is chasing me and I'm running so slow with my bad foot that he's getting closer and closer, and I don't think I can make it. So I try to lateral the ball to Julian, put it right in his hands. But he just hands it right back to me. Unfinished business, he says, and he's gasping for air, maybe because he's exhausted or maybe it's the adrenaline. Ferrara is now within a couple of yards of me. Julian trails behind, his eyes on Ferrara. Five yards from the end zone and I'm pushing as hard as I can. My bad foot hurts because it's just not designed to run this fast, this hard, and I don't think I can make it. I look back and Ferrara is just a couple of feet behind me now, but Julian is right there between us.

Gimpy forty-five! Julian yells at Ferrara. Gimpy fucking forty-five! Then Julian digs his cleats into the ground and plants his legs. He cocks his shoulder and launches himself into Ferrara with a violence and a force that is difficult to describe. I'm right there and I hear the crack of bones, the blast of air expelled from a person's lungs, an inhuman groan. As I cross the goal line, I look back. Ferrara is on the ground. He's unconscious. His left arm is splayed out like the broken wing of a bird. Blood pours from his nose. Julian stands above him, defiant, victorious. He looks like Muhammad Ali standing over Sonny Liston in that famous picture. You know the one?

Gimpy fucking forty-five, Julian yells at Ferrara, at Ferrara's body. He pauses. Gimpy forty-five, he says. Then, in a soft voice, he whispers gimpy forty-five. He whispers something I can't understand. It sounds like *moht*. Years later, I would learn what he said. Mother. He said *mother*, in Russian. And then Julian starts to cry. First, soft tears, then stronger, louder. Gimpy forty-five, he wails. He kneels down and pounds his fist in the mud. And all of us, all of his teammates, gather around him, standing in a circle around Julian. We're quiet, shielding him from the crowd, from the Livingston guys, who are furious and trying to lift Ferrara off the ground, get him medical help. We're respectful of what is happening to Julian. And even though we don't fully understand it, we know it's important.

We wait in that circle for five minutes. We hold hands, real quiet, rock back and forth on our feet. We're patient, awaiting a cue from Julian. Then he rises. There are quiet hugs and pats on the helmets. Not the euphoria of a championship, but a somber satisfaction. It's not a time for celebration. It's a time for reflection, a time for each of us to recalibrate our understanding of the world and the extent to which a person can go when pushed to a limit, the extent to which a person *should* go when he finds himself standing before that line—the line where things really start to matter.

Why Julian cried, Roger says, I don't know. And I never asked him. Maybe it was Ferrara's cruelty. Or maybe having to right a wrong—and using violence to do it. Or maybe it was something else. Maybe it was something entirely different. Maybe he wasn't avenging me. Maybe it was his own rage, his own trauma that he was trying to fix. Maybe this was Julian righting a wrong done to him. His childhood, losing his parents so young. In a way, it didn't matter, *doesn't* matter, because it can be any one of those things. Or it can be all of them, right? It just depends on who you are and how your life goes. If you got lucky or not.

Roger finishes off the beer. He holds the empty bottle up to the light. It's pretty when the light hits it, he says. He holds it up at a different angle near my eyes so I can see for myself. There's a blinking red light above the bar that hits the amber glass and creates a pretty color—and I say it sure is nice when you look at it like that and almost makes you forget that we're in such an ugly place. Roger smiles. I guess so, he says.

He stands up, struggles with his bad foot and I grab his arm to keep him from falling over. He looks at me sort of embarrassed, I'm thinking maybe 'cause he almost fell or maybe 'cause he told me such a personal story, and he leans over and kisses me on the cheek. Nothing creepy, but real sweet like Old Pepe used to kiss me. He says nice to meet you, Perla, but I have a flight to catch. And before he turns to leave, he touches his hand to my cheek, again real sweet and caring, and he says Julian will be back one day, I'm banking on it. And if you could, please be kind to this man. And patient, too. Because things are more complicated than you think. A *lot* more complicated.

135 DEGREES

Julian Pravdin awoke—not to the sound of her choking, and not to a remarkable clearing of the throat, but rather to nothing more than the faintest hint of a gasp emanating from the parched throat of his paralyzed wife. The brain, he once read, has malleable properties. Neuroplasticity, they call it. The injured brain, the weak brain, the brain with diminished capacity can evolve, mutate, compensate for its deficiencies. It can create new neural pathways, new connection points, new wiring. The brain, he learned after the accident, can remap itself.

And so it was, after Sophie became paralyzed from the waist down, that not only did her brain crackle and spark and mutate into a different organ, one that allowed her to exist, to eat, to drink, to brush her teeth, to communicate, to laugh, to grieve— to extract some modest amount of pleasure from a life that had become irreversibly less enjoyable, but so did Julian's own brain undergo a conversion.

In response to her injury, Julian's hearing became acute, animal-like, so that he could now register in the early morning darkness her somnolent gurgle before it occurred. His myopic vision, once the object of Sophie's playful ridicule, could now detect in the lilac twilight a nearly invisible, purplish hue in her calf, a ruptured capillary that foretold a circulatory crisis. And his sense of smell became so acute that, from a distance of twenty feet, enveloped even amid the foul stench of a China-town street in August, the odor of feces from her soiled diaper would rip through his nasal concha and set off his olfactory receptors—prompting Julian to move his wife to a bathroom and clean her up as she grimaced in shame.

And it was these heightened sensitivities that allowed Julian to care for his wife, to keep her alive, to ensure that her reservoir of dignity would remain protected, untouched.

When Julian heard her gasp, a result of the sleep apnea that had plagued her since the accident, he turned and reached for her shoulder—and at that moment of contact, the muscles in the back of her throat flickered and tensed, opening the passageway and again permitting the free flow of air. Julian reached for a pillow. He watched her lips twitch, listened for her raspy exhale. He lifted the pillow and observed the contour of her face, the bump on the bridge of her nose, the beauty mark on her right cheekbone, a pale scar along her hairline—imperfections that perfected her.

As if he were strangling the last breath from his most odious enemy, Julian squeezed the pillow. He calculated the angle of his approach and cleared a strand of hair from Sophie's forehead. Then he lifted her left shoulder and wedged the pillow under-neath her, elevating her upper torso and turning her slightly to the side—a position that drew her tongue away from the back of her throat and allowed her to breathe more freely.

Julian rose and moved to the foot of the bed. There, he checked to make sure that the compression machine was functioning, that it continued to slide up and down Sophie's attenuated legs every five minutes, stimulating the flow of blood, maintaining what little muscle tone remained. Satisfied, Julian returned to bed. He lay on his back and stared at the ceiling. He listened to Sophie's breathing—smooth, metronomic. Grateful, he closed his eyes and wished for a quick transition back to sleep, the opportunity for two more hours before the day started.

Julian reached for Sophie's hand. It was gelid, wet. He squeezed tightly, hoping to transfer his body heat to her. He stared up at the ceiling, at the ornate molding surrounding the room. He recalled their first visit to the apartment, an innocent time when they were propelled forward by a surge of optimism, giddy, buoyant—how Sophie gasped when she saw the twelve-foot ceilings and the intricate molding, how she pressed her hands to her chest and mouthed the word *wow*. Julian had noted his wife's reaction. He turned to the broker and said we'll take it. It's ten million, the broker replied, and they received an offer this morning for the asking price. Then make it ten-five, Julian said. All cash.

The recollection of that joyous day had a soothing physiological impact on Julian. His heart rate slowed, his breathing deepened, his jaw loosened, his otherwise busy mind approached stillness. But then, mere seconds from unconsciousness, a siren roared down Fifth Avenue and the frantic howl created in him an instant mental acuity that precluded sleep.

Conceding the hopelessness of it all, Julian lifted the covers and swung his legs over the side of the bed. He repositioned the cashmere blanket so that Sophie's shoulders were covered. He stepped out of the bedroom and down the hallway—toward the bathroom—in a manner designed to reduce noise and thus avoid waking Sophie: shoulders hunched together and pushed up toward his ears, forearms pressed against his rib cage, and tender steps taken not on the soles of his feet, but on the balls and toes. Still, despite this deft technique, it seemed that each such carefully orchestrated step transferred to the wooden floor the same amount of pressure as any uninhibited step—and as Julian made his way to the bathroom, each step noisily announced his departure.

Sophie's eyelids lifted. She scanned the room, the scope of her vision limited by her immobility—a range of no more than 135 degrees, as she had once calculated from this very same position. A strand of warm drool slid from her mouth. She reached over and felt the empty bed next to her, the perspiration, the dampness left behind by her husband. She closed her eyes.

REALITY NUMBER THREE

Since my injury, I have learned that within a person are multiple levels of reality—realities that may oppose each other, contradictory realities that may appear identical to the person in whom these realities reside, realities that, despite their differences and because of their similarities, may coexist. The two most common are what we know to be true and is true—and then what we know to be true but is false. These are not *views* of reality, not perceptions, distorted or accurate, not hallucinations or altered states of consciousness. Rather, they are realities that carry with them all of the trappings of truth—crispness, clarity, irrefutability, immediacy, pervasiveness.

Sometimes these multiple levels of reality are of equal potency; sometimes one exercises dominion over the other; sometimes that dominion is temporary, transient; and sometimes it is permanent. But it is exceedingly rare, some would say impossible, for one reality to extinguish fully the other, for the weaker of the two (or three or more) has a life that co-terminates with its stronger counterpart: star-crossed lovers toasting goblets of hemlock brew.

For Julian, one reality is that he drove the car in which I became paralyzed—but that it was neither his fault nor mine. In that reality, he wasn't so drunk that his reflexes were impaired—just a hair under the legal limit, the police would determine—and that even if he were stone-cold sober, he still had no choice but to veer hard left to avoid the deer and would have hit the utility pole. That reality is coupled with a necessary assumption—that my insistence on driving instead of walking had no bearing on his decision, that he is not the type of man to be cajoled into doing something he does not want to do. One without the other and this reality is negated.

Julian's second reality is that he drove the car in which I became paralyzed—but that it was entirely his fault. This is a reality to which I do not and have never subscribed. There are, of course, two integral parts to this reality: that he was indeed too drunk to drive and that he allowed himself to be coerced into doing something that he did not want to do. Again, one without the other and this reality is negated.

It is this second reality to which Julian most often attaches and in which he curiously finds some comfort. I asked him once, and only once, to explain why this reality dominates his psyche, and he mumbled something about categorical imperative and certainty, even if faulty, as an antidote to the horror of ambiguity. Now, what this has to do with categorical imperative, I have only the faintest idea, and when he said it I smiled and made an awful joke about *Kant* being a word that should almost never be used, an imperfect homonym that gave us a good laugh. But, really, maybe what he meant by it was that taking sole responsibility was, for him, a moral obligation that might free me from my own guilt.

My first reality goes something like this: it was not Julian's fault and it was only partially my fault, because even though I shouldn't have pressured him to drive, especially knowing how much champagne he had that night, how could I possibly have anticipated that a deer would leap out from nowhere on a quiet sandy lane and guide us straight into a utility pole at no more than twenty-five miles per hour, and that all of this would have happened? What are the odds that such a thing could happen? Infinitesimal, I have been told.

My second reality is that it was entirely my fault, and it is this complete accountability that is the most unpleasant of my realities. Why had I not agreed to walk home with Julian on that lovely summer night? Would not most women have done anything for the chance to walk with this man along a winding, seaside lane through the nectarean air? What compels a woman to make a foolish decision that puts everything at risk? Is there a root cause of such a decision, some unresolved childhood conflict? A trauma? The belief that any good fortune is undeserved? Or is it something else? Maybe there is no root cause at all. Just a silly decision, random and impulsive, that changes the course of many lives.

My third reality (yes, I have three) is the most beneficial to my well-being. But sadly, it is the most elusive, accessible only in my darkest moments—an option that becomes apparent to me only when I think about the limits of my life; about the near-sexless existence my condition has imposed upon me and Julian; about the body not as a mechanism for joy, pleasure and action, but nothing more than a mushy, sloppy host that houses my intellect and my dwindling soul; and about my infertility, the internal injuries suffered in the crash that made it impossible for me to have a child. It is at these dark moments that I eye the bottle of pills on the side table and wonder what it might be like to take the leap. The deep sleep.

This third reality is one that Julian refuses to entertain. In fact, it is one at which he recoils and rejects as delusional folly. To him, my third reality is the antithesis of reality. It is pure fantasy. For it is in this state of sublime belief, of sublime relief, that I know with every ounce of my transmogrified being that it was no one's fault. Rather, I know that it was the will of God. It was a decision made by some vague, constantly shifting higher power— not a decision that I should be paralyzed, for the will of God was not that I should suffer so, but that once I was, once I could do nothing but crap in diapers for the rest of my life, bear witness to the wasting away of my body and develop bedsores on my ass, once I was forced to face the shame of my permanent impotence— a life stripped of its tactility and redomiciled in a smelly, abstract realm—only then could I have some weird freedom.

What I have is the freedom to take all of that horror and turn it into something good, to be of service to another, to navigate through this mess. I cringe when I hear people say that things happen for a reason. I don't know about that. I mean, what reason could there be for any of the horrific things that happen in the world? What I do know when I am in this third reality is that things don't happen for a reason, but once they do happen it's up to me to find the meaning, the purpose, in them.

And that's what I (sometimes) have every intention of doing. During these fleeting moments of divine inspiration, I believe that somehow I'm going to turn this catastrophe into something spectacular, something joyous and unexpected. I don't think I will ever get to the point where I say fuck, I'm grateful that my spinal cord was severed, but there just may be a way that Julian and I can still squeeze a bit more pleasure out of this life.

But most of the time I'd rather die.

A SUCKER FOR A
MAN WHO CRIES

It's five of nine and I'm sitting on one of those soft chairs near the side of the stage and I got a napkin unfolded on the fabric 'cause who knows what kind of germs are on that seat. And I'm hardly wearing anything over my pussy, so a girl's got to be careful. I look in my purse, check the bills in my garter, and it turns out I only made ninety-seven dollars all shift. And that means I'm three bucks in the hole 'cause the house fee is seventy-five, Schultz and the boys get a twenty-dollar tip and the DJ gets five so he plays my favorite songs when I'm onstage. That's how it goes around here sometimes, especially during hurricane season when you don't get many snowbirds and all you get is locals who come in for the free wings at five, have a couple of beers, a slap on the ass, maybe a buck or two in the garter, then back in their F-150s and off to wherever they live.

I've got five more minutes and I'm out of here. And I'm thinking about having a shower and dinner with my mom. She sent me a text saying she had a good day at the diner, a tour bus broke down right in front and fifty hungry people from some place in the Midwest came piling out and boy did they eat. And not bad tippers, it turns out. So a lucky day for her, and for me I guess, but not so much for the tourists. And 'cause my mom made a few bucks, we're going to celebrate with some shrimp and rice and her amazing sweet plantains.

I stand up and the napkin sticks to my ass, stuck to the sweat on me I guess, dangling like some sort of funny tail from a kid's game. There's an old lech in the corner—way off, but harmless— and he sees the napkin hanging from my ass and sticks out his tongue like he's going down on a girl, flicks it real gross, and I give him the finger and get the hell out of the club.

I'm sitting in my car in the back lot and send my mom a text saying be home soon. But damned if I can't find my keys in my purse and I'm pushing around all the crap inside, the makeup, some tampons, old lottery tickets, some condoms—not that I get a chance to use them much these days—a photo of my dad that I keep in a little plastic holder, a bunch of phone numbers on scraps of torn paper. I'm going through all this stuff and I get that little panic you get when you think something's lost. The heart beating real fast and a bit of sweat under my arms is the way I feel it first. And I'm wondering how I could've lost my keys. Then I remember that I had them in my jacket pocket and maybe they fell out somewhere, maybe on the way to the car. Then I wonder how it was that I got into the car without my keys. And I realize that the door was unlocked, which is something I never do, leave the door unlocked.

So I go to open the door, but before I can pull the handle, there's a knock on the window just a few inches from my face.

My heart jumps and I look out the window. Turns out there's a man standing there but I don't know who 'cause his head's above the window and he's pressed real close to the glass. But I can tell from the arms and the pants that it's a man. And now I'm a little panicked and I try to open the door but the man pushes back and closes the door real aggressive. He stands there for a few seconds, doesn't move or say a word, and then there's a rap on the window and I see that this guy's dangling my keys in front of me, and I know it's my keys 'cause they've got a little mother-of-pearl cross hanging from them, a gift from my dad.

And now I'm pissed, 'cause it's one thing to take my keys, but another thing to take something that's got meaning. And I'm scared, to be honest, 'cause even though I'm just fifty feet from the club and Schultz and the boys are right inside, my car's parked behind this row of messy shrubs and some garbage cans and there's not a damn person who can see what I'm dealing with.

Next thing I know, this guy raps his knuckles on the glass, real threatening, takes a step back and walks around the back of the car. I turn around to see what he's doing and sure enough he walks over to the passenger side and reaches for the door. Well, I press the lock button real fast, just before he pulls the handle. Then I see him press the button on the key chain and the doors unlock and he reaches for the handle. But I hit the lock button again real fast before he can open the door. He holds up the keys, hits the unlock button again and opens the door before I can hit my button. And I'm thinking that if it weren't so scary, it would be sort of funny, in a slapstick way, like the Marx Brothers or the Three Stooges, with the two of us pushing the buttons back and forth, back and forth. The door flies open and he plops down in the passenger seat. He closes the door, hits the lock button and turns to me, dangles the keys before me like some sort of hypnotist. These fell out of your pocket, he says, and I'm a Good Samaritan returning them to their rightful owner.

Far from a Samaritan, I say to Julian and grab the keys. You're a fucker, a motherfucker. And he smiles and leans over and gives me a little peck on the cheek. Your signature move, he says. I lean back against the door and take a good look at him. My signature move? Don't even go there being all sweet and charming, 'cause you're a motherfucker and I haven't heard from you in forever, not even a call or a text since Roger came down. He's a lovely guy, by the way, and thanks for the money, really, and now you show up out of the blue all bullshit mysterious and inappropriate. What you want from me, I've got no idea, and it's starting to not be fun but starting to feel a little sad and demeaning and it's chipping away at what little self-esteem I got left.

Julian nods his head and places his hand on mine and ignores what I just said. He tells me he's got five hours before his flight, a layover to Bogotá. So what are we doing? he asks. And I say *we*? What are *we* doing? *We* are doing nothing 'cause *I* am having dinner with my mom. Shrimp and rice and sweet plantains. And Julian says I love plantains. And shrimp, too. What do you say I come have dinner with you and your mom?

I put the key in the ignition and turn on the engine. The radio blasts real loud, a reggaeton station I love, and I turn it off. I don't think that's a good idea, I say. In fact, I think it's a really stupid idea. Julian looks at me all confused. A stupid idea? Yeah, a stupid idea, 'cause what am I gonna say? Mom, I'd like you to meet Julian. He's the married guy from New York I met when I was stripping up in Lauderdale—which she doesn't know about, remember, the stripping. She thinks I'm a waitress at the beach.

So, Mom, we've been fucking in hotel rooms, me and Julian, on and off for months. You got enough shrimp for the three of us?

Lopez, the burlesque girl with the ink, she steps out the back door of the club and behind her is a rich guy who comes by every now and then, a real mean guy, short with a hard, round belly. I danced for him once and that was enough for me. Lopez looks around the back lot like she's casing a bank job and then the guy puts his hand on her shoulder, pushes her down to the ground as Lopez unbuckles his pants and gets to work. Now, I'm not too shocked, 'cause I've seen this sort of thing a hundred times, but I look over at Julian and I can tell immediately that there's something wrong. He's biting his lower lip and there's a twitch in his eye and he leans forward, almost pressing his face against the glass, and it looks like he can't believe what he's seeing.

Julian puts his face in his hands. He rubs his eyes and turns away from me, so I'm looking at the back of his head. And I hear a little sound. I don't know what it is. A grunt? A whimper? Is he clearing his throat? And then I reach over and I place my fingers under the man's chin, turn his face to mine, and I see that he's got tears in his eyes. Now, I'm a sucker for a man who cries, 'cause unlike with us girls it's usually something real. Most men, they're not using tears to manipulate, to get a result. They're just as sneaky as us, of course, it's just that they use different tactics. Anger, threats, lies, but no tears. When they cry, there's something going on. So I pick up my phone and text my mom.

I hope you got enough food for three, 'cause I'm bringing a friend.

SACRED RITUAL

The litany of indignities that I must suffer in our sex life is sometimes too awful to accept—so awful that I have at times considered putting a permanent end to it. The only thing that prevents me from shutting down completely, from refusing to touch or be touched, is the rare moment when Julian and I are together: when our bodies touch; when the upper half of my body feels his weight; when I forget for a moment, as if I am in a dream, that I cannot move; when I see that look of pleasure on his face; when my ability to bring him to orgasm is a validation that, yes, I am still a woman; when my brain triggers a recollection, an echo of my able-bodied self when I once moved freely above Julian, below him, beside him; when I experience not an orgasm in the traditional sense, but something frustratingly close—a vague sensation above my waist, a tantalizing tingling, a flutter and a spreading warmth like a drop of ink on white linen. The brain, I guess, rewiring and adapting and trying to give a paralyzed girl just a little bit of pleasure in life.

Julian enters the bedroom at half past nine. He's been out for dinner with Roger, his buddy from high school with the bad foot, the good heart and a loyalty to Julian that is unshakable. I love Roger. I love anyone who cares for Julian as much as I do. Julian and Roger have been at Clancy's, their favorite little Irish bar on Second Avenue. Julian doesn't drink at all, not since the accident, and Roger only has the occasional beer, but they love this place, what with the antique wood bar and the old Paddy from Shannon who pours well vodka into the Stoli bottles, and the antiquated jukebox that plays classics from The Chieftains, The Dubliners, The Wolfe Tones. They've got shepherd's pie there, corned beef and cabbage, even a wild game menu with quail, ostrich, bison and all sorts of weird, wild things that Julian loves. The hunter's son.

Julian enters the bedroom. He smiles. You good, babe? he asks. I smile in return and, with my left hand, weakly pat the open stretch of mattress by my side. Julian removes his clothing, everything but his boxers. I admire his body—sinewy, lithe, powerful. The body of his youth. Julian sits down next to me. He puts his hand on my shoulder, which is one of the few areas of my body that transmits normal sensation.

In Julian's eyes, there is a hint of his amorous flash, vital and dangerous, that has stirred me since our first night together. Prior to the accident, there was a certain coarseness to Julian's otherwise glorious lovemaking—not violent or mechanical or detached, but instead efficient, controlled, determined, as if his sexuality, his technique, were driven not by a need to dominate me, but instead by a need not to be dominated himself, to defy any submission on his part.

Since the accident, Julian's flash has appeared with less frequency. But he is more tender now, and the crippling of my body has awoken

in Julian a reservoir of compassion, an appreciation of human fra-
gility, an understanding that his aggression could be harnessed,
tamed, maybe even a belief in the possibility that one could be safe
without dominating the world. Julian now expresses his desire for
me in different ways. The playful, painful tug of hair—which had
once been my great delight—has been replaced by the gentle stroking of my scalp. Instead of the pinch of my nipple, Julian now runs
his tongue delicately across my breasts. And rather than a quick slap
on my bottom, there is the long, deep therapeutic massage that
stimulates the flow of blood in my partially immobilized body.

"What do you think?" Julian asks.

"About what?"

"About trying tonight?"

"Tonight?" I reply, alarmed by the immediacy of this proposed intimacy.

"We could," he says reassuringly. "It's been a while. But no
pressure if you're not up for it."

I struggle to recall our last attempt at intercourse. "How
long?" I ask. "How long has it been?"

"Not sure exactly. Five, maybe six months."

I cringe at the length of our dry spell. I pause and consider the
preparation that will be involved. I consider the potential pleasure
of the act, the possibility of achieving a greater closeness with
Julian, the look on his face as he comes inside me, the twist of his
mouth, his post-ejaculatory daze, his surrender, his collapse, the
full weight of his body supported by mine: all beautiful images
that evoke in me not a *current* desire to fuck Julian, to make love
to Julian, but rather a desire that is vestigial, a wistful longing for
a complete romance that is not missing its most essential element.

"You do know how long it takes me to get ready," I say.

"An hour?"

"About."

"I can wait all night."

I sigh and brace myself for what comes next. "Okay, have Norma come in."

Julian kisses me on the forehead. Since the accident, I find this gesture to be patronizing, as if I am either infantile or elderly. Almost immediately upon Julian's departure from the room, Norma enters.

"Yes, Mum, you ready for bed?" she asks, unaware of our intentions.

I pause, embarrassed. We've been through this a few times, Norma and I. And while it's always awkward for me, it arouses in Norma an adolescent jubilation, as if she is back in Trinidad preparing for her first date with the shy boy she met at a church dinner.

Norma accurately interprets my pause. She smiles to ease my discomfort. From the cabinet next to the bed, she removes a pair of rubber gloves. She shakes them, snaps them over her hands, then removes a suppository—bullet-shaped and waxy—and a tube of petroleum jelly. She squeezes out a glob of jelly and coats the suppository, gently turning me on my side.

"I normally don't do this on the first date," she says.

"This isn't our first date," I reply.

She reaches between my legs, nothing more than two floppy ropes, and inserts the suppository into my anus. I wince, not from the pain of the insertion, as that I cannot feel. I wince from the indignity.

"How long does it take? I forget."

"When was your last movement?"

"Midday. Around three."

"Then no more than an hour, Mum. Then we'll get you all cleaned up."

Paralysis raises numerous issues when it comes to sex, the most repugnant being one's inability to control bowels and bladder. For how quickly the inadvertent release of feces or urine can extinguish the roaring libido!

Norma guides me onto my back. She taps the urine bag that is strapped to my midsection. "Half-full," she says. "Maybe three-quarters."

"How's the color?" I ask.

"All good, Mum, not too dark. Perfect color."

She rubs her gloved hands together, warms them up, and then pushes slowly down on my bladder.

"Anything?" I ask.

"Yes, Mum, it's filling up now." Norma watches as the bag swells with urine. "I think that's it," she says, removing the bag by twisting a plastic seal that connects to the catheter tube. Norma wraps a diaper around my waist and tapes it up, careful that it does not tug at the dangling tube. "I can stay here with you, Mum. Or come back when it starts to work."

"Best to come back, Norma."

She nods and lowers the lights. "I'll make sure Mr. Pravdin doesn't come in until we're finished. Keep that man at a distance until you all fresh and pretty."

I stare at the ceiling and wait for the rumbling sensation in my bowels. I snapped the cord clear through, so waist-down I've got nothing. Then there's a few inches above the waist, a narrow, transitional band where I've got some feeling, then above that there's normal feeling, and in some places it is even super-normal.

From the bathroom in the hall, I hear Julian in the shower. He is engaged in his own pre-sex ritual. I hear him humming out of tune. He's the only man I ever met who is so tone-deaf he can't even hum right. Several minutes later, Julian turns the shower off. He moves to the sink, indicated by the tapping of his razor on the marble counter. I know from experience, from listening to his rote ablutions for so many years, that he will shave quickly. Another minute passes and the sink is off.

I close my eyes and imagine him now. He takes a small towel from the rack and wipes his face, clears off the remaining dollops of shaving cream. He moves closer to the mirror. He examines his face. He wonders what it is about this face, with its odd angles and the crooked nose and the scar across his right cheekbone—a busy face—that has such a powerful effect on people. He shrugs his shoulders.

I feel a movement in my midsection, the suppository softening my stool, causing my bowels to contract, expand, contract— and forcing the feces downward through my rectum and then outward, toward the light. My body expelling excrement is one of the few sensual pleasures that remain. I don't get the full experience, though. There's no feeling of climax when the shit squeezes through those final inches and leaves my body. But there is movement within the intestines that I do experience and, when it is finally expelled, a feeling of lightness and detoxification that I enjoy.

I know that the process is complete only when the smell becomes detectable. My diapers could be filled with five pounds of shit, but if by some miracle it were odorless I would have no idea that I'd soiled myself. No idea. It is only the smell that alerts me.

I call for Norma by pressing a button on the side of the bed.

Norma knocks before entering, a gracious, subtle adherence to etiquette that in some odd way helps preserve my dignity.

"Come in, Norma."

"How you feeling, Mum? Ready for a wash?"

I nod affirmatively as Norma rolls the rubberized mattress next to the bed. The mattress is part of a customized, all-purpose bathing unit that has stainless steel channels and protective rails running around all four sides, hot and cold water dials, a shower nozzle, a small rack for soap, shampoo, sponges and scented lotions.

Norma drops the side rail closest to the bed. "Come here, Mum." She places her hands under my arms and slides me, top half first, over onto the bathing cart. Slipping one arm under my hips and the other under my knees, as if I am some tragic, beached mermaid, she guides my lower half onto the cart so that I am now perfectly aligned. "You okay?"

"All good," I say. Norma removes my diaper, taking a quick peek before disposing it in a sealed container by the bed. "How much?"

"Tons, Mum. No need to worry when you with Mr. Pravdin. There can't be a speck left in you."

Norma lights a long wooden match and touches the wicks of the six Cire Trudon candles that fill the room—and have since I first returned home from the hospital. The candles, citric and woody, hide the smells that my body emits. And as if we are in some Eastern temple, the candles have the effect of ritualizing this cleansing. She turns the dials, hot and cold, and tests the water first with her hands, and then—because my lower half has no pain receptors—she checks again with a thermometer. Satisfied, she removes a sterile sponge from a package, soaks it in water and then squirts on some antibacterial soap.

Norma starts with my feet. I look down to see her cradle my left leg, holding my heel in her meaty palm. She tenderly spreads my toes, glides the sponge between them; then, up over my ankle, my calf, under my knee, my upper leg. She repeats the same procedure on my right leg.

Once Norma is finished with my legs, she soaks the sponge, squeezes it out, soaks it again, then applies more soap. She rolls me onto my side so that I am facing her. She lifts my left leg, which, given its dead weight, requires considerable effort on her part. She guides the soapy sponge between my buttocks, cleans out the remaining feces. Several times, she cleans the sponge with water and applies soap. She returns to my buttocks, the area between, until she is satisfied with the results. And then, with the quick flick of her foot on the bin pedal, she disposes of the sponge.

Norma removes a new sponge from the rack, douses it and applies not the antibacterial soap but a mild soap designed for babies. She moves to my vagina—that sacred space that once offered me both a narcotic escape and the promise of children, but that now offers only a sickening reminder of my fallowness, a dry crusty hole.

She works her way inside, cleaning me, careful not to abrade the tissue within. When she has finished, she again discards the sponge and moves on to a new one.

"The worst is over, Mum."

"For you or for me?" I ask.

"There's no worst for me. It's God's work, a privilege. I should be paying you."

"That can be arranged."

Norma laughs and returns me to a supine position. She runs the sponge over my lower belly, along that narrow band where the sensation begins. She cleans out my belly button, moving upward—and I brace for what comes next.

The best way I can describe the change in my sensitivity since the accident is as follows. Let's say that when I was healthy, I had one million sensory receptors on my entire body: from my scalp to the soles of my feet. Now, that's not the real number, it's just for illustration. After the accident, what happened is that the, say, half-million receptors that had been allocated to the region below my waist—my feet, my legs, my hips and vagina—were not eliminated; rather, they seem to have been relocated upward, so that my upper body now has twice as much sensitivity as before.

But it is not as if these half million additional receptors were spread out evenly over my upper half like some pointillist creating richer detail in a painting. Rather, while some of them are placed between existing receptors, thus reducing the distance between point A and point B, the vast majority have been placed *on top of* existing receptors, stacked like poker chips, amplifying the sense of touch. Some areas, like the belly button, are stacked two or three high, thus creating a heightened sensitivity that is only marginally more enjoyable than before. But there are some areas, why they were chosen I do not know, that seem to be stacked as high as the ceiling. The receptors on my breasts are ten high, a thousand percent increase over my prior self. My nipples, twenty high. And here's the strangest of all. My ears—the lobes, the flesh just outside the canal, the ridge—a good thirty high. So high that my ears have become sensualized, almost sexualized.

For reasons that not even my doctor can fully explain (maybe psychological, maybe neurological, maybe a bit of both), my ears have developed a sensitivity to touch, but not hearing, so extreme that I am convinced my nerve endings are raw, exposed to the air, dangling and thrashing like the translucent tentacles of a jellyfish. They pick up everything, my ears, every contact—a wayward strand of hair, the otherwise indiscernible texture on a fine cotton pillow, a drop of rain. The sensations are, unlike those generated in my breasts, not entirely pleasant. I am grateful for them, as any sensation for me is now a luxury, but sometimes it is too much to bear.

I've read books about spinal cord injuries that talk of nonvaginal orgasms, nonclitoral orgasms—the stroking of the breast or some other part of the body causing something either identical to or remarkably similar to an orgasm. That has not been my experience. I get intense sensation, arousal even. I get those moments that used to lead up to orgasm: the slow, steady increase in pleasure, the anticipation of climax, the fear, sometimes a primal terror, that for any number of reasons climax will not be achieved. I get all of that, but I never get the climax. I get that sneezy flutter in my chest, in my brain, without the release, without the closure. I get a big tease that reminds me what I do not have—the nasty prom queen flashing a cruel wink after she steals my boyfriend.

Norma lifts my breasts and slides the warm sponge underneath. As the sponge touches my flesh, there is a feeling of excitement, a tingling, soft and warm, first on the outer layers of my skin, then, as if it is burrowing, deep into the core of my breasts—then down into my chest, where it seems to coalesce and concentrate. The feeling is not quite sexual, but it is, rather, a pleasurable and welcome sensual experience, one that far exceeds the sensation I felt in my breasts prior to the accident. Here it is, I think, the brain remapping, rewiring, creating neurons and receptors where they once didn't exist, or if they did exist, were not so finely tuned. Norma now moves up to my neck, under my chin and carefully dabs the skin on my face, making sure that the soapy water does not enter my mouth, my nose, eyes, the canals of my ears.

Norma moves to my hair. She fills a pot with water and pours it over my head, shielding my eyes with her hand. Into my scalp, she massages a lavender shampoo from France—for years, my favorite. I love the feeling of her strong fingers pressing into my scalp, stroking my hair, stimulating the points at which each shaft of hair enters my scalp. She finishes, and I ask her to keep going a little longer. Norma obliges.

She then refills the pot and washes the shampoo from my hair. She lifts two towels off the electric warmer. She wraps one around my wet hair and drapes the other over my body, from my neck down to my shins. As if she is kneading bread, she pushes and folds the towel on my body and thus both lifts the water from my skin and accelerates the flow of blood.

Once I'm dry, Norma removes from my dresser drawer the lingerie that Julian bought me last Christmas, and which I have not yet worn. It's a beautiful, plum-colored ensemble from one of those old shops on Madison that sells sexy stuff even though it's been around for fifty years: bra, panties and a baby-doll top. Norma lowers the rail on the shower bed and slides me back on to the mattress, propping me up so that my back is upright and pressed against the tufted headboard.

She arranges my legs before me. From this angle, I have observed my legs many times over the years—and they have taken numerous forms. There was the time Julian and I traveled to the Cayman Islands, when he wheeled me out onto the beach and laid me out on a chaise, placed a straw hat on my head and a silk scarf over my legs. I recall waiting for Julian to fully immerse himself in the sea before pulling the scarf off my legs, revealing them to the blazing sun, watching them for a half hour as they turned from deathly gray to a salmon pink. At least there is some part of these legs, I thought, that still works.

Before we put on the lingerie, though, there is the matter of lubrication that needs to be addressed. For despite my young age—thirty-eight—my vagina is as dry as an octogenarian's. The paralysis has somehow impacted this part of my physiology as well. It is as if the body is telling me that I am not to even think about reproducing. And while there is almost nothing too intimate for Norma when it comes to matters of the body, matters of *my* body, this is where she and I both agree that the task is mine. Norma hands me a bottle of lubricant. She turns her back, pretending to arrange socks in the dresser drawer.

As if I am resuscitating the engine of some rusted Model T, a tremendous amount of lubrication is required for me to have intercourse. I've got to slather the labia, inside and out, the clitoris, the first couple of inches of the vagina. But even that is not adequate to prevent tearing, so I squeeze several globs of lubricant into a plastic applicator—causing a mess in the process. I feel around for my vagina and insert the applicator. I push down deep, so that my entire canal is drenched in goo. And that's still not the end of it, because Julian's got to put it on his dick too.

"Okay, Norma," I call out. "I'm wet as a twenty-year-old."

Norma closes the drawer and turns around. "At least one of us is."

With a soft towel, Norma wipes the excess lubricant from my hands, my upper thighs. She lifts my right leg and guides my foot through one hole of the panties. When she gets it up to my knee, she does the same thing with the left foot and, when she reaches knee level on that side too, pulls the panties up to my waist. She takes a step back, and we both stare at the panties, at the contrast between the silk's deep purple and my pale skin. I nod, and Norma lifts the bra with two hands, spreads it out so we both can see it. "Mum, this wouldn't even hold *one* of my titties," she says. "Maybe half a tittie."

I laugh as Norma reaches for my shoulder and pulls me forward, away from the headboard. "Arms up," she says, and I comply with some difficulty. She drops the bra around my outstretched hands and then, after I lower my arms, she wraps her own around me—her huge breasts pressed up against my face—and fastens the bra in back.

"Stay right there," she says, reaching for the silk baby-doll top. She drapes it over my head and pulls it down over my shoulders, over my arms, down to my waist. She takes a step back to admire me. "Time for your hair," she says, plugging the blow-dryer into the socket. For ten minutes, Norma works my hair like she is arranging flowers—with numerous permutations, angles, shadows. Finally, she settles on something feral, wanton and holds up a mirror for me to see.

"Not even when I could walk," I say, "did I ever wear my hair like that. You directing a porn video tonight?"

The final part of the ritual is the perfume. Norma walks over to the dresser on which a dozen bottles sit on a sterling tray. "Which one do you want, Mum?" There are so many beautiful scents, and the bottles too are gorgeous.

"Anything," I say, "I like them all." Norma hands me a bottle, frosted and smooth, that I have not touched in months. I examine the top to make sure that it is pointed in the right direction and shoot one test spray into the air. I inhale the bergamot, saffron, nutmeg. I spray twice between my breasts. The atomized perfume settles on my skin and triggers a surge in anticipation. Careful to avoid my ears, I spray once on my neck and then a quick wave that sends a fine spray over my upper thighs.

After returning the bottle to the dresser, Norma lifts my left leg and crosses it over my right at the calf. She pulls down the baby-doll so that my cleavage is revealed, then pushes the shower bed into the corner and turns to leave. "Thank you, Norma," I say.

"An honor, Mum. Now you give that man a ride."

A minute or two passes and Julian knocks on the door. He, too, has embraced the formality of knocking before entering, but for different reasons than Norma. For Julian, his consideration is necessitated by an awareness of my self-consciousness, a diffident state that plagued me in my adolescence, caused me to cast my gaze to the floor, cover my body in baggy pants and thick sweaters, but that lifted soon after Julian broke my uncle's nose, a brave and principled act that awakened in me a confidence in my body, my curves, the possibility that justice exists— only to return the moment I awoke in the hospital and learned that I could no longer walk.

And even though Julian has seen everything when it comes to my physical degradation—the feces, the vomit, the urine, the necrotic skin, the bedsores—I just can't bear for him to see me when my hair is a mess, my lipstick smeared, crust in the corner of my eye. Despite all that has happened, I still want to look like a lady for him.

Julian enters, wearing nothing but his boxers. When he sees me dressed up in my beautiful lingerie, bathed in the soft light of the candles, he stops and smiles, shakes his head. "You're a hot piece of ass, you know."

I loved Julian's sweet vulgarity when we first began to date, and I'm grateful that he has not given up. "Still?" I ask.

"Still."

He sits down on the bed next to me. He, too, admires me. And he does so sincerely and without a hint of pity or regret. He pushes a strand of hair off of my forehead. He lifts the baby-doll at the waist and places his hand on my left side, within that transitional band of flesh. He guides the shoulder straps down over my arms and tugs down until the fabric encircles my mid-section. Julian leans over me and kisses me on the lips, and when he does so, his chest touches my breasts and an intense sensation ripples through them. I giggle, in part out of the discomfort of so much feeling, of so much *good* feeling, and in part out of shame. My nipples become hard, pushing back into him, bringing me great pleasure. It is a pleasure that, sadly, I know cannot be fully consummated.

Julian kisses me deeply, presses his fingers against my jaw—careful not to touch the finely tuned flesh on my ears. With his left hand, he reaches around my back and deftly opens my bra clasp, and I enjoy the release that follows, the unpinching of the flesh under my arms, the dropping of my breasts, the slight expansion of the rib cage. When you are as confined as I am, a few centimeters of freedom are pure heaven. Julian lifts my bra, gently kisses my nipples, rubs his chin over them. And there it is, the rapid firing of thousands of stacked receptors; the oil heats, crackles, elates me, terrifies me with its power.

With my right hand, I reach down and tug at his boxers, rub my hand over his dick. I am relieved, flattered to see that Julian is still aroused, almost instantly, by my touch. He groans, pulls his boxers down over his thighs, and I hold him in my hand. I squeeze him tightly, too tightly, and he winces in pain. "Sorry," I say. "It's been a while." There is something adolescent about our foreplay: the awkwardness, the speed, the clumsiness, the mutual concern.

"You sure you want to do this?" he asks.

"After all the work Norma and I had to do, you're damn right I want to do this."

Julian nods and looks down to my legs. He stands by the side of the bed. His boxers fall to his ankles. He slips one foot out and, with the other foot, flicks the boxers across the wood floor. I admire his erection. Julian runs his fingers from my hip down to my upper leg. He reaches the knee, taps once, twice, three times, then along the ridge of my shin, to my ankle, which, as if to measure its circumference, he momentarily wraps his hand around and, finally, over my foot. I feel nothing. Absolutely nothing.

Julian moves to my panties. He pinches the side straps and pulls them down over my hips. The panties get stuck under the dead weight of my ass, so Julian slides a hand underneath, lifts me an inch or two off the mattress, and frees the panties. From there, he removes them with ease.

Julian reaches across my body, puts his right hand under my calf and his left hand under my thigh. Gently, he lifts my right leg, and it is from this perspective that I have a good view of it. My leg is pale—paler than my arms, which are more often exposed to the sun. There is a blotch of red on the kneecap, which is where blood seems to gather. I can see my foot—thin, drooping, curved inward. Julian spreads my leg out to the right, maybe ten or twelve inches from center. He lifts my left leg, the one where I had the bedsores last month, and this time I do not look. I do not want to see. Spreading my left leg out the same distance, he repeats the preparation. I extend my arms to the side, so that they are parallel to my shoulders, and I imagine that from above I might look like some sickly Canon of Proportions, one drawn by a novice art student. Or a surrealist.

Before Julian can ask where the lubricant is, I nod over to the nightstand. He removes the cap and squeezes a large amount into his palm. "You know, we would have needed this in fifty years anyway," he says.

"That's all *I'll* need," I say. "But you're going to need a whole lot more in fifty years. Like some pills. And a defibrillator."

"Good point." Julian rubs the lubricant over his dick, which has retained its tumescence throughout this clinical process. "That should do it."

I watch as Julian inserts his penis into me, observing not with the trembling anticipation of my youth, but with a curious, almost zoological interest in his insertion—as if I am watching a nature film documenting the curious mating habits of some rare primate. And where Julian inside me once elicited a glorious range of secretions, contractions, spasms, emotions, orgasms, it now offers nothing of the sort. Still, despite the limitations that we now experience, there is some pleasure I get from this, from surrounding Julian with my flesh. Maybe it is the joy of pleasuring another, albeit in an imperfect manner; or the pleasure of being of service to one we love; of receiving love over the objections of one's own shame; of re-creating a better past, even though we both know that the re-creation is nothing of the sort—that it is nothing more than nostalgia, a longing for things to be the way they once were.

Because I have no sensation in my vagina, my first inkling that we are having intercourse is when Julian presses his hips into me, drives deep into me and thus moves my body upward, toward the headboard.

"You okay?" he asks, and I hate that he has to ask.

"Yes."

Julian runs his hand along the band above my hips, and I feel his fingertips on my skin. He then leans down and presses his chest carefully on my breasts. The warmth of his skin activates the supertuned receptors on my nipples, sends a jolt down through my core and into the upper part of my spine.

"Oh, Julian, Julian. That feels good."

Julian smiles, kisses me on the lips. The heat of his body combines with mine and in no time I start to sweat—not gym sweat or stuck-on-the-subway sweat, but sex sweat—slippery and brackish. I start to forget my self-consciousness, how peculiar my body looks, how limited its range of motion. I kiss Julian, sliding my tongue into his mouth, along the roof of his mouth, then back out and across his lips. I am here with him, cojoined and, yes, content.

The band above my waist flutters, its receptors attempting—unsuccessfully—to replicate an orgasm, getting tantalizingly close but not close enough. Julian makes love to me. Sadly, the days of fucking are over.

"I love you," he says.

"I love you, too." I wrap my right arm around his back. "Does it feel good?"

"It feels great, baby."

"Good," I say. "You know, you know I wish . . ." Julian places his hand over my mouth, stops me from continuing.

He brushes his fingertips across my nipples, and the sensation is now too much to bear. I shake my head. "Too much, it's too much." Julian understands and stops, kisses me on the forehead. I'm feeling tired now, as I no longer have good stamina. My endurance suffers in all areas of my life, including sex, and I can last only about five minutes, ten at the most. And then my body starts to break down. Forced to do all the work, my arms and shoulders will fill with lactic acid and burn. The inner lining of my vagina will begin to lose its lubrication and expose me to tears in the mucous membrane. And although I cannot feel it, I know that the attenuated skin on my upper thighs will begin to chafe and crack from the friction created by Julian's body; the remnants of bedsores on my left leg will pulsate, redden, and threaten to reemerge. Sex, at this point, is not as a vehicle for reproduction or transcendence—but sex as a path to decay, death.

"You can come now, babe," I say.

"Okay," he responds, trying to hide his disappointment.

Julian's thrusts grow deeper, quicker, more decisive. I await his release. I've been with this man long enough to know when he's close. A few more, I think, and Julian will reach orgasm. Prior to climax, there will first be that exaggerated curl of the lower lip and a squint of the eyes. Then his face will go flat and serene, as if he is floating—a moment of quietude before ejaculation. And then the spasm of ecstasy that every woman loves to see in the man she loves: a mad grimace, as if he is lifting some heavy object, the primal groan, the convulsion, his hands tightening around my arms. And finally, the surrender, the fusion—the full weight of his body falling onto mine, *into* mine.

"Come, babe," I whisper.

"I'm close."

And then it happens. At first, there is the smell—vile and

disturbing. My paralyzed body always expels a blast of noxious gas prior to defecation. I guess it is God's way of sending up a warning flare. I notice it first, a split second before Julian. I pray that my body will behave, that it will allow Julian to finish before I soil myself. Prompted by the smell, Julian picks up the pace, thrusting faster and harder. But then the sounds follow: the rumbling of my bowels, the rush of feces through me.

"Hurry, babe," I implore.

"I'm trying," he responds, exasperated.

And then the final indignity. An awful sound interrupts our lovemaking—a splatter followed by a gurgling, and then a prolonged hiss. Julian stops and looks down. He sees that the bed is covered in shit, that we are covered in shit—a hot, viscous fecal stew.

My tears are immediate. My rage is immediate. My self-loathing is permanent, etched now into my genetic code.

But rather than withdraw from me, Julian stays inside. He falls back onto my chest, drapes the full weight of his body back onto mine. Here we lie, in my shit—in *our* shit. And as we hold each other, something odd happens. The olfactory receptors in my brain start the process of remapping, refusing to accept painful stimuli, converting them not yet into pleasurable stimuli but into neutral ones. I inhale deeply, searching for the smell of my crap. But I smell nothing other than Julian, the candles and the brackish sex sweat.

Julian strokes my hair. "I love you," he whispers.

"I love you, too." I tighten my weakened arms around his back—and there we lie.

"I'm going to get some towels," he says after a few minutes, "clean you up." Julian pulls out of me and stands to the side of the bed. I turn away, careful not to observe the dark mess on his skin.

"Don't you go anywhere, I'll be right back."

"Where the fuck do you expect me to go?" I ask and give Julian a wink.

I use my arms to turn myself over onto my right side. Given my disability and the fatigue of intercourse, I struggle but succeed. On the bedside table is a photograph of us from before the accident. Julian and I are on a sailboat in the Peconic Bay, in the choppy waters between Shelter Island and Greenport. The wind whips in from the south, and you can make out a dark cloud in the background hell-bent for the North Fork. Julian slips on the wet deck. He loses his sense of direction and stands just as the boom shoots across the boat, cracking him across the cheekbone.

I lean a few inches closer to the photograph to get a better look. He's got blood running down the side of his face. He's not badly hurt, just a short, shallow gash on the cheekbone that will require eight stitches. But it's his ego, not his face, that takes the brunt of the blow. I've got my arm around his shoulder, kissing him on the cheek. I'm laughing because it's a relief to see this man finally make a mistake. In the corner of the photograph, just above Julian's head, Roger mockingly holds out a live lobster—its claws grasping wildly for Julian's ear. Julian's got a sheepish look, and, relieved to be fallible, he touches his fingers to the wound.

I use my right arm, push and return to my back. I inhale, hoping to detect nothing. I am not disappointed. The brain remapping; I smile and close my eyes.

TAP, TAP, PAUSE

This time, the first time since I met him, Julian actually calls me *before* he comes down. Sure enough, I'm in the mall one day with my girlfriend. Rebekah's her name and she's what I call a Juban, a Jewish girl from Cuba. Yup they exist, but there's not many of them left. She's real smart, studying to be a lawyer at UM and just got through her first year, which they say is the hardest. I'm so proud of her 'cause she's one of my girls from the neighborhood and she's had it just as hard as me. Came here when she was real young and lost her dad too, who was a secret rabbi in Havana, and it's just her and her mom now. And she's my only friend who knows I've been stripping, and I love her 'cause there's no judgment from her, just pure love. She even came to see me dance one night and the look on her face when I hit the pole was something I'll never forget. She could barely look and almost fell off the chair she was laughing so hard. After I got off the stage, she said guys pay you for *that*? No wonder you're broke!

Anyway, we're looking for some cute sandals, me and Rebekah, 'cause that's what we love to do when we want some retail therapy but don't want to spend too much money. Just then, I get a call on my phone and it's a number I don't recognize. Normally, I'm not answering a call like that 'cause who knows who's on the other line. Maybe a bill collector or an ex-boyfriend or some girl from the club who wants me to cover her shift. And I don't want any of those calls.

But something makes me take that call and who's on the other line but Julian, and boy, am I surprised to get a call from him, and that's exactly what I tell him. Boy, am I surprised to get a call from you. And he says I'm surprised I'm calling you, so that makes two of us. You calling 'cause you want to marry me someday? I ask, all joking, but only half joking, I guess, 'cause sometimes I really do have feelings for the man. There's silence on the phone. Or you in town and just want to get laid? There's more silence, so I repeat you want to get laid? Still nothing, then he says yes. All right, then, now we're getting somewhere, and I'm having a good time with him 'cause he's real fun to tease. Same hotel, same room? I want to know. Yes, again. Am I getting a burger and a ginger ale in exchange for having sex with you? Well, not in exchange, really, but yes, he says. And how about fries? Sweet potato fries? Another yes from Julian. Then I'll see you there at eight.

Rebekah wants to know who it is and I tell her it's the guy from New York. She knows all about Julian, 'cause I told her about him that very first night when he made me come and I fell asleep for a few seconds on his shoulder. Now, most girlfriends would say Perla, don't you spend one second thinking about that man, but Rebekah listens to me describe how he touched me and how good it felt, and she knows how rare that is. She's more of a romantic than I am, maybe 'cause I dance for a living and she doesn't, so she just gives me a big hug and says happy for you girl, that sounds real nice.

Rebekah and I say good-bye, waving our new sandals in the air. I get in my car and figure I've got a couple hours to go home, have a shower, put on some nice clothes and then get up to the hotel, which is a good hour from our place. But as I'm pulling on to A1A, I get a call from my mom and she sounds all frantic and overwhelmed and I say what's wrong? Turns out she got a burn on her hand at work, spilled some water in a frying pan by mistake and the cooking oil shot up and hit her wrist, not too bad but real painful. They got it all bandaged up and she'll be fine to work in a couple of days, but still that's two days without work and the diner won't pay you if you don't work. No paid sick days or worker's comp at the diner.

My mom's been providing for me and her for so long, she's so proud and self-reliant since my dad died, that anything that keeps her away from work—anything that maybe gives someone else a chance to take her job—anything like that makes her real afraid and nervous, stirs up tons of fear and she gets seriously emotional. And that's not all, Perlita, she says, 'cause we got no water, something's wrong with the pipes and it's a few days until we can use the shower, the toilet, the sink.

Great, I'm thinking. My mom's hurt and that makes it hard for me to leave her and go enjoy a few hours with Julian. And also we don't have any water, which makes showering pretty damn hard. Impossible. And 'cause I'm all sweaty from walking around the mall with Rebekah, I don't know how the hell I'm gonna be ready to get into bed with that man. Fuck it, I think,

I'm just gonna cancel Julian, go home and help my mom, tell her everything's fine and we'll be okay.

When I get to the house, Mom's on the couch and she's drinking a cold beer, which she almost never does, and she smiles when she sees me and says oh, baby, it's been a bad day, one of the worst. So I plop right down next to her, lift up her burned arm and look at the white bandage around the wrist and say girl, what the hell were you doing within even five feet of a frying pan? She shrugs her shoulders in a *damned if I know* way and points to a bottle of aspirin on the table and a couple of Latin gossip magazines with pretty Colombians and Venezuelans from the telenovelas.

I look at my watch, six thirty-five, and think about Julian. I stare off into the distance, through the window and out to the mango tree outside, to the house where Old Pepe lives, just looking out at those mangoes and thinking about Julian and the club and that bitch Lopez, then Jade and her big old hips and on to my dad. And I'm wondering what the hell kind of life I made for myself?

It's like some sick joke, where you start out in Cuba, not even enough food to eat half the time, but there's great music and dancing and lots of love from your family. So there's misery and there's ecstasy, and you really do get used to the misery, don't even know it's all around you, up to your knees, under your fingernails, in your hair. It's everywhere, so it's really nowhere. And then you get over here and all you're supposed to get is the ecstasy without the misery, that's the propaganda that the States tells the world or that the world tells about the States, or a bit of both. But the truth is there's just as much misery here, but a different kind.

The misery here is worse 'cause it's relative. There's enough people here who aren't struggling that you can't go half a day without being reminded how bad you got it. It's not like that in Cuba, where everyone's got the same. Nothing. And the funny thing about the States is the highs aren't as high as I thought they'd be. I'm still dancing like I used to. Not salsa and merengue with my dad, but a different sort of dancing, joyless and mercenary. *Mercenary.* That's a word my dad taught me, and if I used it with Julian or Roger, those bastards would raise their eyebrows all surprised. Julian's a condescending fuck sometimes, but boy, does he make me feel good.

My mom pops an aspirin and says don't you worry about me, Perlita, my hand's gonna be fine and I think I'll just stay at Felipe's until the water comes back, maybe a bit longer. I'd invite you to come stay with us, she says, but Felipe's got a small place and his cousins staying with him for the month. I guess I look sad, and when she sees that my feelings are a little hurt, she says Perlita, you can probably come over and use the shower if you need. I tell her it's all right, thanks for the offer, but I can go shower at Rebekah's or Carolina's until the water comes back.

Felipe is my mom's boyfriend. They've been together now for a few months and she's been staying at his place two or three nights a week, so I haven't been seeing her as much lately. For years, it's been just me and her, so this is a real hard adjustment for me. And having her separate a bit like this is bringing up all sorts of feelings, none of them good, and making me miss my dad even more. Anyway, this Felipe's a Cuban guy and compared to the other guys she's been dating since my dad died, he's not half bad. He's got a repair shop in Little Havana, car rims, tires, mufflers, that sort of thing. Best thing is that Felipe doesn't seem to get too drunk and he's not asking Mom for any money. Most of the other men she dates are either abusive or drunk or gambling all their money away. They're out chasing girls, sometimes leering at me like they want to fuck me. But this one's fine, just a regular nice guy. Nothing like my father, who was real special and smart, with a smile that made you feel like he was the happiest man in the world—which I think he was.

Now, Julian's all the way up in Lauderdale, so it's a long drive up 95 and I better move fast if I'm gonna make it by eight. I got lots of failings, but being late isn't one of them. I'm a punctual girl, always have been, always will be. When I have a shift that starts at one, I'm there at ten of and never a second after. That's one of the things my dad taught me—that one of the most respectful things you can do for another person is be on time. 'Cause what's more valuable than one single minute in a human being's life? Time is finite, he used to say, the most precious and limited resource.

Speaking of precious and limited resources, there's no water in the house, so I figure my only option is to shower at the hotel. I jump in my Mini, put on a salsa station I love and they're playing one of my favorites by the Fania All Stars. I'm tapping a beat on the steering wheel, thinking about dancing to "Ella Fue" when I was a little girl, the whole family dancing and laughing in the backyard. I get on 95, there's hardly any traffic for a change and I'm up at Sunrise in no time. Once I'm off the exit, I head east toward the beach, green lights all the way for maybe the first time in my entire life.

I pull into the parking lot and take a look at myself in the rearview mirror. The streetlight fills the car, and it's a mean light, cold and white, that reveals every flaw in my face—not like the lights at the club, all dark and warm, that wrap me up and make me look like a movie star. I move closer to the mirror and examine a fine line, two really, that extend from the corner of my right eye. I turn my head and see the same lines on the left side. It's near impossible for anyone else to see them and people always tell me I got perfect skin, but I know they're there, the lines, and I know where they're going. I'm pretty sure I know where all this is going.

And there's also the start of a pimple on my right nostril, and I remember that I'm getting my period soon. I hope it's not tonight, 'cause that would be too embarrassing. And then there's the scar under my chin, from when I hit the dashboard as a little girl, and for some reason it looks different in this light, from this angle, waxy and smooth and more oval than I remembered. And, of course, I got that little strip of white hair in the back. I'm starting to feel sad and insecure with all these little flaws. And just like I do when I start to feel too good with a man, I shut it down. Can't get too high or too low. So I snap myself out of that state and jump out of the car. In the lobby, I wave to the proper girl behind the counter, get in the elevator and hit the button for the fourteenth floor.

I stand in front of Julian's room and take a deep breath. I wonder what am I doing. Where's this going? It's just the same old stupid Perla, I think, getting hooked on a married man, setting myself up for a fall. I knock and Julian answers the door, looking fine as always. His hair's all messed up the way I like it, fashionable and sort of cool. He gives me a kiss on the cheek and says Perla, you look beautiful. And I'm thinking *boy, you are one lying bastard, 'cause right now I'm a hot mess.* I kick my sandals off and say I'm gonna take a quick shower. I toss my purse on the counter and turn on the water. It's nice and warm, and I love it under the nozzles. I shampoo, soap up my body, especially my feet, my underarms, between my legs. I'm out of the shower in two minutes, even though I could've stayed there for hours. I towel off, put a dry towel around my body. A couple of sprays of perfume on the wrists, the neck, and I'm ready to go.

I step into the room and toss the towel to the floor. It's freezing with the hotel AC blasting out of the vent, and I make a run for the bed and dive under the covers. Within seconds, I feel Julian's warm body pressed hard against mine, and in an instant I'm so wet that I can feel it all the way down on my thighs, the wetness. And then, before I can even moan, whisper in the man's ear, Julian's inside me. I close my eyes. I try to have a little pleasure for once, try not to get too far ahead of myself or too far behind. I tap a beat on his shoulder, but he's too busy to notice. Tap, tap, pause. Tap, tap, pause. It's a nice beat, a simple one that calms me down. Tap, tap, pause.

JE VEUX PASSER MA
VIE AVEC TOI

On the terrace outside our apartment, there is a solarium with hundred-year-old glass, original lead mullions and an oxidized copper crest that runs along the peak. The doors are open, the side vents nudged ajar, and the autumn air washes past us, soft and with a hint of that back-to-school wistfulness that will likely plague me for the rest of my life, long after my final matriculation. The late afternoon light is rich and pearly and, despite the difference in season and location, it reminds me of the East End in July, when we hit the pole, when the sun near the beach stands tall and confident, infuses the warm seawater and browns the shoulders—and it looks to some like the air is filled with dust particles or pollen, but what it's always looked like to me is millions of tiny crystals that shimmer and rotate like the sparkles on a movie star's gown.

Julian and I sit at the table in the solarium, I in my wheelchair. It has been two weeks since my bowels betrayed me in bed. Our love for each other is as strong as ever, but our sex life has become so complicated by my predicament, so infrequent, so calculated and prone to disastrous outcome, that we have both withdrawn to unreachable places when it comes to physical intimacy. Sure, there are kisses and hugs, stroked hands and cuddling in bed—but that's the extent of it. We've been through these periods of distance before. They might last a few weeks or months. We always recover and give it another shot, but something about this distance seems different, as if we have reached some inflexion point in our relationship where there is no choice but for us to move forward at different trajectories, different speeds. It's as if we have finally given up the fantasy of having a normal relationship.

We look west out over the park—the museum to the right, Sheep Meadow in the distance, the two-spired monsters on Central Park West that mock us with their blinking red eyes. Julian strokes my hand, which is something that he has done habitually from the very first day we spoke, when we sat by each other in class; when I told him about my uncle, when he comforted me and first offered me a glimpse of his majestic brutality.

From a straw in a plastic cup, I sip cool blush wine—one of my few remaining pleasures. Julian has mint tea in a tall, perspiring glass. To the west, a small plane, a prop, glides up the Hudson River. For a fraction of a second, as if in a lucky photograph taken with an old Brownie, the plane is frozen, framed between the Choragic towers of the San Remo. Then it continues north, crosses the George Washington Bridge, dips its shoulder and swoons low and smooth over the Palisades.

"How are you?" I ask.

Julian stirs his tea with the tip of his index finger. "Fine, I guess. You?"

"All things considered, I'm well."

Julian picks up on my clue and turns to me. "All things considered?"

I take a sip of wine from the straw and swallow. I take in a colossal breath, feeling the expansion of my diaphragm. I hold the breath as long as possible and then exhale. I enjoy the relief of this release. "I've been thinking," I say. "You know, it's been six years." I tap the wheels by my side.

"Doesn't seem that long."

"Speak for yourself." I smile and give a little tug on Julian's pinky.

"I'm not even sure I was speaking for myself."

"Then who were you . . ." I pause and, with a bit of pretension to which I sometimes resort when anxious, I correct myself. "For *whom* were you speaking?"

"I don't know. How about the god of denial?"

"Yes, dear, yes! The god of denial, he's my God too."

Julian squints at me with mock skepticism. "I thought you were Lutheran."

"Wrong again," I say.

"That's the beauty of a marriage," Julian jokes. "Always learning things about your spouse you never knew before. Peeling layer after layer."

"Like an onion."

"Or the matryoshka dolls."

"Matryoshka?" I ask.

"The Russian dolls. Wooden, with smaller ones inside."

"Oh, yes."

"We had one at the orphanage. Missing a couple of pieces, but we kept it right there on the shelf. Very colorful and sweet. Petrov brought it with him when he arrived."

"Petrov . . ."

"Petrov . . ." Julian repeats.

We again gaze west over Central Park. There's a patch of red just to the south of the museum, a sugar maple in full bloom. "I've been thinking," I say, not fully prepared to continue. I struggle to place my wine cup on the table. I've got the bottom pressed on the edge of the table, but I'm feeling particularly weak today and just cannot get it over the edge. I turn to Julian. He reaches for the cup and places it on the table. Then he holds my hand, my fingers clasped tightly together, flipper-like.

"Look over there," he says, pointing to a huge cluster of balloons—dozens maybe—elevating to our left, just north of the zoo.

"You think that's a celebration or a catastrophe?"

"The balloons getting away?"

"Yes," I say. "Happy or sad?"

Julian thinks. "I'd like to think they're up there on purpose, that the birthday boy released them at the end of the party. So I'm going with celebration. You?"

"Me, too. Celebration." I lie, imagining a child pointing at the sky, wailing, screaming. Come back, come back.

"So . . . what have you been thinking?" Julian asks.

I reach for the plastic cup and lift the straw to my lips; I feel like a child. I take a sip of wine, a big sip. I'm feeling a delightful buzz from the alcohol. "Well, what I've been thinking is that maybe it's time we start living like the French?"

Julian turns to me. "The French? Yes, yes, a place in Paris. Is that what you're thinking? Or in the south? I'd love that. Get away from New York for a while."

I shake my head. "I'm not talking location. I'm talking state of mind."

"State of mind?"

"Mistress," I say.

"Sorry?"

"I've gotten pragmatic over the last few years, Julian. Paralysis will force your hand like that." I look down at my legs, my feet curved inward, my weakened hands. "There's just limits to what a person can do, you know. You start giving up on stuff, start giving up on things that . . . There's some things that, no matter what, we just can't make happen."

Julian reaches for my cup and again places it on the table. "What do you mean?"

"What I mean is that I can't fuck you the way I want, the way *you* want."

Julian pauses before responding. "It's different now, and that's okay," he says, and I know he wants to mean it. "Sickness and health and all that. It's life."

"It's not life, actually. It's the *opposite* of life. Shitting while fucking is not life. That's death and degradation. That's just us limping toward obsolescence while we obey some convention that never contemplated anything like this." Frustrated, as if I am about to escape, I disengage the brake on the wheelchair. "Sickness and health and all that? Nonsense, fucking nonsense."

"It's not nonsense," he assures me.

"You're telling me that in all these years you haven't slept with one single girl other than me?"

Julian does not answer. Instead, he positions his feet on the seat of an empty chair. "What do you want?" he asks.

I have rehearsed this next part of the conversation *ad nauseam*, and I thus deliver it without hesitation. "What do I want? What I want is for you to have a mistress. What I want is for you to stay with me, to love me, to care for me. What I want is to stay married to you, to love you, to fuck you the best I can, infrequent and *shitty* as it might be. What I want is to see you happy, to see you fuck like crazy . . . not to actually see it, of course . . . but to know that you are having your needs met by someone who rings your bell. But what I do *not* want is for you to fall in love with someone else, that would be too much for me to bear. Just for you to find someone who fucks you good, that's all. Like I used to."

I believe everything I just said, but not without great reservation. Julian looks at me. His face is oddly serene, and I cannot tell if his expression suggests disbelief or relief. We sit in silence as another plane shoots north up the river, but this time it's a jet that rapidly makes its way over the bridge and out of our view. "Well, then," he says, "the truth is, this French thing has already started."

I reflexively grab the wheels of my chair and re-engage the brake. "I figured," I respond, surprised by a titillating, prurient interest that Julian's revelation elicits in me—and at the same time working to suppress a piercing ache of jealousy that I'd assured myself would not arise. "Tell me about her."

Like a prickly little boy who's just been told to do his errands, Julian kicks his feet off the chair. "You want me to tell you about her?"

"Yes, but first I want you to fill my kiddie cup with some more blush."

Julian lifts the bottle out of the ice bucket and fills my cup.

He places it in my hand. I pull on the straw, take down half the cup. I'm loopy and ready for Julian's lurid confession.

"Where do you want me to start?"

"Hmmm. I'm not sure it matters. Name? When you met her? When you slept with her the first time? What she looks like? Hot, I assume. Age? I'm guessing she's barely out of high school."

"You've got all the answers, don't you?"

"I always do, so let's hear it."

"Well, I met her down in Florida when I was there for work. Must have been, I don't know, maybe six months ago."

"And where did you meet her?"

"Just around, nowhere special."

"Ju-li-an." I draw out his name in an admonishing way.

"In a strip bar."

"Ooh, how tawdry." I feel a vaguely erotic sensation in the band above my waist.

"I was bored and was just driving through Fort Lauderdale one day, saw this place on the side of the road and figured what the hell? Just go in for a lap dance, get my mind off work for a half hour and that's it. So I go in, and it's a trashy place, not like the one you and I went to in Vegas years ago. Remember that place? With the tropical fish tanks and all those Greek columns?"

"I do remember. That was a fun night. And the ridiculous blonde who wanted to come back to the room with us? Good call on our part to decline the offer."

"I think that was *your* call, not mine," he reminds me.

"Good point. Anyway, continue."

"So I walk in and I'm looking around for a cute girl to give me a dance. Next thing I know, this Latin girl comes out from behind a curtain, sees me and walks right over to me." Julian pauses to dry off his wet glass. "Most of the girls in these places are pretty aggressive, but this one, Perla's her name, Perlita, she's a bit shy and sort of proper. Normally, the first thing they do is ask you to buy them a drink, and next thing you know you're paying twenty bucks for a beer. But Perla offers to buy *me* a drink, which is pretty damn clever, and I started thinking that this girl's got some business smarts to be pulling a stunt like that. So, we sat and talked for a few minutes. Turns out she was raised in Cuba, came over with her parents when she was young. Her dad died, she loved him like crazy, and she lives with her mother down in Miami." The intimacy, the familiarity of the phrase *she loved him like crazy* makes me cringe.

"What's she like, physically?" I ask.

"You want it straight?"

"As an arrow."

Julian squirms in his seat and prepares for the next level of disclosure. "She's beautiful, young. Twenty-three. Dark skin, a nice body."

"Her tits?"

"Excuse me?"

"How are her tits? Are they fake?"

"No, natural."

"Cup size?" I ask, bordering now on extreme drunkenness.

"Sophie, are you serious?"

"Very."

"You know how bad I am with that stuff."

"Compared to me, then . . ." I cup my hands under my breasts.

Julian looks at my chest, sizes me up. "About the same, maybe a little bigger. But not much."

"So a B cup?"

"I guess."

"Did you fuck her that first night?"

Julian makes a jerky motion with his hand, an upward motion toward his mouth—a sign, I think, that he is startled by my directness. "That's crude, Sophie. Please."

"Julian!"

"Not the first night, no. That night I just got a lap dance in a private room."

"And you liked her?"

"I don't know if I *liked* her, but I found myself very attracted to her. She's smart, street-smart. And there's something sweet about her, almost wholesome."

"Wholesome and smart?" There's some skepticism and mockery in my voice.

"Something like that."

"So you started to see her every time you went down there for work?"

"I'd stop by, go in the back and get a dance. And then one day, I just invited her back to my room and . . ."

"And?"

"And I'd rather not continue," he says weakly, aware that his wishes carry little weight at this time.

"Please continue."

"We had sex."

"How was it?" I ask, and I really do want to know.

Julian squirms again and kicks his feet back up on the chair. "Fun, I guess. It felt innocent. There's no drama with this girl. She expects very little, which I guess is sort of sad."

I smile because Julian's arrogance has again gotten the best of him. "That doesn't sound sad to me at all. In fact, it sounds exceedingly healthy. Realistic." I want to ask Julian if Perla is a hooker, if he pays her for sex—but I know how sensitive this particular topic is for him, so I do not ask. In light of his mother's painful life, I would be astonished if Julian ever paid for sex. Although he's paying for lap dances, so I'm not sure where the dividing line is. "Do you enjoy her?" I ask. "Your time with her?"

"Sophie . . ."

"Do you?"

"It's just sex."

"It sounds like it's a tiny bit more than just sex," I snap, cursing myself for my broken state, my inability to satisfy Julian.

"Maybe."

I take another drag on the straw and suck the remaining wine out of the bottom of the cup. I slurp from the bottom like a kid and make a grotesque sucking sound. I'm drunk—the first time I've been truly drunk in years. It feels as though my wheelchair is moving, which it most certainly is not. I'm feeling loose and uninhibited, giddy. I used to love this feeling; I used to love fucking Julian when I felt like this.

But I'm also feeling furious. I'm furious at myself, at my *sexless* self. I'm furious at Julian, who manages to be both blameless and guilty. And I'm furious at Perla, too, the little slut with the B cups who has been fucking my husband.

"I need you to do me a favor," I say.

"Anything, babe."

"Anything?"

"What is it, Sophie?"

"I'd like you to bring her to me."

"Bring her to you? Bring *who* to you?"

"Perla," I say. "Bring her here."

LOOKING GLASS

I've had guys ask me to do just about every sick, twisted fetish you can think of. I don't do any of them 'cause I got boundaries, but some of the girls will do anything for a buck, especially that skank Lopez and the ones that are hooked on drugs. They've got no dignity, those girls, no limits, and they will do anything, *anything*, for some cash. So I guess it's just natural that when a guy meets a stripper, he assumes she's a whore too.

So I've had guys ask me if I'll piss on them, which is sick, shit on them, even sicker, stick my finger up their asshole, my *fist* up there too, if I'll smoke a cigarette all sexy and let them jerk off, let them come on my feet, hit them, jam a dildo in their ass, my tongue in there too, dress up like a schoolgirl, simulate rape, you name it. One guy, get this, wanted me to put on fuck-me pumps, crush a baby mouse under my heels and make a video of it. A crush video! I mean, how sick is that? Have you *ever*? One of the things I've learned stripping is there's really no end to sexual pathology, no end.

But the sickest thing I ever heard, well, not as sick as crushing the mouse but pretty close, was when that clubfooted messenger, Roger, walks into the club one day and says have I got a strange request for you. And I'm thinking, here we go, all that friendship stuff is out the window and Roger wants to fuck me. And I'm half thinking of doing it just to piss Julian off 'cause I haven't heard from the man since the last time we were in the hotel and he doesn't even have the decency to let me know he can't see me for a while. I'm at the end of my rope with Julian 'cause there's no hope of it being any more than just an occasional lay. It's getting a little boring and empty and I'm getting to the point where I think I'm looking for a little more out of life.

So Roger limps over to the bar and he's looking real uncomfortable and all the compassion I had for him comes right back, 'cause how could you not feel bad for a guy with a clubfoot? Although I once read about some Nazi guy who had a clubfoot, so I guess you can't feel bad for *all* of them. Anyway, Roger settles into a bar stool. I give him my signature peck on the cheek and get him a beer. Okay, he says, in the event you thought it couldn't get any weirder, it's getting weirder. He takes a swig of beer and a deep breath and says Julian sent me down here and he's got a favor to ask you. And before he can tell me the favor, I want to know why the hell Julian didn't come down here and ask himself. Julian's a tough guy, Roger says, and a stand-up guy. When he says this, I raise my eyebrows 'cause I'm not so sure Julian's the definition of a stand-up guy, whatever the hell that even means. But he just can't stand rejection of any kind, Perla, never puts himself in a position where he can fail in the eyes of someone he cares about. He's real tough in some areas, not so much in others, I guess. So he sends me down here to ask you an important question.

Roger finishes off his beer and waves real wild for another one. I'm laughing 'cause Roger is no big drinker, you can tell, but he's knocking them down today. You know that Julian's married, he says, and I nod yes. Well, his wife, Sophie, she knows all about you. When Roger says this, I all but fall off the chair 'cause the last thing I want in my life is drama, some crazy bitch who can't satisfy her husband showing up at my place of work and threatening me. And I also don't want to be the home-wrecker type. If I'm going to be fucking a married man, the last thing I want is for her to find out about it. Roger sees how concerned I am and he puts his hand on my arm and says don't worry, Perla, it's all good.

It's all good? I ask. How the hell is it all good? It sounds *all bad* to me, and I jab my finger in Roger's chest, not too hard but hard enough to make a point. Roger flinches when I touch him and I realize that he's a gentle man, afraid of aggression and afraid of a fight. And that's why he loves Julian so much, 'cause Julian is just the opposite and he's got Roger's back.

It's all good, Perla, he says, because Sophie wants to meet you, wants you to come to New York. What? I ask and say there's no way, Roger, no way that I'm doing a threesome with Julian and his wife. That is just not cool. I say it real slow. That. Is. Just. Not. Cool. Roger smiles and says please listen to me, Perla. Remember when I told you that things were more complicated than they seemed? I nod yes and out of the corner of my eye I see Lopez running and stumbling over her high heels, turning her ankles, chasing a Hollywood guy who comes in a few times a year and throws around hundreds like they're nickels—and I'm thinking how can I ditch Roger and get across the room before Lopez is on the ATM's lap. ATM, that's what I call a real rich guy who tips huge and doesn't ask for any extras. With the best ones, you can make a thousand bucks in an hour and all you have to do is dance and whisper some sweet things, push a few buttons and the money spits right out. But Lopez is fast tonight and she's on his lap in no time. And she looks over to me and gives me a cocky wink, that bitch.

So, Roger, tell me why a girl like me would want to go up to New York and meet my customer and his wife. How does that make even the tiniest bit of sense? I want to know. Roger looks down to his bad foot and moves it so that it rests on the brass rail that runs along the bottom of the bar. He puts his hand on my hand. And he says 'cause Sophie's paralyzed, waist-down, and can't ever walk again, and Julian loves her. And Sophie has some desire to meet you, *why*, only she can explain, and that's why I'm here.

Roger takes out an envelope, just like he did last time, but this one's got a plane ticket and five hundred bucks for travel money. Show up whenever you want, the ticket is always good, he says. You don't even need to call first, just show up. He drops his bad foot with the thick shoe onto the floor and pushes himself off the stool. I hold his elbow so he's stable and we stand and look at each other, him in his funny cripple shoes and me in my five-inch pumps. He puts his hands on my shoulders real sweet and looks around the dingy club, at the lights, the girls, the smoke, and he says make the trip, Perla, 'cause who knows where it takes you. Maybe it ends up worse than this, that's a possibility. Or maybe it takes you through the looking glass, he says, clear through to a place unexpected and great.

ENOUGH

My mom's over at Felipe's again. I usually get home from the club at around ten, and that's when we used to catch up. Have a late dinner and do our nails together, reminisce about Dad and Cuba, listen to music, maybe play some cards. But now when I get home it's empty most nights and it's just not the same. I just turn on the TV and eat takeout and do my own nails. I sleep late, maybe Mom comes by in the morning to change her clothes or pick up some things for the day, and we chitchat for a few minutes and then she's gone. It's been lonely without her around as much, real lonely, and I'm thinking maybe it's time I just tell her she doesn't have to worry about me anymore, that she can move in with Felipe full-time and I can get a roommate, see if maybe Rebekah wants to move in with me.

So I'm in the club and feeling lonelier than usual. I'm on the stage, wondering what I'm gonna do when my shift is over, what the hell my life is about, no man, no respectable job, and I'm dancing on the stage, rubbing my pussy against this disgusting pole. I'm staring off into the distance for I don't know how long and I lose track of where I am. I forget that I'm in the club, forget that I'm naked, that there's twenty gross men staring at me. My body's moving to the beat of the music, moving without me giving it any orders. This happens to me sometimes, my body and my mind doing different things. I once went to a psychologist a couple of years ago, when I was feeling real depressed and frightened and missing my dad so bad. The shrink thought that maybe the depression was one of the reasons I got on the pole in the first place—and maybe the reason I couldn't get off it.

Anyway, I told the shrink about these episodes, where my mind and my body go in different directions, and she said I was *dissociating*. She described it all technical, but I think what dissociating means is that sometimes your life sucks so bad that the brain has no interest in being around and says thanks for the invite, but I'm gonna sit this one out. Or the other thing it could be is not my brain reacting to a shitty life, but maybe it's some screwed-up wiring in my brain that *caused* this shitty life in the first place. Cause or effect? Who knows? It's better if it's effect, I think. Effect is easier to fix.

So, I'm dissociating right there on the pole and I don't hear Schultz on the loudspeaker calling Lopez up on the stage and telling me it's time to get back on the floor. And the only thing that brings me out of this dopey state is Lopez tapping me on the shoulder saying Perla, Perla, you okay? And something about the way she taps me, real gentle and concerned, something about that changes the way I feel about her, makes me think that maybe she's had a real hard life too and she's doing the best she can. And that beneath all the toughness and the ink, beneath all that, maybe there's some decency under there.

I make it down to the floor and it takes me some time to come back to reality, to *re*associate, like the shrink used to say. I start recognizing things and people, and one by one the picture gets put back together. There's the Champagne Room, I recognize that. The VIP Room. There's Schultz and Jade. There's the lawyer who got disbarred. I know that strobe light, that curtain, that sticky leather couch. And finally the picture's complete and I'm *back*.

I sit down and Jade brings me a bottle of water. A guy walks over to me, sort of sweet-looking, attractive. He's dressed in expensive clothes, not flashy but nice. His hair's combed and he looks like he smells good, which is real rare in a place like this. I check his left hand and sure enough he's got a wedding ring, and I think at least here's an honest guy, at least from the view of a stripper. He sits down and tells me his name is Jed, which makes me laugh 'cause it doesn't seem like a real name, and he says let's go to the Champagne Room. That's two hundred, you know. And I say that 'cause sometimes they've got no idea how pricey it is. Turns out he's fine with it. When we get in the room, he sits down and I take off my top, tell him he can touch my tits but no kissing and no touching me down there.

Well, we're half a song into the set and I'm straddling him and doing my thing, trying to be present but not *too* present. I can feel his hard dick through his pants, pressing against me. I got no problem with a guy having a hard-on 'cause that's what they're here for, right? A few more songs, I think, and I get my cash and maybe I'll tell Schultz I don't feel good and get out of here early tonight. But next thing I know this guy slips his hand under my panties and I grab it real fast, pull it out and remind him no touching down there. He nods okay and I go back to doing my dance. But sure enough his hand is right down there again, but this time he pushes real hard and I feel his finger on my pussy, reaching around to get his finger *inside* me.

I grab his wrist and try to pull his arm away, try to get up off him, but his arm's around my waist and I can't move. He's pushing his finger deep inside me, and I'm not wet at all so it hurts bad and I know this is gonna cause a tear and some bleeding. And I'm sure his hands are dirty so I'm already thinking infection. He's got one finger in, then he puts another and another—and I think it's three and it hurts like hell.

I scream out Schultz, Schultz! And thank God he's standing right on the other side of the door. He hears me and runs in, pulls me off the guy, smashes the guy's face into the wall, and then Schultz and the other bouncers take him out to the back lot and get rid of all the frustration that's been building up in their lives. After that first punch, it's got nothing to do with the guy breaking the rules. After the first punch, it's the closest Schultz and the boys are ever gonna get to a shrink's couch.

Schultz comes back after a few minutes and he's holding his hand, which is red and swollen. He hands me a hundred bucks that he pulled off the guy. You okay, Perla? And that's the second person in the last half hour who asked me the same question, and when two people in a shit-hole like this ask if you're okay, then clearly you're *not* okay. Schultz tells me to go home, get some rest, and says maybe go see a gyno doc if your pussy's sore. That's exactly how he says it, *go see a gyno doc if your pussy's sore.* I give Schultz a hug, 'cause he's a big, sweet oaf and he's got my back.

I'm in my car driving down 95 and my pussy *does* hurt. I'm

mad, real mad, but mostly at myself. I knew a recovering alcoholic once and she kept hanging out in bars with her drinking
buddies even though she was trying to stay sober. And then one
day I saw her and she looked like shit, been drinking again.
When I asked her how she ended up boozing, she said Perla, you
keep hanging around in barbershops long enough, eventually
you're gonna get a haircut. That's how I feel about my pussy
right now. It was just a matter of time.

I look down to the center console and reach for a pack of
gum. Underneath, I see the envelope that Roger gave me. There's
no cash in there 'cause I already spent that on rent and some
new sandals. But the plane ticket is still there and it's been peek-
ing out of the envelope for weeks, just one little corner, teasing
me and eyeing me and begging me to do something outside my
comfort zone for once in my life. I remove the ticket from the
envelope and pick my teeth with it, 'cause I think I got something stuck in there and it's driving me a little nuts. I'm wondering how an open-ended ticket works. Does that mean I just show
up at the airport and I get to go on *any* plane? Fly to Caracas?
Or Milan? Or just to New York?

There's traffic on 95 and it looks like a big wreck ahead, so I
pull off at Hallandale Beach Boulevard and start taking side
streets south toward Miami. It's going to take a while to get
home and I want to be in a shower so bad, soap up and wash
away the stench of that guy's fingers. I'm thinking maybe I'll
hang out with my mom tonight, play some cards with her, heat
up the rice and fish that's left over in the fridge.

Then I remember that my mom's with the boyfriend tonight
and I'm gonna be all alone again. I look over at that envelope and
boy, is it seductive. And I think *fuck it, I'm not gonna lie on the*

couch alone and eat Cuban food and listen to music. Instead, I'm gonna go home, take a shower, pack a bag and take a trip to New York City—maybe walk around Times Square and Greenwich Village. And maybe, if I have enough courage when I get there, maybe I'll stop in on Julian and his paralyzed wife. 'Cause I don't know what's on the other side of the looking glass, but it sure as hell can't be worse than having some asshole stick his fingers in your pussy.

CLOVE GUM

'm home alone with Norma, and Julian is out for a late dinner with his friends: Roger and the Russians. After Julian made his first of many fortunes, he turned his attention to expatriating Petrov and Volokh from their dreary lives in Siberia. His two friends had remained tight after their expulsion from the orphanage at the age of sixteen, and their lives since then were defined by grueling manual labor, poverty and petty crime. It took Julian five years, several trips to Moscow and Washington, and countless millions to get them, their wives and children to the States. And now he's got them right here in the city, and they are about the closest group I've ever seen. Thick as thieves. And with this group, there might be a bit of truth to the idiom.

Since Julian amassed great wealth, his interactions with others have changed in such a way that his insularity has been reinforced, for no longer are people genuine in his presence. In the orphanage, when he had nothing, they were real—either kind or brutal or indifferent, but always real. But with his wealth now extraordinary and well known in this gossipy town, he no longer enjoys truly honest interactions with strangers.

His friends in the inner core, however, have managed to express their reverence and unwavering loyalty and have coupled that with playful ridicule. It is the ridicule, good-natured, that Julian misses most—the therapeutic effect of being forced not to think too highly of oneself, not to buy into the myth that wealth, the *creation* of wealth, assigns to that person a wisdom, a morality or a competence that exceeds those who are less successful financially. The great American myth, Julian calls it.

I'm right in the middle of this group, cozy and safe under its protective cloak. There are others who dance along the perimeter, people who for any number of reasons are not fully embraced by Julian; it could be a shameless self-promotion or the hint of pathological narcissism or a nauseating deference that will cause Julian to keep someone at a safe distance. And I guess that Perla is somewhere near the periphery now, a tiny, curvy figure in the distance. But I can feel her moving closer to us. And I wonder, if she makes it here, will she be additive or displacing?

After Norma works her magic to get me properly positioned, I sit in a fluffy chair in the living room. I am as comfortable as my condition will permit, and I can't decide if I want to read yet another rock-and-roll memoir, a genre that I've been loving lately, or if I should close my eyes for a few minutes. While I am considering my next move, Norma stands in front of the window and looks out to the park.

"Pretty night," she says. "The museum's all lit up and a nice moon. A *crescent* moon."

I lean forward and to the right to get a better view of the sky.

"I can't see," I say, frustrated by my inability to view the moon from this perspective. "What does it look like?"

Norma studies the moon. "It's thin, real thin, just a little bit of light on the side. It's got color, which you don't see much. Orange, maybe even some red, with streaks going across it." Norma looks at me and understands that her description, while lovely, leaves me ungratified. "You want me to get you back in the chair?" she asks, nodding in the direction of the wheelchair— a weird vehicle that sickens me with its simplicity, not much more than two engorged bicycle wheels bolted to a beach chair. "What do you think, Mum? Get you close to the window?"

I eye my wheelchair in the corner of the room. I think about the snugness that I feel in this wingback, the effort that will be required for me to transfer, and I decide that, sadly, my aversion to inconvenience exceeds my desire to witness beauty.

"No, thanks," I say. And as I'm thinking about yet another joyous thing that gives me no joy, an intrusive thought emerges without warning or context; I think about Julian making love to another woman, to Perla—his commitment to her orgasm, his strength, his surrender upon release. There's a surge of jealousy, searing and unexpected, that floods my bloodstream with stress hormones. "Open the window, please," I say, my body temperature rising. "I'd like some air in here, some *fall* air." With only the slightest flick of the wrist, Norma guides the perfectly crafted window upward.

The wind pours in from the west. It's cool and crisp and there's a hint of something sweet that surprises me. It's not the autumnal sweetness of apple cider or pumpkin pie or a rural leaf burn. No, it's something vague and alluring. "You smell that, Norma?" I ask.

As if she is a curious terrier, Norma makes a sniffing motion with her nose. "Smell what?"

"Something sweet," I say, reaching to the side table for a brilliant memoir by a poet and musician, a memoir about her love affair with a photographer and their life in New York. By mistake, I knock the book to the carpeted floor. "You don't smell it?"

Norma sniffs again, this time with an exaggerated motion that contorts her entire face. "No, Mum, there's nothing but the air."

I reach for the book on the floor, but it is well beyond the tips of my fingers. Norma notices my struggle and crosses the room to pick it up. I close my eyes. I inhale. And there it is—that sweetness, an eclectic sweetness, paradoxical, like clove gum or a charred fig.

THE RUBICON

The last time I was in New York was with my father when I was nine years old and it's one of the few childhood memories that's just like I remembered, but now they print the calories on the menus, which seems odd, and there's no smoking in the bars and the taxi driver told me that you can't even have a cigarette in Times Square or Central Park. *Outdoors!* Which is something that just cannot be true, can it? In Florida, the government pretty much stays out of your hair, which is something that means a lot to us Cubans, 'cause God knows we had enough people telling us how to live our lives, and down in Florida you can do just about anything you want, carry a gun and strip fully nude and have a big fatty milkshake and probably smoke in the middle of a library if you really want. Cubans, we don't like having one man with all the money and all the answers making up laws that's supposed to be in our best interest. My dad used to call that *paternalismo*. And he used to say

Perla, you already have one father, and you don't need another one telling you what to do.

I'm standing on Fifth Avenue and Seventy-sixth Street, and there's a gorgeous old building on the corner. I look at the address on the envelope and sure enough this is where Julian lives, with his paralyzed wife, I guess, and maybe some other people that I don't even know about yet. I cross the street so I can get a good peek into the lobby. There's a guy in a uniform standing in front of the door and he looks like a soldier, an officer from one of those World War II movies—not one of the smart officers, but one of the goofy German guys everyone's always fooling even though he thinks he's in charge.

I look again at the envelope to see if there's an apartment number or a floor, but there's only the address. I look up at the building and count the stories. It looks like there's fourteen, maybe fifteen, and I wonder if these people are so rich that they have more than one floor. I start to shake a little and I'm thinking that maybe I'm not too comfortable being away from Florida. Maybe I should just go over to the Doll House, 'cause I know a couple of girls from Miami who work there and I can crash at their place for the night. But I hear they're getting in trouble lately, dabbling in drugs—meth and X, which is a really strange combination I think—and they've always got sketchy boyfriends, tough guys from places like Albania and Serbia who scare the crap out of me.

On the tenth floor, there's an open window and it's the only open window in the building. I can see an arm hanging out, a woman's arm, dark-skinned and thick. That must be somebody's maid, I think. But then I get real angry at myself for thinking so racist, 'cause I'm a Cuban girl and I know what it's like when fools make assumptions about you based on nothing. And why *can't* a black girl own a fancy place like that? It's a possibility, right? I'm watching her arm and it's so still that I wonder if it's real or a mannequin. But then her head pops out of the window. She's wearing a uniform, sort of like a nurse, and I guess that means she works there, 'cause no way a nurse can afford a place like this. Or maybe she just happens to be a really rich black nurse. Or maybe she does live there and her husband's got a nurse fetish, likes to have his temperature taken from behind.

My mind's racing now and coming up with so many crazy ideas, each one canceling out the last, that I'm getting anxious and afraid I'm gonna have one of those dissociating moments again. I think about my comfort zone now and how I'm already so far out of it and so uncomfortable that I don't think I can take much more. I figure I'll walk over to the next avenue, which turns out to be Madison, and get a snack and settle myself down.

Turns out there's not much going on at night on Madison, but I find a deli a couple blocks down and get a little bite to eat. And when the guy behind the counter tells me how much a soda, an apple and a bag of chips costs, I'm thinking that people up here are totally nuts. 'Cause if an apple, chips and a soda cost almost as much as a lap dance, you got a serious problem on your hands. A serious problem with *society*. I pay the money, but give the cashier a mean look just to let him know I don't approve, not that he seems to care one damn bit.

I walk back toward Julian's building and stand across the street. I look up again for that open window, but all the windows are closed now and I don't remember which one it was. The doorman stands in front of the building and he's leaning against the brass pole under the awning and he's smoking a cigarette in a way that says he doesn't want anyone to see that he's smoking a cigarette. He's holding it in his cupped hand behind his back, and I laugh 'cause I've seen *that* move before. He looks across the street in my direction, and I try to look away before he sees me, but too late. He nods to me. I just stand there all still, nervous and feeling silly. He squints at me like he's trying to get a good look at my face. And then he holds up his cigarette, above his head, and yells out *want a smoke?*

I'm not a smoker, but I shrug my shoulders and walk across the street toward the man. I walk right up to him all confident, even though I'm not. He says *evening*, nothing sketchy or sleazy, but real sweet like he's bored and so happy to have contact with someone that he doesn't see every day of his life, someone he doesn't work for. Good evening, I say, and he pulls out a pack of cigarettes and offers them to me. Smoke? he asks. No, thanks. And we both stand there by the side of the awning with the brass poles, just like the ones at the club, but these are shinier and they must get polished all the time. I take a look at him and I'm guessing he's mid-fifties—a little puffy with a gray moustache and the funny uniform that's got to make a man feel like he's being dressed up like a clown for someone else's amusement.

He bends back a bit at the waist, hands on hips, then points to the sky and says cool moon, huh? I look up and there it is, crescent and hanging low to the right. It's got a reddish look to it, orange, which is something that I'd figure you see in a desert or in the Caribbean, but not right here in the middle of New York City. It *is* a cool moon, I say. And he smiles a bit and I can tell that he's happy a young girl is talking to him and seeing the same beauty he sees and that I don't think he's just some nostal-

gic old man. We stand there for a few seconds, just looking up at
that funny-colored moon, and I say does Julian live here? Julian
Pravdin?

The doorman stares at me. He takes another drag of his cigarette and flicks it with his middle finger and thumb into the
street, a perfect shot so it lands right in the center of a puddle
and fizzles into nothing. You Perla? he asks, all matter-of-fact.

Well, I'm not sure I've ever been so shocked in my life, but I
try to act real cool and nod yes. He opens the front door for me
and tells me come on in, we've been expecting you. I enter the
lobby, and he points to an elevator at the end of the hall and says
tenth floor, Perla, I'll send you up.

INNOCENCE

I get a bit of a chill and ask Norma to close the window. Again, with the tiniest flick of the wrist, she slides the window downward. She approaches me and looks at her watch.

"Let me take a look at your bag," she says. She leans over and unties the sash around my silk robe. She opens the robe and looks at my midsection. "Almost full," she says, removing two rubber gloves from her pocket.

"How's the color?" I ask.

"All good."

Norma twists the clasp and removes the bag. One drop of urine, warm and slick, lands on the band above my waist—and I enjoy the sensation. Norma wipes it from my skin and then disappears into the bathroom. She returns five minutes later with a clean, empty bag that she attaches to the tube. Then she lifts the memoir off the armrest and takes a look at the cover, at the black-and-white photo of the author and her lover.

"I know him," she says. "*Knew* him."

"You did?"

Norma pulls the book closer to her face and examines the photograph. "He took a photo of my cousin, you know, in the eighties. He's passed. Mikey." She crosses herself. "The same thing that got most of those boys back then, damn shame. They had no idea, no one did. All so innocent, every one of 'em. My aunt still has that photo, black-and-white just like this one."

After six years together, Norma continues to reveal herself to me episodically. I guess that I do the same with her. "Really . . . I'd like to see that photo one day."

"One day, Mum."

"I'm tired," I say. "Let's get ready for bed."

Norma places the book on the side table, then leans down and places her wrists under my arms. She spreads her strong legs shoulder width apart and prepares to lift me off the wingback and into the wheelchair.

"A one . . . and a two . . . and a . . ."

Norma pauses before she gets to three—not a long pause, but an almost undetectable hesitation, as if she's got a tickle in the back of her throat. And in that hesitation, that briefest moment of suspension, there is a knock at the door.

HALLWAYS

I'm standing at the front door for what must be five minutes, so nervous and wondering what the hell I'm doing here. And I'm pacing back and forth and peering *into* the peephole to see what's going on inside, but of course that's ridiculous 'cause they're designed so you can only see *out*. Finally, I just think *fuck it, I've come this far, so I might as well see it all the way through*. It can't be worse than getting fingered in the club.

I knock on the door. One tap, two taps, three taps. Tap, tap, tap. I straighten up and get as tall as I can. I hear voices on the other side of the door, women sounding sort of surprised and confused. I look around to see if I knocked on the right apartment, looking for another door, but this is the only one on the entire floor, except for one at the end of the hall that says STAFF in real old letters. And then the lock clicks and the door opens, and there's the dark-skinned woman from the window, looking real protective and tough. She takes a step to the side so she's not blocking the view, and what's there before me is the biggest, most beautiful home I've ever seen, like a museum in Paris or Rome. There's high ceilings and antiques and even a fancy old pool table with green felt so smooth and perfect that it looks like a putting green. And sitting right there in a chair in the middle of the room, in a pretty silk robe, is one gorgeous and seriously paralyzed woman.

SUPPLICANT

Why the doorman did not announce Perla's arrival is something that I do not understand, and it's also something about which I never felt the need to question. Maybe it was at Julian's prior instruction or a momentary lapse in the doorman's judgment, or maybe the doorman was so taken by Perla's beauty that he lost sight of his responsibilities. Whatever the reason, Perla's knock caught me and Norma off guard. Had I known she was coming, I would have prepared a bit, done my hair, put on a nice dress, some jewelry. I also would have set the place up for her—some food and drinks.

Perla stands in the doorway, and we stare at each other. "It's okay, Norma," I say. "I believe this is Perla?"

She extends her hand to Norma and then approaches me. She stands before me in tight jeans, cute silver sandals, a pink cotton sweater and a short leather jacket. It's apparent that the girl is uncomfortable, and who wouldn't be? I sure as hell am. And so is Norma, who is beyond confused. Perla is in an opulent apartment and, at the risk of sounding like a damn snob, it's probably unlike anything she's ever seen before—and people can get awkward in the presence of wealth. People also get awkward in the presence of the disabled. They either treat you like you're some delicate egg and overcompensate with excessively slow, careful motions and soft voices (I'm paralyzed, not deaf), or they try so hard to show you that they think you're just like everyone else (which you most certainly are not) that they are casual and brusque to the point of danger. And, of course, people get painfully awkward in the presence of the wives of the men they are screwing. And who knows how awkward people get in the presence of the *disabled* wives of the men they are screwing? I can only assume that's worse yet.

The mind creates mental images of the things it has never seen. I would guess that there is something evolutionary about predictive imagery. One can envision a hunter returning to his small village and warning his fellow tribesmen about the warriors he has just seen amassing over the hill. To assess the threat, the villagers will ask him to describe the threat. How big are these men? How many are there? Do they have bows and arrows? Knives? Spears? Shields? Are they wearing face paint? If so, what color is it? The villagers will process the data, create a mental image of the threat and respond in a manner consistent with the perceived peril. Our ability to create a preceding mental image that comports with the actual image depends upon our own experience, our powers of imagination, our emotional intelligence. Sometimes we get close. Sometimes we are so far off that we wonder what the hell we were even thinking and thus begin to question our own judgment, the effectiveness of our survival instincts.

As I observe Perla, I am relieved by the accuracy with which I had imagined her. The skin. She has a perfect complexion. I look for something, for some imperfection: a faint birthmark, a mole, a pimple, a broken blood vessel, a tiny hair on the upper lip. But other than what might be a pale sliver of a scar under her chin, I see nothing. Her skin is a shade or two darker than I had anticipated—and she could have as easily been Creole or Indian, which I guess is logical given the heterogeneity of the Caribbean. Her hair, dark chocolate brown but lightened in streaks by the Florida sun, is cut shoulder length and wrapped over her ears. When she turns to the side—a quick glance to break the tension of the moment—I notice that she has a thin white streak of hair in the back.

Perla removes her jacket. Her pink sweater clings tightly to her body, revealing both the broadness of her shoulders and the contour of her breasts. Julian is right, she does have B cups and thus does not fit my mental image of a stripper: a thin wisp of a girl sporting hydraulic DDs that threaten to topple her forward. Instead, here's a girl who is sticking with what God gave her, and something about her resistance to convention humanizes her in my eyes, reveals a stubborn, proud character, a refusal to let go of something important that I do not yet understand.

Her face. Her face is lovely. Not model stunning or head-turning, but just plain lovely. There are the green eyes that contrast so sharply with her skin that they suggest a penetrating eagerness, as if she is in a constant state of forward, bounding motion. Her mouth is wide, her lips full and glistening in a sweet-smelling gloss that only a girl of her age can wear, her chin smoothly pointed.

Perla stands before me, and there is a moment during which

neither of us know how to behave. And then, as if I am some decrepit but revered queen, she dips her right knee into a deep curtsy. I'm alarmed and touched by her display of deference, and I can only think that her mother—or a nun—must have taught her this gesture when she was a little girl. I hold out my right hand to shake Perla's. She reaches out but does not shake it as I expect. Instead, she clasps it with her two hands, cups my hand in her palms; she rises closer to me and presses my hand against her cheek. I feel the sensation of my palm, my fingers, against her smooth skin—which is so hot that I'm afraid the girl has a fever.

Perla's eyes water. "I'm sorry," she cries. "I am *so* sorry."

SERENDIPITY

There's something about seeing Sophie stuck in that chair and how she struggles to lift her hands—and the fact that here I am screwing her husband, and she's just about as courteous as a woman can be. And then I bend down like I'm bowing before the nuns at school and why I do that I have no idea. But I bow down and reach out and hold her hand, which you can tell is not as strong as a normal hand, and I press it against my face. It's cold, her hand, and something about how it feels all cold and stiff, something about that does something to me, brings up some emotions that have no business coming to the surface. Maybe it's being so close to the woman I betrayed. Not direct, but an indirect betrayal, 'cause I slept with her husband even after I knew she existed and us girls are supposed to look out for each other, not stab each other in the back. And she can't walk, and that makes me feel even worse, makes me feel real bad for her and for Julian, too.

So I'm crying, and where so much feeling comes from I'm only just starting to get a better clue. I'm thinking that maybe I disappointed all the people who ever cared about me. And maybe it's from the pain of disappointing the people I love, 'cause is there anything that feels worse than that? Anything worse than disappointing the people we love? I'm one of those fools who believes in the afterlife, and I don't make any apologies for thinking there's something beyond this earth. And I'm thinking that wherever he is—heaven, I'm sure—my dad sees how I'm living my life, the cheapness, the lies, the bad men, and he's sad it turned out like this. And Old Pepe, too. How this is not what he wanted when he taught me how to feed Chico and Chica and said to find a man who feeds me first and gives me the firewood, whatever that means. And I'm sad that my mom's still waiting tables, which I guess is better than *dancing* on them, and I'm happy she finally found a man who's good to her. But it also means I'm going to see a whole lot less of her and that makes me feel so alone and hopeless.

I put my head on Sophie's shoulder and she lets me cry right there, without pushing me away or making me feel even worse. I'm getting her silk robe all wet and I feel bad about that. The shrink I once saw would have called that projection. Or was it transference? I forget. But she would've said that it was something else I was feeling bad about, not messing up her robe. I think it can be both. I think I can feel bad about her robe and also feel bad about a bunch of other things.

I'm tired, drained and wondering why I'm here. Why I'm *really* here. I'm wondering about serendipity. I love that word, 'cause it sounds exactly how it means. There's a word for that, too, when a word sounds like it means. But I can't pronounce that one. So I'm wondering about serendipity, wondering how it is that certain people get drawn to each other, how they cross paths and build relationships, make real deep connections. I'm wondering why I'm *really* here.

I lift my head off Sophie's shoulder and take a good look at her. She's a beautiful woman, Sophie, and she looks like an actress from one of those old French films, the kind who doesn't wear makeup but just looks so simple and elegant that you think she could roll out of bed, tie her hair in a ponytail, jump on a bicycle with a basket on the handlebars and ride into town for bread and cheese. And then later on you see her at a dinner party and the only thing that's different is now her hair's down and she's got a pair of earrings on and every guy at the party wants her.

I look at Sophie's face and she's got a beauty mark on her right cheekbone, a little dot that's in the perfect place and makes her look so cosmopolitan, and ooh, I wish I had something just like that. Sophie wears a short pearl necklace. And when I see her pearls, real, beautiful ones, I panic and reach for my ears to remind myself what I'm wearing. Little gold hoops, so thank God I didn't put on my fake pearls today, 'cause that would've been embarrassing. I look down to Sophie's chest, just a quick glance 'cause I don't want her to think I'm staring, and it turns out she's got small boobs just like me. And something about that, me and Sophie both having small boobs, something about that makes me smile.

Sophie asks if I'm hungry or thirsty, and I say no. She asks me if I'm tired. And when I don't answer, when I can't answer, when I'm feeling so drained it's near impossible to speak, she says Perla, I think you need some sleep. And then she turns to

Norma, who's standing a few feet away and nods, and it occurs to me that these two women spend so much time together that they communicate like porpoises. Norma motions me to follow and I do, 'cause I don't have the energy to resist. And just before we turn a corner down a long hall, I look back to Sophie and she tries to lift her left hand to wave, but it's too hard for her, so she waves good night with her right. I ask her if Julian's here, wondering what's happening, what's really going on. He's out, Sophie says, won't be back until late. So best to get some rest and see him in the morning.

Norma leads me to a room that's bigger than any bedroom I've ever seen and it's decorated with pretty things, glass paperweights and an Oriental vase with fresh-cut birds-of-paradise and a silver tray with ruby-red glasses all lined up in a row. There's beige wallpaper with branches of flowered trees and red, blue and pink birds. I close my eyes, and I think of Pepe and his parrots. I picture the mango tree behind his house and the birds bouncing from branch to branch.

I take off my bra, pull it out through the sleeve of my sweater, and toss my jeans to the floor. I get under the sheets, which are made of the smoothest, most luxurious fabric to ever touch my body. I get on my side, rest my face on the pillow—and the next thing I know, it's morning.

SOMETHING AMISS

Julian arrived home from a late dinner with his friends. At the restaurant, Julian ate too many slices of Clancy's famous chocolate pie; Roger consumed far too much Chablis and tried, despite his drunkenness and bad foot, to dance with the curvy hostess from County Cork; Volokh and Petrov, as always, enjoyed their expatriation, telling bawdy Russian jokes and eating with a ferocity intended to obliterate their childhood privations.

Val, an avuncular Montenegrin who had worked in the building for close to forty years, stood under the awning and greeted Julian. "Evening, Mr. Pravdin," he said, opening the lobby door, unaware that the doorman working the earlier shift had sent a female guest up to the apartment.

Before opening the front door, Julian looked at his watch and was surprised to see that it was half past midnight. Inside, the apartment was dark and quiet. He turned on a wall sconce that created just enough light to illuminate the main parlor, but not so much that Sophie would be awakened if her door were open. Julian looked around the grand room. There was something different about the place, but he did not know what. The sofas, the chairs, the tables were all in the same place. The artwork was exactly where it had been that morning when he left for work. The vase of white roses sat, as always, on the credenza along the far wall.

Hanging over the arm of the wingback was the silk sash from Sophie's robe. Julian walked over to the chair and lifted the sash. He wondered why it was there, why Sophie had left it behind, whether it had slipped from her robe. He feared that she was not feeling well and that Norma had rushed her to the bedroom. Or maybe it was nothing so dramatic; maybe it fell off while Norma was transferring Sophie into the wheelchair and neither of them noticed. Julian put the sash in his jacket pocket.

Walking down the long hallway, Julian passed Norma's room on the right—the door slightly ajar as usual so she could hear if Sophie called out for help. The door to the guest room was closed, which was not atypical. Julian slowly opened the door to the master bedroom, careful not to push past forty-five degrees, at which point the hinges barked and might startle Sophie from her sleep. The bedroom was dark, but washed in a wan, ambient light from the street that had managed to slip under, around, through the thick curtains.

Julian listened. There was the pneumatic hissing of the compression machine on Sophie's legs; there was her raspy breathing; there was the insectile buzz of the night-light by the floorboard. Julian removed his clothes and stood naked. As he had done every day in the orphanage, he carefully folded each piece of clothing, including his socks, and placed them on the dresser—and he did so despite the fact that they would be gathered in the morning by the housekeeper and cleaned. He lifted Sophie's robe from the reading chair in the corner of the room and threaded the sash through the loops.

Julian inhaled, taking in the residue of the candles, the tart orange blossom to which he had become accustomed. But on this night, another smell lingered and mixed congruously, logically, with the candles' scent. It was a smell that to Julian was familiar but elusive: sweet and playful. Julian slid under the covers next to Sophie. He lay on his back and, with his right arm, reached over to her. Gently, he placed his hand on her left breast, delivering a warm shiver that penetrated her sleep but did not withdraw her from it.

Sophie blinked, a recognition, a relief that Julian had returned. She felt his lips on her cheek. In the other room, Perla slept soundly.

A wrinkling in the corner of Sophie's mouth—not a full smile but something close—further indicated that at this moment in time, swaddled in a diaper, her legs compressed by some weird machine, Perla in her crosshairs, she had everything she needed.

ESCAPE ARTIST

wake up with no idea what time of day or night it is. But it seems like it's morning, 'cause there's some natural light in the room and my body is telling me it's morning. I spend a few seconds trying to get myself oriented, reminding myself what happened last night, why I'm here, how I ended up in this bed. Just like some hungover drunk trying to remember the night before, but of course, I don't drink. I'm doing the same thing, though, trying to put all the pieces of the jigsaw puzzle together. There's the birds on the wall and the vase with the flowers and there on the floor is my bra and jeans.

Turns out there's a bathroom *in* my room, which I didn't notice last night, and that's a relief 'cause that way I don't have to go out to the hall to get ready. I'm standing in front of the sink and looking at myself in the mirror, and something's a little different about the way I look. I don't know if it's the nice lighting in this bathroom or the fact that I got a good night's sleep for the first time in weeks or maybe something else. But I look like I gained a few pounds, which of course I didn't in just one night, and I look healthier and a bit more like a woman instead of a silly little girl.

I brush my teeth and straighten my hair and I'm just about to start with the makeup—rouge, lipstick, mascara—and then I think about Sophie and how beautiful she looked last night, and without even a speck of this stuff on her face. So I toss my little bag onto the counter, the pink bag with Hello Kitty on it, and I tie my hair in a ponytail and pull off my sweater. I'm standing there pretty much naked, except for my panties, and I look at myself in the mirror. And again, I don't know if it's the light or what, but my skin looks different to me, thicker and pinker. I put on my bra and my jeans and take one more look at myself in the mirror. From my travel bag, I take out a cute periwinkle V-neck that Rebekah got me for my birthday, and I pull it over my head, shimmy it down and now I'm ready to go.

I'm in front of the door, about to make my move, but I'm frozen in place and can't seem to grab the doorknob. I'm real nervous 'cause who knows what's happening on the other side of that bedroom door. Maybe everyone's gone and I can just slip out real quiet and get back to Miami and see my mom and Rebekah, get back to Paris Nights and make a few bucks. Or maybe Sophie and Norma are out there having breakfast. And then what? Or maybe, and I think this would be the worst, maybe Julian's there with them. The three of them having breakfast and me coming down the hallway all uncomfortable and feeling out of place.

I put my Hello Kitty case in my purse and toss my travel bag over my shoulder. I look around the room one more time and wonder if I'll ever be in a room this pretty again. I'm still stand-ing in front of the door and I'm dreading what's gonna happen next, cursing myself for getting on that plane, for coming over here, cursing myself for letting Julian make me come that first time in the Champagne Room. I stand up tall and get some good posture and remind myself that I've been in worse situations than this, 'cause at least no one here's trying to hurt me—best I can tell. But I'm real frightened. And then I just think *fuck it*. And I reach for the doorknob.

BREAKFAST FOR THREE

was a drama major in college and not only do I love acting out a drama but I love *creating* a drama, too. I love knowing things that others don't know and setting up players and scenes, triggering a series of events, a chain reaction among the unsuspecting, directing them without their knowledge. I do all of this not for some weird thrill, a perverse rush of omnipotence, but rather out of my affection for those who just need a gentle nudge in the right direction, for those who don't know that the answer is right there on the other side of the curtain. There's also something empowering about all of this scheming—especially when viewed in light of my otherwise disempowered state.

Julian and I sit at the table in the breakfast room, which is a sunny, high-windowed space off the kitchen that faces southeast and thus welcomes the morning light. The table is set for three, and Norma prepares breakfast in the adjacent kitchen. Because Norma joins us for breakfast on occasion, the third place setting does not attract Julian's attention.

"What time is your flight to D.C.?" I ask Julian.

Julian looks at his watch, a reflexive response that can in no way inform his answer. "Noon."

"Private or commercial?"

"Private."

"And back tomorrow morning?"

"Back in the morning," Julian says. "I've got meetings today, then a black-tie dinner tonight. A breakfast tomorrow at one of those horrible clubs, then I'm on my way."

"Any way you can get out of it?" I ask, knowing that Perla's unexpected visit will create chaos around here.

"Sadly, none," he says. "They have me meeting a bunch of government people. And the president of the bank. It's a whole dog and pony show, took them months to get it arranged."

I extend my left hand and reach for Julian. But midway through my extension, my strength wanes, and my arm drops to the table in a thud. Julian jumps up. He lifts my arm, cradles it in his palms and examines it for damage. "You okay?" he asks. "Do you need some ice?"

"Yes to the first question. And no to the second," I respond. Julian kisses my sore hand and places it gently on my lap. He runs his hands through my hair, and when his fingertips inadvertently tickle the blade of my ear, I am sent into a state of heightened stimulation that is too much this early in the morning. I shiver and wait for the sensitivity to pass.

Norma emerges from the kitchen and places a plate in front of me—egg whites with parsley and specks of salmon, roasted potatoes dusted in rosemary and two links of spicy merguez. She then places a similarly adorned plate in front of Julian. Finally, she places the third plate—with a metal cover—in front of the empty chair and returns to the kitchen. Julian looks over to the empty setting and waits for Norma to return, to join us for breakfast.

"Hurry, Norma," he calls out. "It's getting cold."

Norma pokes her head out of the kitchen. "You get started. I already ate," she says.

Julian looks at me. He is confused and shrugs his shoulders. And as I sit before my food, observing Julian in his gentlemanly restraint, I revel in the superiority of my prescience—for I know what is about to transpire. And so does Norma. I'm thrilled, superpowered, awash in my great advantage, for is there anything more exhilarating than knowing the future?

I don't know exactly how things will unfold, of course, but I'm confident the following will occur. At any moment, the guest room door will open, and Perla will emerge. Julian will hear noise from down the hall, footsteps in the corridor. Rather than his being frightened that an intruder may be in our home, a look of curiosity will first cross his face. He will turn to me, seeking reassurance that I either did or did not hear the noise, the advancing footsteps.

Julian will watch the bend in the hall, wondering what, who, could be the cause of the creaking floorboards. Meanwhile, Norma will emerge from the kitchen, lean against the doorjamb and watch as the theater unfolds. Perla will turn the corner and see before her a table set for three. Whether she turns the corner with trepidation or stumbles eagerly into the trap, I do not know. But when she emerges, she will see Julian sitting before her. She will see me sitting in my wheelchair next to Julian, my excitement within masked by my deportment without. She will see Norma standing in the doorway with a look of motherly compassion on her face.

Everything happens as I expect. Perla turns the corner not with exuberance but with mouselike trepidation. She stops and takes in the scene before her. This morning, she wears a sheer periwinkle shirt, jeans and sandals. Her hair is pulled back in a ponytail, so I get an even clearer view of her delicate face. She stops a few feet from the table and nervously pulls her tight-fitting shirt away from her breasts. She places her bag and her purse on the floor beside the empty chair.

"Good morning," she says. "Sophie. Norma. Julian."

I watch Julian as he watches Perla. What has crossed his face is something different than shock or horror; yes, there is some of that, but there is also wonder. And when he turns to me and sees that I am not surprised, when he sees that I am actually enjoying this moment, his wonder turns into awe. Unsure what happens next, Perla stands behind the empty chair and places her hands on its back. She swings her hips anxiously, while Julian remains seated, bolted to the chair.

"Well, don't just sit there like a damn fool," I say. "Get up and greet our guest. She's come a long way to see us."

Julian gives me a look that asks *you sure?* And I nod yes. He pushes his chair back, braces his hand on the table and stands before all of us —exposed and defenseless. He walks over to Perla so that he is just a foot away from her. Then, as if he is greeting a colleague at the office, he extends his hand. Perla stares at his hand. And so do I and Norma. And I know that we're all thinking the same thing. *What the fuck is this guy doing?*

Well, Perla looks at me and at Norma, and we both chuckle. And that's all Perla needs to break the tension—a good laugh—and she throws her arms around Julian and kicks her feet in the air like a little girl, and she rests her face in that little nook between his neck and his shoulder. And while I can't see Julian's face from this angle, I can see a part of hers. I see tears of relief, as if she has reached a fortified sanctuary after a long, difficult journey. I know this sanctuary, too, for that is where *I* am with Julian, where I have always been with Julian. And that's where Roger is, too. And Petrov and Volokh. And where Julian's mother was for too brief a time. I know how it feels when someone will kill for you.

Julian guides his right hand up Perla's back. He tugs gently on her ponytail, pulls her head away from him. He wipes the tears from her face, careful not to scrape her flawless skin. I turn to Norma, and she makes a pitter-patter motion on her chest—which has the effect of irritating me, evoking in me not only a jealousy of Julian's affection for Perla but of Norma's affection for *them*. I turn back to Julian and Perla. He guides her to the chair, pulls it back a foot so she can sit down and, once she is settled, slides it forward.

After removing the metal cover from Perla's plate, Julian returns to his seat and reaches for my hand. I offer it without resistance, without bitterness. Norma returns to the kitchen while Julian, Perla and I eat in silence, verbal silence; there are the taps of sterling on china, the sipping of coffee, linen folded and unfolded, but no words. Unlike the austere, repressed meals of my youth, however, this silence is not uncomfortable. Rather, it is akin to the silence of the elderly couple sitting across the table from each other, enjoying—each in their own minds—the ambiance of the restaurant, the clatter of plates, the fusion of a hundred voices, the past, the shared memories, wondering how long they will both live, who gets the short straw and must outlive the other; it's the silence of the elderly couple that chooses not to speak because they've either said it before, or if they haven't already said it then there's a damn good reason to keep it quiet.

I am at peace. I look to my right, to my left. And I know there's only one way this whole thing can go, maybe two.

(MIS)FORTUNE

The gods smile upon me today.

After several minutes of peaceful quiet, I ask Perla about her life—careful not to touch upon those subjects, like stripping, that might cause her some discomfort.

"Julian tells me that you're from Cuba?"

Perla folds her napkin in half, then in half again, and places it on the table. "That's right. My family is from Matanzas, a town on the coast that's east of Havana. We lived there for a hundred years. Not me and my parents for a hundred years, of course, but all of us, our ancestors, generation after generation."

"Do you still have family there?" I ask with genuine interest.

Perla pushes the plate a few inches away so she has more room for her arms, more room to talk with her hands. "I do. My uncle lives there, my father's brother. He's a fisherman and has a little shop that sells what he catches. So it's my uncle and also a couple of cousins I haven't seen in forever." Julian listens, and the calm look on his face suggests that he has heard all of this before—and his deep knowledge of Perla's life reveals an intimacy between them that is greater than I had realized.

"And your parents?"

"My parents? Me and my mom, we live together in Miami and we got a cute little place in Little Havana, which is filled with Cubans." Perla smiles bashfully and hits her forehead with the palm of her hand as if to say *stupid me*. "Obviously, or why else would they call it Little Havana? It's not like it's filled with Swedes." Julian and I both laugh and turn to each other; Julian's wink says *I told you so*. "But she's got a serious boyfriend now, Felipe, and he's not half bad compared to the losers she usually dates. So I don't see her as much, which is pretty crappy." When the word *crappy* escapes, Perla reflexively covers her mouth. "Sorry," she says, "that's not too ladylike. Sometimes I forget where I am and I get a little dis-so . . . sometimes things just come out of my mouth, and sure enough . . ." Perla trails off, surrenders the rest of the sentence.

"Don't worry about being ladylike around here, Perla. We can get pretty crude, right, Norma?" Norma pokes her head out of the kitchen, gives me the middle finger, and then returns to her work. "And your father?" I ask, forgetting for a moment that Julian told me he died and remembering only when it is too late, when my regret is sealed.

Perla looks down and crosses herself. Then she sits straight up, as if she is sitting on a church pew, and looks at me. "My father died when I was fourteen. He was a great man, humble and poor but real smart and filled with lots of love. And gratitude. He had lots of that, too. But he didn't have much money or success in his job," she says, and looks around the apartment, at the grand space, the artwork, the furniture. "But he had lots of faith in God, faith that we'd be taken care of, me and him and my mother, and faith that I'd turn out good, too."

I can see that Perla is getting emotional, shaky. "Well, then," I say, "it looks to me like his faith has been rewarded."

Perla shakes her head as if I have proposed something that is too painful to accept. "You think?"

"Yes, I think so."

"Maybe."

I look over to Julian, who in turn looks at his watch and taps the glass face, indicating that he must leave soon for the airport. There are a few more moments of silence, but this time it is not so comfortable. "So, Perla, what would you like to do today?" I ask.

"Me? What would I like to do?" she responds, surprised, and turns to Julian for guidance—which is not forthcoming.

"Julian's off to D.C. now, back tomorrow morning. He's useless to us, at least for the time being. So what do you say?"

"I don't . . . I don't really know, to be honest, and I'm not sure what I'm doing here or what you want from me." She eyes her bags on the floor. "Or what made me come up here in the first place, which is something I'm still trying to figure out. I'm just real uncomfortable, and that's obvious, I guess." Perla pulls her shirt away from her skin, now damp with perspiration, and then crosses her arms over her chest. "I got a return ticket that takes me back tonight, so maybe the best thing is for me to get my bags right here and go meet my girlfriends, they work downtown at the . . ." Perla catches herself, for she has realized that to continue would reveal something that causes her shame. "Just go meet my girlfriends and thank you, thank you for . . ." Flustered, she straightens the knife by her plate. "And just be on my way."

I am disappointed, as I am beginning to experience a bit of affection for Perla. "How about you stay for a couple of hours?" I ask. "Just a couple of hours. We can go for a quick walk in the park. It's beautiful outside." I slap the sides of my wheelchair. "Come on, you can walk and I can roll."

Perla again eyes her bags. There is a flare of the nostrils, a scrape of the lower lip that reveals her conflict.

"I don't know," she says. "Maybe just a couple of hours. Get some fresh air and then I can head back tonight."

Gleeful, I turn to Julian. "Honey, Perla and I are spending the day together. So I will see you back here in the morning." I use my arms to rotate the wheels of my chair in such a way that I move back away from the table and then around to Julian's side. I drape my arms around his neck and give him a kiss. After a quick, self-conscious glance in Perla's direction, Julian hugs me tight and kisses me. He whispers *I love you*—and I know that he does.

But for Norma, whom I shall exile shortly, I've got Perla just where I want her—alone, on my turf, away from her support system.

ANGEL OF
THE WATERS

If you asked me to make a list of my most favorite things about
New York—and it's a very long list—there's a sublime stretch
in Central Park that is at the very top. I cannot even think of a
close second. Maybe the Frick or the Guggenheim or the pool
room at the Four Seasons.

On this warm autumn day, Perla and I cross Fifth Avenue
and walk south along the park's edge. Unlike the paved sidewalk
on the east side of Fifth, the sidewalk that runs along the park is
made of bumpy, hexagonal stones and is thus, despite the determination with which I work the wheels, difficult for me to tra-
verse. Perla notices my struggle. She steps behind me, grabs the
handles in back and pushes.

Just north of Seventy-second Street, my front wheels dip
into a depression caused by a couple of missing stones, and the
chair comes to an abrupt halt that causes my upper body to
lunge forward. The seat belt cuts into my waist, and although I

cannot feel it poke at my skin, I do feel its impact on the band above my waist, pulling it downward, stretching it.

"I got it," Perla says.

I can't see what Perla does now, but I understand the physics and can thus imagine her movements. Perla squeezes the handles and pushes down on the rear wheels, taking pressure off the front of the chair. She then extends her right leg backward and braces it on the ground. She leans forward and pushes hard. When the chair does not budge, she leans even lower so that now her chest, her breasts brush the back of my head. Perla's body is upon me, if even for just a split, fully clothed second.

"One, two, three," she calls out. And then the wheels release, up and out of the hole—and we are on our way. At Seventy-second Street, we make a right into the park, and then another quick right, where we descend downward to Conservatory Water. The path down to the pond is steep, and there is no way I alone can control the chair on the descent.

I look back at Perla as we both peer down the sloping path. "You got this?" I ask.

"Got it."

Again, I cannot see what Perla is doing, but the physics dictate that she is now leaning backward, her left foot forward and just under the edge of the chair, her shoulders turned a bit to the right so she is generating a bit of torque that allows her to lower the chair slowly down the path. About halfway down, her left foot gives way on a patch of gravel, and we—me, her and the chair—accelerate at a scary rate. Perla stomps her left foot on the pavement. Her foot bounces a few times before she can plant securely and assert the necessary counterforce.

We continue our deliberate journey downward with Perla

controlling the pace. I now comprehend the physical strength of this girl. I picture her on the pole, suspending herself, her muscles twitching. I imagine her making love to Julian, the strength of her arms, the arch of her back. I imagine her on top of Julian, using her strength to fuck him. These thoughts are bittersweet for me. There is, of course, great pain, but there is also some pleasure.

We stop in front of Conservatory Water, a small, man-made pond that accommodates not real boats, but rather radio-operated toy boats with crisp white sails that cut gracefully through the still water. Along the edge of the shallow pond, children hold the controls, protruding antennae directing the boats. The occasional duck glides by, glances at the boats with bemusement and moves on, careful not to come into contact with the lifeless creatures.

Perla and I do not speak. We watch the boats, the faces of the children, their wonderment that the mere flick of a finger can move an object. Right, left, forward—but never backward. The only way they can go back to where they started is to make a series of rights or a series of lefts. They have power, these kids.

"Let's go this way," I say, pointing west. "There's another pond, a lake really, with real boats."

We move north along the edge of the toy boat pond. On this flat, paved walkway, I work the wheels with ease. We pass the Alice in Wonderland statue on our right and go under a stone arch, stopping when we reach the park drive. A peloton of recreational cyclists flies by in a blurry whoosh. Noting the danger of crossing the busy road, Perla steps behind me. She looks both ways, then again. And she runs me across the drive with a powerful burst.

The next body of water, the lake, always reminds me of a Seurat painting: couples in row boats, the men working the oars, turning their heads to avoid a collision, the women sitting on the opposite bench with a full view of what is to come, wincing when a stray boat comes too close. On this day, the lake is algae-rich and has an emerald hue. There are many ducks and two swans, a couple I assume. A huge turtle swims past us, slow and unconcerned, just below the surface of the lake's water. Perla and I settle by the southern edge of the lake, a few feet away from the glorious Bethesda Fountain, the Angel of the Waters. Across the plaza, a gospel singer—off-key—sings "Oh Happy Day." On the ground before him is a hat with just a couple of coins in it.

There are a few minutes of stillness, a few minutes during which Perla and I try to process every detail of this stunning, encircling tableau—one in which I guess we both participate. The singer finishes the song, and Perla and I move in his direction. Perla takes a twenty out of her purse and drops it in the hat. She then turns to me. "The best way to show a person you value their talent," she says, "is to pay for it." She smiles, and I believe this is her elegant way of acknowledging an obvious but unspoken fact: that I know she's a stripper.

"Agreed," I say, admiring both her generosity and her subtle candor.

Perla looks around the plaza. "Where now?" she asks.

I spin my wheelchair around and point south, toward the forty or so steps on both sides of the arcade. We cannot scale so many, so I point to the path on the far left, a good forty-five-degree incline that leads up to the band shell. As I look at the daunting hill, I consider that this is my fifth test of Perla. So far, she has passed the previous four. To start, there was the invita-

tion to see us in New York, the invitation that I strategically
encouraged Roger to deliver on my and Julian's behalf; the second was the invitation to sleep over; the third was the offer to
take a walk in the park; the fourth, the decline to the pond with
the toy boats; and now the incline above the Bethesda Terrace.

We stop at the base of the hill and consider our strategy. "I
think we gotta get some speed going before we hit the hill," she
says. Perla stands behind the chair and reverses about twenty
feet. "Hold on." And like a sprinter taking off from the blocks,
Perla runs. Within about ten yards, we've got speed galore. And
by the time we hit the incline, Perla has generated enough
energy to keep us going at an admirable clip until we get three-
quarters up the hill, where we reach a set of steps. Perla stops a
few feet away. "You buckled up?" she asks.

I check my belt and tighten it. "All set."

Perla slowly spins me around so that I am now facing north
toward the lake. As I grip the armrests, she pulls me backward
until the wheels bump against the first riser. Then step by
step—all nine of them—she pulls me up to the crest of the hill,
and there we stop. Exhausted, Perla pants and bends over at the
waist, hands on her knees. I turn to her. And when her breathing soon regulates, she stands up and looks at me. Her sheer
shirt is now wet with perspiration and clings tightly. But unlike
earlier in the apartment, she is no longer self-conscious. She
glances at her breasts, and rather than cross her arms over her
chest, she smiles, spins and elevates to get a look at the fountain,
the lake, the people below.

I now take the lead as we continue south, and Perla walks
closely by my side. To our left is the empty band shell; before us,
the grand American elms, haunted, twisted and gnarled. We

cross a small patch of gravel, and the crunch of the stones under Perla's feet reminds me of strolling through the Tuileries with Julian. Perla and I make our way south through the bench-lined corridor between the elms, and then we make a left, turning east for the final few hundred yards of this transcendent stretch.

We pass under the Willowdell Arch, a short stretch of musty darkness that smells of urine, and then emerge back into the sunlight. We stand before the brass statue of Balto, a sled dog from Alaska—heroic and lauded—whose back has been buffed and shined by the seats of thousands of children who have jumped on top for a photo. Then we move down a short, rock-lined path to the Delacorte Clock and arrive just in time, half past the hour, to watch the animals—a monkey, penguin, hippo, bear, elephant, goat, kangaroo—dance and make music. Tourists gather around the clock, taking photos, little kids dancing along with the animals. Children, too, are bittersweet for me. In light of my situation, I have mixed feelings about them. I experience a subtle change in mood in the presence of these children, these families, these symbols of my loss. I go from this moment, which was until now a great moment, to someplace in the past— a place where I was ambulatory and fertile.

Perla observes me; I can feel her gaze upon me. I can feel that she has detected my shift in mood. "You ready to go home?" she asks. Perla has passed her next test—one that I had not planned, one that has arisen by chance.

Relieved, I look back to her. "All ready," I say.

CLOUD ON A STICK

Well, it's a perfect day to take a walk through the park, sort of warm even though it's fall. I don't think I could have a better tour guide than Sophie, 'cause she knows just about everything there is to know about the park—the toy boat pond, a beautiful fountain—Angel of the Waters, it's called—the band shell, these crazy-looking elms, even why the back of a brass dog is all shiny and bright. After the walk, I looked up this Balto dog and it turns out he brought medicine, antitoxin they say, and saved lots of people in Alaska a long time ago. And now the real Balto is stuffed and in some museum in Ohio, which is sort of weird. It's weird that he's stuffed and it's even weirder that he's stuffed in Cleveland.

It's good exercise for me, too, 'cause I don't get much down in Florida. I'm on the pole, but that's not really exercise. That's just holding on for dear life. So we're walking around the park, and there's a lot of up and down here, and sometimes having to push

Sophie in that wheelchair wears me out, but in a good way. I'm all sweaty and my tits are on display, and even though they're not too big, every guy who passes me is taking a look. And it gets so obvious that Sophie turns around when I'm pushing her and says you think they're looking at the cripple in the chair or the wet T-shirt contest you got going on back there? And I laugh and say maybe a bit of both. But what I'm really thinking is that if these guys have any sense at all, any idea what pure beauty looks like—crippled or not—then Sophie's the girl they should be staring at.

We're standing near a clock tower and there's animals on top, funny ones holding instruments, and next thing I know there's music. It's a kid's song, and the animals are dancing and spinning around in a circle to the tune. *Frère Jacques, frère Jacques.* There they are, up on a stage, dancing to the music, children and their parents watching, some lovers too, and of course me and Sophie. And as I'm watching this, the dancing animals make me think about me, 'cause that's exactly what *I* do. I get up high and dance and people have their eyes all fixed on me. And even though they're just metal figures dancing up there, I'm pretty sure they're more alive than I am.

There's a family standing near us, a big family with four or five kids and parents who look so young it's hard to believe they have even one kid. But they're a sweet family, tourists I think, and the kids get crazy when the animals start dancing. The little one, she can't be more than four or five, she's got cotton candy in one hand, a big fluffy pink cloud on a stick, and she's pointing at the animals with the other.

The girl's so amazed that she keeps moving, step by step, toward the clock, like she's being drawn to it. Next thing I know, she's broken away from her pack and she's standing alone next to Sophie and the wheelchair. She's doing a little teeter-totter thing with her feet 'cause she's so excited and she holds on to the big rubber wheel on Sophie's chair. She looks at Sophie and smiles and points to the animals with her cotton candy. She doesn't say anything, just holds on to the wheel all comfortable and natural.

The music ends, and the girl lets go of the wheel and runs back to her family. We watch her jump on her daddy's back, and then she's gone. I look down at Sophie and I can see in her face that something's wrong, that maybe this little girl being so close and sweet and intimate, maybe something about that got to Sophie. Maybe a memory? Or a fantasy? Or maybe it's something different. It's too early for me to tell, 'cause I hardly know her, but I can read a girl, and I know it's time to get her the hell out of this park.

WHO'S THE FOOL

Sophie and I are back in the apartment and I think she's finally settling down from seeing that little girl with the cotton candy. Like I said, I've been in some really weird situations in my short life, and having an asshole finger you in a booth is one of them, but sitting in a fancy apartment in New York with my customer's paralyzed wife and a take-no-crap Trinidad maid is way beyond weird. And just when I think it can't get weirder, just when I have my escape plan all worked out, something happens that makes me even more nervous.

Julian's off to D.C., so now it's just me, Sophie and Norma. Sophie says to me hold on for a few minutes, and then she spins her wheelchair around like a top and goes into the kitchen with Norma. Now I can hear them talking, whispering who knows what, and it's clear as day they don't want me to hear what they're saying. There's a point where it almost sounds like they're arguing, but still whispering, which is real funny. When people argue but keep their voices real soft.

Sophie comes back out of the kitchen, and boy is she good at racing that thing around, moving her arms, weaving in and out of chairs, through doorways, and never bumps into anything. She's back at the table for just a few seconds when Norma comes out of the kitchen holding her chest like she's having a heart attack, all dramatic, and says Mum, I got an emergency on my hands, a big one. My cousin, my cousin, she's in the hospital and I'm her only family so I got to get down to Saint Luke's right away.

Now, the way she says it it's real obvious that either her cousin's not sick or maybe she doesn't even have a cousin at all, and she's just trying to get out of the apartment. Sophie puts her hand on her chest, all fake and dramatic too, and she says oh, no, Norma, what happened? And I'm thinking does everyone up here take the same shitty acting course? *Here we go,* I'm thinking. These two bitches are setting me up to be alone with Sophie, God knows why, and there's no fucking way that's happening. She seems to move real good in that chair and of course she's got a phone in case there's an emergency and enough money to hire an entire hospital for a house call.

Sophie looks at me with a fake-sincere look on her face and she says Perla, Norma has to run and Julian doesn't get back from Washington until the morning, and I'm wondering if there's any way you can stay here with me until then. I don't mean to impose, she says, but it's just one night.

Now, a few hours with this woman is about all I can take, but *another night?* Norma's looking at me, waiting to see if I'm fool enough to take the bait. And Sophie, too. I look around the apartment, then I think about that shitty club and my mom spending almost every night at Felipe's and how lonely I'm gonna be down there.

Of course, I say. Happy to stay.

I HATE MYSELF AND
WANT TO DIE

Perla and I have just finished dinner, and we're alone in the apartment—Norma having ostensibly left earlier to visit her very sick and very nonexistent cousin. It is nine at night, and I am tired both from our long walk in the park and from the intensity of this day. I ask Perla if she can help me onto the bed. I position my wheelchair at a slight angle to the bed and, despite my fatigue, use my arms to push the entire weight of my body off the chair. My legs dangle and swing like those of a jolly marionette, the tips of my toes brushing the wood floor. I can hold myself up for a few seconds, but I need someone, Perla, to guide me the foot or so over to the mattress. Perla leans forward and ducks her head low. She wraps her arms around my waist, then slides them up under my arms. It occurs to me that she has experience with this, that she is not a novice; Perla has loved someone who was either quite sick or hopelessly drunk.

Again, I am impressed by Perla's strength. With neither a

grunt nor a wobble, she transfers me to the bed and rests me tenderly on my back. She covers me up and stands before me, her own fatigue apparent.

"You mind if I go to sleep, too?" she asks. "In that guest room from last night?"

"Of course, Perla." She leans down, puts her arms around my shoulders and gives me something approximating a hug. Then she stands up straight, kicks her right heel in the air and, from just a couple of feet away, waves to me—an odd but adorable gesture from someone standing so close.

"Good night," she says. "See you in the morning."

"Good night, Perla." And as she exits the room, I watch her move away from me—a sexy swagger in her gait. I think about Perla's keen observation, how she noticed the impact that the little girl with the cotton candy had on me, how she extracted me from that painful setting. I think about Julian's arms around her waist, about the pleasure that she—and not I—can give the man I love. I look down to my useless legs and curse myself for destroying not just my own life, but Julian's too. For what kind of stupid girl declines a beautiful walk down a beautiful seaside lane with such a beautiful man? What kind of stupid fucking girl does something so fucking stupid?

There are times—and now is one of them—when I hate myself and want to die. Never have I had the courage to kill myself, to take the necessary and affirmative steps to ensure my own death. But tonight, I will do something that may guide me further along the continuum and, in the process, determine what type of girl this Perla really is.

I set the bedside alarm for one in the morning. I close my eyes and, as if I have not a single care, I pass seamlessly into sleep. When I am later awakened by the soothing chime of the alarm clock, I reach over to my left and lift a pillow. I toss it to the ground beside the bed. I then grab another pillow and drop it to the floor next to the other pillow. I do this two more times until there is an imperfect, cushioned row on the floor. The pillows are misaligned and there are gaps through which the wood below is revealed. Still, there's some cushion below extending the better part of the bed's length. I eye the expensive jewelry on the dresser: my watch, earrings, a diamond-and-sapphire brooch.

My plan is this. I shall push myself up onto my right side. It will take me some time to do this, as turning on my side—for reasons having to do with angles and leverage—is harder than maneuvering out of the chair. Once I am on my side, I shall peer down to the pillow-covered floor below. With my left arm, I shall push off, creating momentum that carries my body toward the side of the bed. I shall rock back and forth several times, gaining speed as I go. Eventually, I shall pass that tipping point and my left shoulder will rotate forward, carrying the rest of my body with it. I shall fall off the side of the bed and crash to the ground, the pillows partially breaking my fall, but my body, my head, my face may be exposed to the wood between and around the pillows.

Depending upon which part of my body misses the pillows and hits the floor, I may feel pain. If it is my lower body, then there will be no pain—just bruises and scrapes and possibly a broken bone. If it is my upper body that hits, I may have those things as well, but accompanied by severe pain. There I shall lie, in a paralyzed crumpled mass, awaiting Perla's response to this manufactured tragedy. I wonder if she will seize the opportunity of my total incapacitation to rob the place. Or will she take no action, just sit in the chair and watch me die, thinking about how she's going to redecorate the apartment once she has replaced me? Will she recoil at the pathetic horror of my deformed body in its soiled diaper and, rather than assist me, gather her things and flee? Will she make a sincere effort to help, then cradle me while calling emergency, comforting me until the medics arrive? Or will she do something else? Something entirely different.

Using my left hand, I push down on the mattress and lift my shoulder off the surface, extending my arm stiff and straight until my body has turned over on its right side. I rock back and forth, back and forth, riding along the fulcrum that is my shoulder and hip, until my body gains enough speed and carries all of my weight over the edge of the bed. My body hits the ground in an odd way, such that my head and shoulders go first—which is the opposite of what I had hoped. The right side of my head misses the highest pillow and cracks with terrific force into the floor. My skull bounces off the wood like a bag of fruit and lands again on the floor. My shoulder slams into the hard surface, and the pain drives across my neck, across to the other side of my body. Soon, my legs follow, and I watch the two lazy ropes of wet dough slide off the mattress and land in the center of the pillows below.

My right cheek rests on the cool floor. I am in agony. I moan loudly, a signal for Perla to save me. I open my eyes and wait, but I see and hear nothing. Where is she? Where are the sounds of her movement? Surely, I think, she would have heard the crash and my call for help. And then a terrifying thought occurs to me, one that I foolishly had not considered prior to this dangerous stunt: Perla is already gone, escaped earlier in the night. Smart girl. Julian was right.

I look over to the phone, which is beyond my reach, and I wonder if I have suffered internal injuries. I wonder if I am bleeding from within, if I shall die before Julian returns from D.C. I wonder if my death will be ruled an accident or a suicide. Or if—something I had not foreseen—Perla will be suspected in my death. And I wonder if the circumstances of my demise will, for any number of reasons, prevent Julian and Perla from being together. Or if they will now be free to share a spectacular life.

BROKEN DOLL

'm sleeping so deep in the comfy bed and I'm having a dream about what looks like Cuba, but could really be anywhere, and what happens but I get woken up by a big noise. I'm not used to this city, so who knows what it could be. I'm wide-awake now, staring at the ceiling and a little scared. I listen real close for another big boom, but it's quiet now, so I figure it's just nothing and try to get back to sleep. Then a few minutes later I hear something else. I hear a groan and some crying and I think *oh, fuck, Sophie's hurt*. That's the first thing I think, and I'm out of bed and in her room in a second and what I see is horrible.

Sophie's on the ground and her body's in a real odd shape. Her upper half is going in one direction and her lower half the other, and it looks like she's a broken doll. She's wearing a top but her bottom's naked and I guess her diaper got knocked off in the fall, 'cause it's right there next to her on the floor, open and filled with her stuff. I kneel down next to her to get a good look, brush the hair away from her face. She's got blood running out of her nose and her lips are swollen and I have no idea if she's still breathing. I put my fingers on her neck, right under her jaw, and it turns out she's got a pulse. Not much, but still a little beat.

I look around the room. On the dresser there's a sculpture of a lion, it's made of green stone, jade I think, with jewels in the eyes, and next to it there's Sophie's fancy watch and some jewelry, gold with diamonds and blue stones that must be sapphires. I look at Sophie and her eyes are still closed with blood all over her face. I look back to the dresser, then down to the end table where the phone is.

I jump up and grab the phone, call 911 and tell them I just found Sophie hurt bad, she's paralyzed from the waist down, but that was from before, and I'm alone in the apartment and need some help real fast. I hang up the phone, hold on to her hand and pray hard that she doesn't die. Now, there's lots of reasons I don't want Sophie to die. I don't want her to die 'cause it wouldn't be right for Julian to suffer any more. And also 'cause I sort of like her, even though I've only known her for a day and a night. And I don't want *anyone* to die, except that guy who fingered me at the club.

I'm holding on to her real tight. Sophie, Sophie, I'm begging. I start screaming help as loud as I can, hoping maybe a neighbor hears me or the doorman or someone who works in this goddamn building who's not too fucking busy polishing the brass poles. But I guess 'cause the apartment's so big and the walls so thick, nobody can hear me. In my neighborhood in Miami, everyone's right on top of each other, the windows open, music playing, kids laughing. So there's not much privacy, and that's the way we like it. Real social. But nobody's coming to help me now, and I think that's one of the problems with being so rich—nobody can hear you scream.

There's blood all over the floor. Sophie's eyes are open now, flickering real fast, and I'm nervous 'cause that's exactly what you see in the movies right before someone dies. I don't know how long it's been since I called emergency, could be a minute, could be five. And then I hear some noise in the hallway, a door opening, and I scream help, help, we're in the bedroom. Someone's running toward us now and I turn around to the door, and standing right there just a few feet away is Julian. Now, he's not supposed to be back until the morning, so boy, am I happy to see him.

Thank God, I scream, thank God. Sophie's hurt, I don't know what happened. I just heard a big noise and ran in and she was right here on the floor. I hold up the phone—there's blood all over it—and say I called 911 and they're on the way. Julian runs toward me, toward us, and I stand up to get out of his way. He kneels down next to Sophie, throws himself down to the floor next to her really, and cradles her head with one hand, wipes the blood from her face with the other. He presses his lips against hers. Baby, baby, he's weeping.

Then he puts a pillow under her head and lays her down real careful. Give me the phone, he yells, and I hand it to him. But it's all slippery and covered in blood and he drops it on the floor, picks it up real fast and calls 911, says we've got an emergency, I need an ambulance and the police. Then a pause, and Julian says to the operator oh, you already got a call? I don't say a thing, but I'm thinking that I already told him I called emergency, so maybe he didn't hear me right. And I'm also wondering what we need the cops for. Julian hangs up the phone and strokes Sophie's face, just keeps saying baby, baby, and I'm standing a few feet away not sure what to do with myself.

As he's holding her, he turns to me and tells me to get some towels from the bathroom and fill up a few plastic bags with ice. I'm out and back in a flash and I got a stack of fresh towels and two bags of ice. Julian pats the cuts on her face with a towel, then wraps up the cold bag and holds it to the bump on Sophie's forehead. I'm squatting right next to them with a washcloth in one hand and ice in the other, and that's when something strange happens. Julian looks at Sophie, then at me, and there's a change in him. I can see it on his face first, then he says real accusing, what happened, Perla? What did you do to her? What are you even *doing* here?

Well, I look at him for a sec, then stand up and back away 'cause even though I'm not sure where he's going with this, I don't like his tone. What did I do to her? I didn't do anything to her, Julian. We went for a walk in the park, then Norma had to go 'cause her cousin got sick and Sophie asked me to stay until you got back. I was sleeping, *we* were sleeping, and then I heard a big noise and came running in here. Sophie was right there on the floor, *right there*, blood everywhere, and the first thing I did was call emergency. Then you walked in.

Julian shakes his head like he's disgusted and tells me to grab a couple of pillows, slip them under Sophie's legs while he lifts them up. And just as I get the pillows positioned right under her legs, a radio goes off loud in the hallway—a police radio—and the whole emergency crew pours in. I jump up and clear out of the way, right against the wall, so they can get to her. There's two guys working at the same time, checking her pulse, her eyes with a little flashlight, strapping an oxygen mask to her face. Those medics are so fast and they get her on a stretcher in no more than a couple minutes. And as they're taking her out of the room, Julian gives me a stare that's all blank and distant and maybe even final. Then he points at me and says officer, you'll want to talk to this woman because I don't know what she's doing here at this hour, alone with my wife, and there's a damn good chance she's got something to do with this.

Well, that's the last thing I'm expecting, and I gasp real loud. But before I can even get one word out, Julian and the medics are out of the room and rushing Sophie to the elevator. Next thing I know, a cop steps toward me. I hold up my hands, which still have a bit of red from the blood, and say easy, easy, I didn't do a thing. He says I just want to ask you a few questions. Your name, date of birth, home address, your occupation. I tell him everything except my job, and when he finishes writing down all my info he says again, your occupation? What's your *job*? I'm in the entertainment business. What kind of entertainment? I pause. Dancer, I whisper, and he gives me a little smile, which is real inappropriate given what's going on.

So tell me, ma'am, what happened? I explain how I was staying over, how Sophie asked me to spend the night, how I heard a big noise and ran in, called 911. Then he asks me how I know the Pravdins. The truth? You're not supposed to lie to the police, he says. Which is sort of funny 'cause the only people who think you shouldn't lie to the police are the police. Me and Julian got a little thing going, I say. *Had* a little thing going. And that's when his eyes light up and they might as well be a big neon sign that's blinking *motive, motive, motive*. I know enough people who got in trouble with the law to see where this is going, and I can feel myself getting sweaty and a little pissed off that I even have to explain myself.

You were alone when Mrs. Pravdin fell? Yes. And when you called emergency, was anyone else in the apartment, other than her? Just me, we were alone. He sizes me up and down, not like a construction worker when you walk by a site, but like some-one who's trying to make a decision. Okay, then I think you're going to have to come give a statement, he says, explain all this to a detective, and he reaches for my elbow. Now, I don't like a man touching me, unless it's on my terms and I'm getting paid for it. And I'm in a bad state with everything that's happening, and something about him reaching for my elbow when I'm in the right makes me feel a little violated and angry and without thinking, just pure impulse, I pull my arm away and say don't you dare, don't you fucking dare!

Well, that's all a cop needs, just a little hostility—failure to obey an order, they call it—and he pulls a pair of cuffs off his belt, dangles them in the air. Why don't you just turn around real slow, he says, and it's clear to me that this guy isn't fooling around. So I do just that, turn around real slow and press my palms together behind my back, like I'm praying to the ground. I'm the one who called 911 in the first place! I plead. And the cop laughs so loud, like he's heard that line a thousand times and says to me lady, lots of times people call it in themselves just to make it look like they're innocent. Now, with my kind of job there's no end to the amount of stupid shit you hear, no end, but this idea about reporting a crime to get *out* of a crime is just about the dumbest thing I ever heard. And I'm about to tell him just that, how stupid that sounds, but I figure now's not the time to get into a big debate.

I feel the cold metal against my skin, then the click of the cuffs. I look around the room and see the pillows on the floor and the jewelry on the dresser, that shower bed in the corner and a smudge of blood on the wall. I close my eyes and picture my dad. I pray to him. Forgive me, Dad, forgive me. 'Cause I fucked up good this time.

THE TOMBS

Here's all you need to know about the way this fucking country works. If you're rich, people assume you're telling the truth and they give you a free pass. Maybe 'cause they figure you'll give them something in return or maybe they figure if you made it big then you've got to be on the up-and-up. Who knows? But if you don't have money, if you're nothing more than some poor spic stripper, then you're pretty much fucked. If you're just an immigrant who shakes her tits for a living and they catch you standing over the body of a crippled rich chick who happens to be the wife of the guy you're fucking, then you got motive *and* opportunity and you're screwed. And they could hook you up to the best lie detector in the world and you'd pass it perfect, straight A's, and still there's no way you're walking.

It's five in the morning and I'm in the fucking Tombs. There's four girls in my cell, bull dykes every one of them. Fat as shit with ink all over, their ugly mugs pierced and dressed up in denim and flannel shirts like they just raided Paul Bunyan's closet. And yes, Julian, wherever the fuck you are now, I know exactly who Paul Bunyan is and I know he's not real, just a myth. Though some people think he's a composite of several real people. Anyway, I have interests that go beyond today, that go way back and into the future and all over the world, you patronizing fuck.

These dykes, they've been eyeing me, acting all tough, but they better back the fuck off. 'Cause in the mood I'm in right now, I will go Cuban on their ass and it will not be pretty.

DAMAGE CONTROL

awake in a private room in Mount Sinai Hospital. I am alive. And yes, I am relieved. Julian sits by the side of my bed. He holds my hand.

"Welcome back," I say.

"You, too."

"What's the damage?"

Julian surveys my body, from my toes to the top of my head. "A fractured rib, split lip and your nose got banged up, but nothing permanent. You've got some contusions on the lower legs, your hip, and a pretty bad concussion."

I pause to consider my injuries, then hold my right arm up to the light. An IV is taped to my forearm, just above the wrist. "Could have been worse," I say.

"That's for sure."

I slowly lower my arm to the bed. "Where's Perla? Is she okay?" I ask, concerned.

Julian appears surprised by my question, my tone. "Perla? They took her away."

"Who took her?" I ask, not sure what he is talking about.

"The police. They took her away, arrested her."

"Perla?" I try without success to push myself up with my arms, but I am too sore, too weak. "She's been arrested?" Of the several potential outcomes, Perla's incarceration is one that I selfishly had not considered until after the fall. "You've got to get her out, Julian."

"Get her out? Why would I get her out?"

"Because it wasn't her fault."

Julian rubs my shoulder in a manner that borders on condescending, and if I weren't so injured and so paralyzed, I'd smack him in the face. "You're not thinking clearly, babe. Why don't you close your eyes, take a nap."

"Julian, listen to me. She didn't do anything wrong, nothing at all to harm me. I did it. I hurt myself on purpose, rolled myself right off the side of the bed. It was Perla who came to help, Julian. Perla. And if it wasn't for her . . ."

Julian places his palm over my eyes, priestlike, as if he is delivering last rites. "Take a nap, sweetheart."

"Get her out now, Julian. Get her out." I close my eyes and imagine Perla's incarceration. I see her standing alone in a cell, frightened and confused. I wonder if they let her keep her clothes, her sandals. Or if she is being further degraded by some horrible orange jail uniform. I see Perla kneeling before me the first time we met: her tears, her supplication. I recall her kindness in the park, the little girl with the cotton candy—and my rot sickens me.

I lift my arm and again look at the IV and its network of

tubes, needles and tape. I inhale the oxygen through the tube in my nose. I try to push myself off the bed, but Julian places his hand on my shoulder and guides me back down.

"There, there," he says. "Just close your eyes."

I am exhausted, cloaked in a fatigue so dark and dense that I am losing sight of Julian. "Now," I plead to a form that is now nothing more than a tenuous blur. I close my eyes and fall into a fitful, febrile sleep.

I wake up several hours later wrapped in damp bedding. The clock on the wall says that it is nine in the morning. His head down, trying to sleep, Julian sits by the bed. When he sees that I have awoken, he smiles and reaches for my hand, careful not to pull on the complex system of tubes that run in and out of different parts of my body. I look around the hospital room, and it takes me some time to recall where I am, to recall the conversation that Julian and I had earlier in the evening—but once I do regain my mental footing, I am again gripped with shame and the need to right my wrong.

"Okay, Julian," I say, grasping his hand as tightly as my depleted state will allow. "Now listen to me clearly, and no superior shit from you this time. My mind is fine, just fine. I'm groggy, obviously, but I've got my wits." I give Julian a steady look to convey seriousness. "Go ahead, ask me anything." Unprepared for my challenge, Julian hesitates—and before he can produce a question, I offer proof of my clarity. "How you proposed to me?" I look to my left hand and see my rings, partially swallowed by the engorged flesh. "On a raft going down the Delaware River, just north of New Hope, when we got stuck on some rocks." Julian smiles. "That was a dangerous place to pull out a ring," I remind him, and he nods in agreement. "The meal that Irina always made on your birthday? Her *best* meal? Brisket with boiled potatoes and carrots, drenched in gravy. And that soup with the mushrooms, the olives, the cabbage. I'm blanking on the name of it, not because my mind is messed up, but because it's Russian."

"Solyanka," he says.

"Solyanka! Of course. You need more? How about that awful stomach bug you got on our honeymoon—I *knew* those scallops were bad—and how you spent a good two days on the . . ." He holds up his hand to stop me from continuing. "My mind's clear, Julian." With the index and middle fingers of my left hand, I tap my temple. "Crystal clear."

Julian has no choice but to concede that my thinking is sound and it is this understanding that terrifies him—because this means that I have told the truth about Perla, about my involvement in this mess. As if he does not recognize me, he removes his hand from mine and leans back in his chair.

"You did this?" he asks.

"I did."

"You tried to kill yourself?" Julian is now confused, and I know that his confusion will soon convert into rage.

I reach for his hand—but it is too far away, and Julian, unraveling before me, does not appear eager to close the gap. "I prefer to call it existential indifference," I say. Julian stares at me, exasperated. I wiggle my hand, imploring him to touch me. Reluctantly, he rests his hand on top of mine, but now there is no enveloping curl of the fingers, a slight difference in physical contact that, to me, is worse than no contact at all. "It's complicated," I say. "Maybe I hate myself. Hate myself for fucking everything up for us." Julian shakes his head as if to deny my culpability. "And part, I guess, was to see what kind of girl she really is, what kind of girl you fell for." I lick my lips, then chew on the inside of my mouth to get the saliva flowing. Julian reads these signals and, with his free and trembling hand, lifts a glass of water to my mouth. I take a few sips and continue. "And maybe," I admit, "maybe I just wanted to be damn sure I was leaving you in good hands."

Julian looks disgusted. He slams the cup back onto the table, causing me to flinch. "You almost killed yourself to see what kind of girl she is? To test her character?" Yes, I nod. "There's easier ways to do it, you know." With his fist, he pounds his thigh. Once, twice, three times; his face twists from the pain. "And I *told* you what kind of girl she is!" His fury, as expected, has now surfaced. "And what about *her?* What about what you did to Perla?"

I wince. I slide my hand out from under his and place it over my chest. On the way, the nasal tube glides across my right ear. I brace myself for the unbearable sensation that will ripple through my ear. I wait. But to my astonishment, I feel nothing other than the normal sensation of a piece of plastic gently stroking the skin. The brain rewiring.

SISTERHOOD

got these bull dykes lined up all docile on the far wall. I tell them you step across this line—and I draw a fake line with my foot in the middle of the room—you take one step across this line and we are having problems. Now, there's no way they could really be afraid of me, every one of them a good two hundred pounds, but I'm hoping that maybe something about the way I say it makes them think I'm not worth the trouble.

But then one of them, the fattest one of all and the only blonde in the bunch, she takes a big step over my imaginary line. She looks at me for a second, sizes me up and asks what's wrong, sweetheart, in a deep voice that sounds like she's been smoking unfiltereds her whole life. Then she shrugs her shoulders and takes a step backward, over to the other side of the line, just to show me she gets to decide where the line is and who gets to cross it. And she smiles—I can't tell if it's sweet or evil—and says why so confrontational, sweetheart?

Well, for some reason that's the moment I give up on the *tough little Latina* act, 'cause right here, in this cell with these huge dykes, that's all it really is. An act. So I say if you really want to know, truth is I've had a bad fucking day. And I start to cry a bit, which I don't think is a good idea in jail, and I rub my foot back and forth over the fake line like I'm erasing it.

The dykes stare at me and shake their heads. Next thing I know, a guard comes by the cell and screams my name, says Perla, you must have some big sugar daddy looking after you, 'cause you're free to go. Well, I got no idea how I'm free, but I'm not asking any questions. Just get the hell out of this place as fast as I can. I turn to the dykes and they line up and start walking toward me. And I'm thinking there's no way they'll beat me up right in front of the guard, is there? I look at the guard and give him the *hurry up* sign with my hands, and he just smiles 'cause he doesn't give a shit. And I'm thinking this day just can't get any worse. It makes getting fingered a walk in the fucking park. The dykes form a circle around me, and they're so big and broad that I can't even see the guard. *Here we go*, I'm thinking, and I put my head down and wait for the first punch.

I feel a hand on my shoulder, a big hand. And then an arm around my back, and another. And I realize what's happening. I'm not getting shivved. Turns out I'm getting a group hug. And one of them whispers in my ear with the sweetest, most feminine voice. And where did *that* voice come from? She says sister, time to let go of all that anger. And also time to take a chance. Maybe do something different, mix it up.

I put my arms around the women next to me, not *around* really 'cause they're so big, but on their backs. We stay like that for a few seconds, maybe ten, and then they step back and leave me standing there all exposed. One of the women calls out to the guard and screams *she's all yours, motherfucker.*

They make me do some paperwork on the way out, give me back my wallet, my keys, my cell phone and my Hello Kitty bag—stuff they let me take when I got arrested. I check to see if those fuckers stole my money, but sure enough it's all there. That's a surprise to me, 'cause you get arrested in Cuba and they steal all your stuff. And the only reason I know that is 'cause I had a cousin who got arrested for fighting in Havana and they stole all his stuff.

I stop in front of a window and use it as a mirror, straighten myself up with a bit of lipstick and brush my hair. For normal me, I look like crap. But for Perla-who-just-got-out-of-jail, I look damn good. And then I'm out in the lobby looking around, and sure enough Julian's standing there looking like shit, looking like he's the one who just spent a night in jail. I walk right up to him and give some real serious thought to punching him in the mouth. But instead, I say how's Sophie doing? And he says she's hurt pretty bad but she's going to be fine in a few weeks.

And before I can make him apologize to me, he says baby, I'm sorry, I didn't know. He says my wiring's all fucked up, has been since I'm a kid, and sometimes I look at a picture and see something that's not really there and then I go blank. And sometimes there's a huge disconnect between what I see and what everyone else sees, a gap so big that it's hard to explain.

I think about that for a second, how maybe the eyes are getting information from all sorts of places, not just what they're looking at, but places deep inside a person, and how that can change what you see, how you see it.

I smile and give Julian a little peck on the cheek. And then I make a tight fist and punch him in the face, right across that Irish boxer nose of his, hard enough to hurt but also ladylike.

I wait until he straightens himself up, gets over the shock, and then I say I want to see Sophie. Now.

EPILOGUE # 1

At this moment, I am a man at peace. My rage appears to be in a period of remission; my ferocious ambition has, for the moment, abated and has permitted some sort of strange and vast contentment; and tonight, for the first time in years, I'm not afflicted by the ache of my childhood. I'm sitting at a corner table with Roger, Petrov and Volokh, and the restaurant reminds me of Frankmann's place in Siberia—mahogany paneling, brass rails and Oriental rugs. Perla is with us, too, and she sits between me and Roger. Perla and Roger adore each other, and their burgeoning friendship is beautiful to watch. We are at a midtown restaurant, a fancy one chosen by Petrov, and we are celebrating my addition to a list of the wealthiest people in the city; it's a good thing, I guess, to qualify for such a list, but a bad thing to actually be on it.

My friends have given me a gift in honor of my accomplishment. It is a plaque—silver on cherry wood—and on it the following words are inscribed: I'M A RICH DOUCHE BAG. I love this gift. I hold it up to the light. Read it, read it out loud, my friends exhort. I relent. I'm a rich douche bag, I proclaim. And my friends howl and hold their glasses up to toast both my success and their joy in my success, their pride in me. They are also toasting the honesty, the integrity of our friendship that grants them the freedom to mock me. Most people I meet these days subordinate themselves to my wealth, obsequious to the point that I feel disconnected. But not so with my inner circle, my core. To be mocked is to be accepted, to be equal. So right now, I am at peace.

Sometimes, though, I get depressed. And when I get depressed, which happens intermittently, I find myself attaching to a negative narrative. Or maybe it's the other way around; maybe I get depressed because my narrative turns sour. Either way, my negative narrative goes something like this: my father was an adrenaline junkie who was so reckless, so ego-driven that he got himself killed, depriving me of a father and my mother of a husband; my mother was a heroin junkie and prostitute who abandoned me; I watched my mother give Krepuchkin a blow job; I murdered a man; I lost my best friends for almost twenty years; my wife got paralyzed, and I believe that, despite what Sophie maintains, I played a role in that; I've been an angry man, violent and intolerant; I have at times suffered from feelings of inadequacy; I broke my marital vows and took up with a stripper; and I am so obsessed with financial success that there never seems to be enough money to fill the void.

But when I fall into this narrative, there is always my inner circle to set me straight. Personal narrative, one of them will invariably say, is a choice. You can go with that story, the one with the junkies, the blow jobs and the shitty orphanage, or you can tell a different story—just as truthful, but a lot more uplifting.

The positive narrative goes something like this: my father was a brave and powerful man who supported me and my mother and inspired an entire village; my mother suffered when the love of her life died, and, in her desperation to care for me, she made many terrible mistakes; my mother's addiction was not a result of weakness or moral failure, but of disease; my mother rebuilt her life and saved me, heroically, from the orphanage, sacrificing her own dignity for her child; I was blessed with the opportunity and the will to kill the man who degraded my mother, and God exonerated me accordingly; she cared for me every day thereafter and, when she could go no further, put me in the hands of a good man; that man, Frankmann, instilled in me toughness and guile and positioned me to survive, to prosper; when I arrived in America, I was cared for by a loving couple who, despite their age and accumulated fatigue, provided me with a safe home and a fine education; I fell in love with Sophie, a spectacular woman who has tried in the most creative and unusual way to liberate me from the burden of my culpability; I have Roger, tough and loyal; I have earned many fortunes; I amassed enough money and corrupt connections in Russia and the States to get Petrov, Volokh and their families over here, carrying the good parts of my past into my present; my past is thus selectively over, as I have the freedom to choose what stays and what goes; I have choices; I love; I am loved.

As I sit in this restaurant, my story is overwhelmingly positive. Is it possible for a life to be more beautiful? I cannot imagine it ever being otherwise. But I know that there will be a time when the story shifts, when I shall again be seduced by negativity and view my life through a corrupted filter. That is when my rage will resurface, when the impulse to kill justly may, given the opportunity, return. What will trigger such a shift, there is no way to know. It could be something huge, an existential threat to me or someone I love. Or it could be something so trivial that I cannot explain its impact: a reminiscent scent, the peculiar angle of the wind, a branch of deadened ivy. And when that happens, as it absolutely must, I shall fight for the strength to change my tune. Perspective, for me, is a constant battle.

Sophie enters the restaurant. She glides toward us in her wheelchair, and we all rise to greet her. Tonight, she is transcendent. She appears comfortable with her place in the world. Nice plaque, she says. You *are* a douche bag.

I would say that for the first time in years, Sophie is truly happy. And for the first time since the accident, we are both happy at *exactly* the same time.

EPILOGUE #2

Eight weeks have passed since my fall, and we are still work-ing out the logistics of this unconventional arrangement. Perla has moved into the guest room, which we no longer call the guest room. It is now *Perla's room*. Most nights, Julian and I sleep together—he on his right side, his left arm draped across my waist and his right tucked under my pillow. Some nights, especially when I am feeling weak and retire early, Julian moves to Perla's bed. Following most of those nights, he returns to our bed before daybreak. But there are nights when he sleeps with Perla all the way through to morning, entering our bedroom only after I have arisen. For now, I am comfortable with that short distance—merely the width of one plaster wall.

I don't want to hear them fuck. I don't even want to know when they are fucking. They understand this intuitively and are thus careful and discreet. Pretty much all I want to know is that Julian is getting his needs met; that between me and Perla, he's getting *all* of his needs met. And I want to know that Perla is safe and loved. And me, too.

So far, everyone seems to be getting as much as they give, although the permutations are confusing, and the imperfect timing of when we give and when we get requires us to access deep reservoirs of faith. It could be Julian helping me out of the chair one day and it could be Perla doing it the next. It could be Julian inside me or Julian inside Perla, but never on the same day and always separate. Our sex lives shall always remain compartmentalized and distinct, for anything else—any conflation or overlap—would violate some sacred covenant and destroy a delicate balance.

One unanticipated consequence of Perla's proximity is that Julian and I have been making love with greater frequency and lightness. It seems that Perla's presence has stripped the heaviness from our act, for now the consequences of my sexual failures are not so grave. Sex with Julian is no longer just an impossible reproductive act; it is once again recreational. Perla has had a disinhibiting effect on my sexuality. My thinking now goes that if I shit the bed during sex, I won't feel as awful as I used to, because now Julian can simply walk down the hall and sleep with a very special woman who has no interest in damaging the bond that exists between me and Julian. And because the pressure is lifted, I'm no longer soiling the sheets.

Mind over matter, so to speak.

And, of course, there's Perla. Dear Perla. What she gets out of this, I am only just beginning to understand. But I am afraid that whatever Perla does get will not be enough. I fear, as does Julian, that she will wake up one morning, take a good look around and decide that she wants more than we can give—and that will be the end of it.

EPILOGUE #3

The first time I change Sophie's diaper is about three months after she gets out of the hospital. Julian's at the market and it's just Sophie and me in the apartment. We talk about all sorts of things, me and Sophie. Our pasts, our families, our dreams. I find out that she comes from a working-class family in the suburbs and that all this wealth was something that she never thought could happen and she still doesn't know how it works sometimes. She just figured she'd take a ride with Julian and who knew where it might end up. But even though she didn't grow up rich, Sophie admits she got used to it real fast and that it's easy for a girl to get sophisticated tastes when she's got tons of cash and access to the right shops and designers. I think it's also easy to get real *un*-sophisticated tastes, so it says something about Sophie and her character that she made such a beautiful home. And that she's so respectful to Norma and didn't even say a word when I made a mistake and put a hot mug on the wood table without a coaster.

But it's not all serious stuff. There's silly girl talk, too, like shopping and hairstyles and even sex. I really like to hear the stories about Julian when he was young, and Sophie never lets me down. I hear things that I never knew but that make total sense given what I know about the man, like how he beat up Sophie's uncle. After two weeks of talk and only after Julian says it's okay, Sophie tells me about his life in Russia, about his father, his mom, the orphanage, Krepuchkin, about the special place that Petrov and Volokh and Roger have in his life, how he would do anything to keep them close to him.

I cry real hard when Sophie tells me all this and she puts her hand on mine and tries to give me some comfort. He *killed* Krepuchkin? I ask, 'cause I'm a little confused about this part of the story. With his own hands? And Sophie nods yes, and I get a little thrill in my chest and in my thighs, sort of aroused. And I think to myself damn right, this is my kind of man.

So, it's just me and her alone in the apartment. Norma's back in Trinidad visiting her family and Julian runs out to get some food for the empty fridge. We've got a fill-in nurse coming by later in the day, so we're all covered. But no more than ten minutes after Julian leaves for the market, there's a real loud sound that comes out of Sophie and she looks at me all ashamed and I know immediately that she just soiled herself. And it's not like this is a little bowel movement and we can wait for Julian to get back. This one's so big that it's coming over the edge of the diaper and seeping through her silk pants.

I'm a girl who's all business when I need to be, so I say Sophie, you and me are about to have a moment. And she says you sure? A moment? Yup. And I roll her over to the bedroom and get that shower-mattress all set up and I do my thing. Water and soap and the old diaper in that sealed bin and a new diaper on her and even some talcum powder like you put on a baby. Funny thing is that the smell doesn't even bother me. I mean, it's there and I guess you could say it's real bad, the smell. But when you're out of your own head and helping someone else, not thinking about your own shit and just being of service to another human being who's got it worse than you, then the unpleasant things don't seem to bother you. I get her all cleaned up and get her some fresh clothes and my girl is looking hot and ready to go!

We sit in the living room and Sophie says you mind opening one of the windows, get some fresh air in here. I'm thinking the same thing, but didn't want to insult her, so I'm happy to do it. I open the window a crack and the air swoops in like it's just been waiting there all day for the invitation. The air's cold and it's not something I'm used to living down in Miami. It feels good, refreshing on my skin, and I wonder what it would be like to spend an entire winter in this city, especially now that my mom moved in full time with Felipe.

Just then, while I'm in a little fantasy, Julian opens the door. Me and Sophie, we've got guilty smiles on our faces, and Julian knows something's up. What's going on, he wants to know. You wearing a different outfit, Sophie? Same outfit, she says, and nothing going on but for a couple girls having a bit of fun.

Julian's got a half-dozen bags and he carries them into the kitchen. He puts them on the table and starts to unpack all the things he bought. There's the stuff that Sophie likes, stuff that I don't have a good taste for yet but I'm open to trying. Goat cheese and crunchy French bread, Greek yogurt, a bottle of fancy mustard, poached salmon, almonds, organic blueberries and the kind of eggs you get from a farm. You know the drill, it's an epidemic up here. Then he opens up another bag and says Perla, I stopped by the Spanish place. And sure enough he pulls out a bunch of ripe plantains, some mangoes, a couple cans of beans, a bag of rice, some fresh shrimp, mojo sauce, which I love, and pastelitos filled with fresh guava.

There's also a bundle of pine wood held together with a thick string, and Julian holds it up. He says it's freezing out, winter's here, so I figured it's time to put the fireplace to use. He lays all the stuff out on the counter in front of us, waves his hand like he's real proud of himself and says this is going to take some time, you know—to figure this all out.

Something about all this makes me think of Old Pepe and his birds, Chico and Chica. I remember Pepe's words like he's right here with me, the funny bowler hat and the blue poncho. *Remember, Perlita, when you get older, you look for a man like that, someone who protects you, who feeds you first, who won't take a bite of anything, won't take a single piece of food or clothing or firewood until you've had enough first.* And I'm looking at Julian and all this Latin food, which is sweet and thoughtful but also maybe a little insulting, but I can explain that part to him later. Julian's a little rough around the edges and he's got some learning to do.

I look at Sophie and then back at Julian, just taking them both in. I have to look down to see her and up to see him. They seem a little concerned, nervous, like they know a decision's about to be made and they don't get to make it. I look at my feet, drop my head real low, 'cause I'm nervous too and it's hard to keep the eye contact. And I close my eyes and make an image in my mind, an image of all the things I want out of my life, which is what I do sometimes when I want to travel to a different place, when I don't like where I'm at. I used to think mostly about the past, but lately I'm thinking more about the future 'cause the past just won't work for me anymore. The past hurts. That's what I'm beginning to learn. The past hurts, so I get out of there. Blink, there I go. Blink, I'm back. Blink, gone. Blink, blink. That's how I do it, just a little trick of the mind.

So I open my eyes and look up, and there's Julian a few feet away, bags of food all around. Sophie's holding the wheels on her chair real tight, like she's at the top of some icy hill and afraid to slide off the edge. And I go back to that day with Pepe, when I blew the feather into the air and made a wish, a secret wish that Pepe said was just for me. For me and my God. And I wonder if I deserve something better than this, something normal.

I rub my eyes, then blink, blink. That takes me to a different place. It could be the future, this place. Or maybe even the present. And I wonder if I've got it all wrong, if maybe everything I ever wanted is right here in front of me, but just dressed up different so it's hard to see, with lots of kindness and laughs— and a man who kills for the woman he loves, for the *women* he loves.

I glance over to that bundle of pine on the counter. I don't think Pepe meant it so literal, the firewood, but there it is plain as day. Then I look at their faces—scared but full of hope—and I'm guessing that Julian and Sophie made a wish one day, too.

And maybe I'm it.

ACKNOWLEDGMENTS

I am enormously grateful to so many people, including Susan Cheever; Lisa Berg Selden; Rebecca Ascher-Walsh; Andrea Stern and Kenneth DiPaola; Peter Appel and Polly Appel; Susanne Gabriele; Roger Kumble; Lori Singer; Joe McKinsey; Allan Weinstein; Simon Furie; Bob Weinstein; Vanita Vithal; Laura Bachrach; Katherine Mogg; Henry Spitz; Simon Doonan; Sandra Schmitz; Greg Redford; Sloane Spanierman; Edward Davis; Mark Loigman and Andrea Glenn Loigman; Mark Rabiner and Avi Pemper; and the entire Burrell family.

Every member of my family—the Pelzmans, the Karnetts, the Newmans—deserves a huge hug for their love and support over the years. They're a great bunch and have been my strongest advocates from the very start.

I am indebted to John Gardner, a man I never met but whose teachings guided me through the creation of this book. If you are a young writer (or an old writer or even a middle-aged writer) and struggling with self-doubt (or maybe you are the rare one who is cocksure), then there is no greater tonic than his books on writing—especially *On Becoming a Novelist* and *The Art of Fiction*.

I am forever grateful to Amy Einhorn and her colleagues at Amy Einhorn Books/Putnam and Penguin; simply put, it is impossible for me to have found a better home for this book.

I also owe many thanks to Liz Stein for her patient support during what was, for me, a new and mystifying process.

I'm at a loss to describe my affection and appreciation for Victoria Skurnick of the Levine Greenberg Literary Agency. For many years before this book came to be, Victoria somehow maintained unwavering belief in me and my work. Whenever I lost faith, she got me back on the beam. Thanks, Victoria!

And finally, a few words for and about my son, Simon. For countless hours, he watched as I sat at my desk and wrote—and wrote and wrote. His optimism, good humor, and encouragement have accompanied me from the first word to the very last.

♦ ♦ ♦

READERS GUIDE FOR

TROIKA

by Adam Pelzman

♦ ♦ ♦

DISCUSSION QUESTIONS

1. The narrative is structured in an unusual way: For most of the book, Perla's and Sophie's stories are told in the first person and Julian's is told in the third person. Not until Epilogue #1 does the reader finally hear from Julian directly. How does this narrative structure affect the story?

2. Julian is a man who is prone to violence, obsessed with making money, and unfaithful to his disabled wife. What about his personality, his experiences and actions, makes him an appealing character despite these characteristics?

3. How would the story be different if, instead of being a stripper, Perla were, say, a waitress or a lawyer? Is there any connection between the fact that Julian's mother was a prostitute and Perla is a stripper? Did Perla's job affect your view of her? If so, how?

4. Consider how Sophie's disability has changed her life. At one point she says, "There are times—and now is one of them— when I hate myself and want to die. Never have I had the courage to kill myself, to take the necessary and affirmative steps to ensure my own death." Does she truly wish she were no longer alive? How has being paralyzed affected her: Her mentality? Her personality? Her relationship with Julian? Her relationship with herself?

5. In light of her sexual limitations, Julian is unfaithful to his wife. Are there circumstances under which marital infidelity is justifiable? Or should spouses always be faithful to each other regardless of the circumstances?

6. Is it significant that Julian and Perla come from foreign countries, and if so, why? How does their "immigrant experience" help form their identities? How might the story have changed if Julian and Perla had been born in the United States?

7. Julian is a violent man, but he resorts to violence only when he believes his cause is just. Is his violent behavior justified when he kills Krepuchkin or when he attacks Sophie's uncle? Are there circumstances in which violence is not only justified, but indeed required?

8. Although the book is ultimately about Julian, Sophie and Perla, there are two old men—Frankmann and Old Pepe—who pass wisdom down to these characters when they are children. Consider the influences that the two men have on the lives of Julian and Perla, and how their teachings are instrumental to

the story. What is the importance of having an older mentor during one's youth, somebody (other than a parent) who imparts great wisdom and experience?

9. Julian blames himself for Sophie's accident, even though she does not hold him responsible. How does his guilt affect him and his relationship with Sophie? Why do people sometimes have trouble letting go of guilt even if they are innocent or have been forgiven?

10. Perla is stuck in a dead-end job, Sophie is stuck in her paralyzed body and Julian is trapped by his past. They have all suffered in their own ways, yet their suffering ultimately changed their lives for the better. How have painful experiences in each of their lives helped shape them and eventually led to great joy? In what ways have they been able to liberate themselves? In what ways are they still trapped?

11. The relationship among Julian, Sophie and Perla challenges the traditional model of a monogamous romantic relationship. Is it possible to be involved in more than one healthy, intimate relationship, if all parties agree? What are some issues these characters might face in their unconventional relationship? Do you agree with their decision to have this arrangement?

ABOUT THE AUTHOR

Adam Pelzman has been a software entrepreneur, an attorney and a private investigator. He studied Russian literature at the University of Pennsylvania and received a law degree from UCLA. Born in Seattle and raised in northern New Jersey, he has spent most of his life in New York City, where he now lives with his son.